Zak Fisher

and the
Angel Prophecy

Carl Ashmore

Carl Ashmore

Author Foreword

I had the idea for *'Zak Fisher and the Angel Prophecy'* in 2009. Back then the lead character was called Billy Fisher. This was all to change on the 26th May 2010 when a close friend's son was shot and killed in Afghanistan. That young man's name was Gunner Zak Cusack.

From then on my eponymous hero became Zak Fisher, as a tribute to that twenty-year old man who died serving our country.

I dedicate this book to Zak Cusack's memory, his father Sean, his mother Tracey, our armed forces, and to his family, friends and colleagues.

Cover Design: Damian Trigo

Please subscribe to www.carlashmore.com

Carl Ashmore

For Lisa and Alice and Will

For Kath, Caitlin and Eleanor

For Keith and Barbara

For Julia Slater

For Tim Cooper

Carl Ashmore

CHAPTERS

Acknowledgements

As has become tradition when publishing my books, I would also like to thank the following children / adult readers for their support.

Aunty Anne and John, Ben, SJ, Lola and Jacob Peyton, Mache, Caitlyn, Mr Brazier, Miss Gadsby, Daryl, Stephanie Jay, Davey & Jasmine Ball, Isabella, Lowri, Cerys, Tiana, Sonny George, Skye and Hayden Hills, Isabel and Zac Taylor, Verona and Grayson Douglas, Piran Hillman, Tommy McGuire, Emma Sly, Kathryn Marriott, Haydn, Harley and Libby-Rose Fryer, Libby Filkin, Liam and Elsa Donnelly, Logan Bull, Tre Furnival, Caitlynn Clewlow, William McNicol & Daniel McNicol, Mark and Nicola Drage, Kira Morris, Eric B Thomasma and Emily, Ziggy James Oxford, Dylan and Oscar, Christina and Charlie Meleka, James Rowe, Ellie, Tristen, Phoebe Rowe, Noah and Toby Aplin, Samantha Ashby, Mike Eldred, Thomas & Arthur Vickerstaff, Will and Matthew Landon, Kathy Bracy, Ann Astrop, Sophie and Rebecca Turnbull, Luna and Pippa Galbraith, Penny McIntosh, Jake Brown, Gemma Murphy, Amelia and Isabella Green, Richard and Portia, Daniel Morrissey, Geisel and Seth, Paula and Garry, Cheryl Ann, Joo Stacey, Jo Hutton.

In memory of Bernard Ashmore

Carl Ashmore

- Chapter 1 -
L'Empire de la Mort

Alex Chambers' muscles screamed but he couldn't stop running. Above, he could just make out the sounds of Paris at dusk, the hum of shoppers scouring the boutiques on the Rue des Francs-Bourgeois, the clatter of trams ferrying commuters and tourists alike. But the world down here was so different: the ancient catacombs that buttressed the city like arteries – a two hundred mile web of tunnels, caves and ossuaries lined with the bones of over six million corpses, disinterred from overcrowded cemeteries in the eighteenth century.

A subterranean city of the dead.

Racing through the half-light, Chambers' grip tightened round the hilt of his Magnasword. If only he could stop and fight. He wanted that more than anything… but he knew he couldn't. It wasn't death that scared him – it was *capture*. He glanced back. The tunnel curved into darkness.

Through the gloom, four figures scuttled into view, scaling the walls, their white eyes locked on their prey ahead; monstrous beasts, each had eight limbs that sprouted from their torsos like grotesque human spiders.

Arachnoids.

Alex Chambers forced his aching body on. Even in his exhausted state, he was convinced he could defeat the Arachnoids. They didn't concern him. No, it was the creature that accompanied them that did. Then he heard something that froze the blood in his veins.

A voice purred from the shadows. 'Have you had enough, Templar?'

Drained of all energy now, Chambers' pace slowed and he stopped. He'd nothing left to give.

The Arachnoids clacked to a halt as a towering cloaked figure soared from behind them, before landing deftly and striding forward like a swan across water.

'I suggest it's time we stopped this game. My Arachnoids will not lose you and I doubt your failing body could overcome them, never mind me.'

The creature removed its hood. At first, it appeared almost human, except for its yellow eyes, twisting pointed ears and the deathly white pallor of its angular face.

Discreetly, Chambers triggered the *Lectroflare* in his pocket. Although he knew his Order would never reach him in time, at least the device would record whatever exchange followed.

Then he had another idea.

He turned to face the creature, raised the Magnasword high and turned it on himself.

In an instant, the creature's eyes locked on the sword and it blinked twice.

An invisible force wrenched it from Chambers' grip, sending it flying through the air, into the creature's skeletal hands.

'I don't think it's time for you to die, Templar. Not yet, anyway.'

Chambers knew he was in trouble now. Taking his own life was the only sure way to keep his secrets safe… *and he had so many of them.* 'So who are you?'

The creature smiled, exposing tiny barbed teeth that blazed a chilling white against its thin black lips. 'But I was told Templar Knights were so well informed. Allow me to present myself then: I am *Lord Ballivan*.'

Recognition flashed in Chamber's eyes. His throat went dry. 'I've heard of you – a true scumbag so I hear. So I guess you're Morloch's new Hell Lord?'

'I am indeed his envoy on this accursed earth,' the creature replied coldly. 'And you are Alex Chambers, First Knight of the Order of the Rose. Furthermore, I'm aware you assisted John Kurnan in the killing of my predecessor: Lord Venogant. Let me assure you, I shall not share his fate.'

'Venogant would've said the same thing until Kurnan lopped his head off and he crumbled to dust. He wasn't so chatty after that.'

Lord Ballivan smiled. 'I've heard all about John Kurnan – quite a *slayer* from all accounts. Yes, I'm certain our paths will cross at some point – in fact, I welcome it. But never think to compare me to Lord Venogant. He was a fool and that is why Morloch corrected his mistake by appointing me his successor.'

Chambers knew there was no way out now. All he could do was to extract information for other Templars to benefit. 'So you can fly … you're telekinetic … what species of demon are you?'

'One unlike any your kind has seen before.'

'You'd be surprised,' Chambers replied. 'I've seen more of you scuzzballs than I care to remember. And no disrespect, but you're pretty much the ugliest of the lot.'

He nodded at the closest Arachnoid. 'And that's saying something considering the pretty boys you hang around with.'

'That doesn't interest me, Templar,' Lord Ballivan replied. 'What does, however, is an answer to a very simple question: where are the *four*?'

To most people these words wouldn't make sense, but Chambers knew exactly who Lord Ballivan referred to. 'If you think I'd tell you then you don't know me at all.'

'Perhaps not, but you will tell me that which I ask.'

'I'll tell you nothing,' Chambers replied. 'You can torture me... kill me for all I care, but I won't say a word. I promise you that.'

'We both know your death is inevitable,' Lord Ballivan said matter-of-factly. 'And I don't need to hear an admission from your mouth. You asked what species I am – well, let me enlighten you... I am a *Terroset*. And you should gaze upon me with awe...' His lips opened a fraction and his blood-red tongue inched out. Growing longer and longer, it filled the air, coiling languidly like a gigantic snake.

Frozen with revulsion, Chambers watched the tongue split down the middle and separate, the tip of each half making its way towards his eyes.

Moments later, Lord Ballivan knew all he needed to know.

- Chapter 2 -
The Most Special Boy in the World

Zak Fisher had not had a good day at school. He'd forgotten his dinner money and had to make do with half an egg bap off his mate, Jem, and two boiled sweets for lunch. He'd been given detention for sniggering when Mister Gimble's false eye fell out during a numbingly dull lesson on soil. And finally the bus that ferried him home had broken down in a fit of black smoke and fumes.

No, it had not been a particularly good day at all.

As a rule, Zak liked school. Although only fourteen, he'd attended so many, and this latest one - Saint Quentin's High School - was his favourite by miles. If nothing else, he loved the fact the school took its name from the patron saint of coughs and sneezes.

And Saint Quentin's patronage felt particularly ironic as a severe outbreak of flu currently swept the school like a forest fire. Indeed, over the last month every boy and girl in his year had been struck down with it. But not Zak. He'd never been poorly in his life - no colds, no fever, no measles, no chicken pox, not even toothache. Nothing.

His foster parents, Irene and Sidney Shufflebottom,

5

put it down to him being the most special boy in the world.

Zak just felt the unluckiest.

Once, in a bid to get out of the school sports day, he invented an ailment called Rabbit Fever, which he claimed to have caught on a trip to Colwyn Bay. Irene, however, said she'd only believe it if he grew a bobtail and started to hop.

And that wasn't the only thing that made Zak different from other kids. Although, from a distance, he looked like a normal teenager, up close his eyes were starkly different colours – the left blue, the right hazel. It was a condition called Heterochromia, and he hated it.

Jem thought it made him look cool. But Zak just thought it another in a long list of things that made him strange, a misfit… a *weirdo*.

Zak levelled the baseball cap that flattened his brown hair and turned to face the dusky November sky. After four miles of walking he could finally see the village of Addlebury.

Zak liked Addlebury. In his short life he'd lived in almost every corner of Britain, from a sheep farm in Lanarkshire to a terraced house in Derby, but this small leafy village in South Cheshire was the place he felt most at home. And being an orphan, it was a home he wanted more than anything.

A proper home.

He'd always found his circumstances rather peculiar. Every few years, for some mysterious reason, the authorities would make him change foster parents and he would live somewhere else with someone else. On some levels it had been an enjoyable way to grow up. Each foster parent taught him something new, an unusual, often dangerous skill they excelled in, something most kids his age didn't learn – like sword fighting, parkour, motocross, free climbing, obscure martial arts, even base jumping. He proved to be an incredibly fast learner, mastering each new skill in no time at all. Still, for the most part, all this moving around made him depressed. He wanted to be part of a family, and more than anything he wanted that family to be the Shufflebottoms.

They really were a lovely old couple.

Sidney Shufflebottom was undoubtedly odd. He liked chocolate éclairs and steam trains and collected bottle tops. He pulled funny faces he claimed resembled famous landmarks like Stonehenge and the Eiffel Tower. He'd been in the army, and was covered head to toe in strange scars. He would show them off proudly at every opportunity, but particularly at dinner parties with guests like Florence Potsworth, the Addlebury church warden, whose only passion in life seemed to be poking her nose into other people's business, or Virgil Bunkle, the local butcher, whose entire conversation revolved around offal. However, although Sid seemed proud of these scars he always responded vaguely when Zak asked how and where he got them.

Irene Shufflebottom was equally strange in her own way. She was a quiet, unassuming lady who loved to bake, read historical romance novels and collect brass rubbings. Zak, therefore, always found it highly amusing she was a Taekwondo expert, an exceptional clay pigeon shooter and ran the Kendo class in the Addlebury village hall on Tuesday evenings.

Passing the village post office and the pub, The Magpie Inn, Zak turned left into Halfpenny Lane and spied Fumbletree Cottage behind a line of trees. With its pointed thatched roof and ivy covered walls it looked like something from a fairy tale. As he approached, his eyes lit up as he saw Sid tending to a thick patch of flowers.

'Hi, Sid,' Zak said.

'Hello, son. You're a bit late, aren't you?'

'Bus broke down. Had to walk.'

'Fair enough. How was school?'

'Not great. I got detention again.'

'What for this time?'

'I laughed when a teacher's false eye fell out. I didn't mean to but it was just so unexpected and - '

'- They gave you detention for that?' Sid replied. 'In my day we would've nicked it and used the ruddy thing as a marble. Anyway, dunna worry... if I had a quid for every time I got detention I could afford to buy Bowen Hall.'

It was then Zak spied the strange tool in Sid's hands. 'Why are you pruning with *nail clippers*?'

'Mrs Potsworth has popped round to see Irene, and I'd rather scoop my eyes out with a spoon than spend five minutes with her. I figured I'd spend as long in the garden as I could.'

Zak laughed. He pushed open the gate and traipsed up the side path to the kitchen door. Entering, he saw Irene Shufflebottom standing at the stove, wearing a flowery apron. She held a bulging tray of Eccles cakes, her kindly face flushed red from the heat.

'Hello, Zak,' Irene said. 'I was wondering where you'd got to.'

Zak kissed her cheek. 'Sorry, Irene, the bus broke down and I had to walk.'

Then another voice cut the air like a drill. 'And you didn't think of giving your foster mother a ring? She's been beside herself with worry. I thought all of your lot had mobile phones nowadays.'

Zak turned to see Mrs Potsworth sitting at the table, her plump, puffy lips caked with sugar and currants.

'The battery died on me.' Zak held up his phone as if the sight of it would get Mrs Potsworth off his back. 'I'm really sorry, Irene.'

'That's all right, love,' Irene said, casting him a warm smile. 'At least you're home. Would you like an Eccles cake?'

Although ravenous, Zak had no intention of spending another second in the company of Mrs Potsworth. 'No, thanks. I'm just going to -'

' - Go on, boy,' Mrs Potsworth said. 'Irene's worked hard on them. You're a handsome lad, but you could do with more meat on your bones! You're as skinny as a dog hair.'

Zak forced a smile. Mrs Potsworth had a really annoying habit of giving a compliment with one hand and taking it away with the other. He glanced at Irene, who pushed the tray at him. A glorious waft of buttery pastry filled his nostrils.

'Go on, Zak,' Irene said. 'You know you want to.'

Zak took one. He wolfed it down in two bites.

'Did you enjoy that?'

'Delicious.'

'Don't mind if I have thirds, do you, Irene?' Mrs Potsworth said, taking another Eccles cake without waiting for a reply.

'Of course not, Florence,' Irene replied. 'So what have you done at school today, Zak?'

Zak wasn't about to mention his detention in front of Mrs Potsworth. 'Not much. I had -'

'- It doesn't surprise me,' Mrs Potsworth interrupted, spitting bits of Eccles cake over the floor. 'If you want my opinion education's gone to the dogs. Teenagers are studying too many useless subjects like Art and English Literature, and leaving school only to hang around street corners, shouting abuse at elderly ladies, stealing plant pots and smoking weeds. No disrespect, Zak, but far too many of you lot are simply bone-idle. What we need - and I know the do-gooder lefties would disagree with me on this – what we need is a jolly good war! Bring back the draft… send the beggars off to fight whether they want to go or not. Maybe then they'll actually be of some actual use to society.'

'Or maybe just get killed?' Zak said.

Mrs Potsworth gave a dismissive shrug. 'Then there won't be as many of the little wasters stealing my plant pots, will there?'

Irene was about to challenge Mrs Potsworth when – *BANG* - the back door crashed open. The kitchen shuddered.

A shocked silence filled the room.

Sid was standing there, his face devoid of colour. 'I – Irene. I've just had a call from John Kurnan. He'll be here in a few minutes. He's taking Zak.'

Irene dropped the tray. It landed with a deafening clatter. 'W-what? Why?'

'They've found out Zak's here,' Sid replied. 'Alex Chambers is dead. Mothmen are coming…'

- Chapter 3 -
Mothmen

Zak's head reeled. Go where? Who was John Kurnan? What were Mothmen?

'Sidney!' Mrs Potsworth glared at him as though his brain had leaked from his ears. 'What on earth are you talking about?'

Sid turned to her, grim-faced. 'Florence, you must leave. Now!'

'But I haven't finished my cup of tea,' Mrs Potsworth replied indignantly.

Zak heard a van screeching to a halt outside.

Sid barged past him, leaving the kitchen, only to return a second later. 'They're here!'

'Who's here?' Mrs Potsworth said. 'Sidney, I demand you tell me what is going on!'

Sid moved in front of her. 'Florence, I'm sorry about this, but it's for the best ... and might just save your life.' He drew back his arm and thumped her in the face.

Mrs Potsworth's eyes rolled white. She crumpled to the ground, unconscious.

Speechless, Zak stared at Mrs Potsworth. 'What have you done, Sid?' he asked, horrified.

'Her a favour, but no time to explain now,' Sid replied urgently. 'Hide in the loft, son. Don't make a sound. No matter what you hear downstairs, you *do not* come down. Irene, get the Magnaswords!'

With a nod, Irene dashed from the kitchen. A moment later, she could be heard rummaging frantically through drawers.

Zak, however, had no intention of going anywhere. 'No. Tell me -'

Before his words faded, his eyes were drawn to the kitchen window. A dozen figures in black cloaks had gathered outside, their faces masked by hoods.

Sid looked over at them. 'It's too late,' he breathed, as Irene rushed in holding what looked like two large candlesticks. She threw one to Sid who caught it.

Zak watched with astonishment as Sid's hand squeezed the object's shaft and a blade shot from its tip. Irene did the same.

Sid and Irene Shufflebottom were holding swords.

Zak's gaze flicked back to the window. Two piercing black eyes peered in at them, scanning the room, until they locked on Zak.

'The boy is here!' the Mothman leader hissed.

Simultaneously, the Mothmen cast off their cloaks.

Zak's eyes enlarged with horror. The Mothmen were simply terrifying, with grey, fibrous skin, which clung to their wiry frames. Each had sinewy wings set into their rutted spine, and their bony fingers were curled around a curved black sword.

With a thunderous clicking sound, the Mothmen's wings fluttered and they took to the air, hovering inches off the ground.

'RUN, ZAK!' Irene cried.

CRASHHH – the window exploded. Through the fog of shattered glass, the Mothman leader flew in, his sword directed at Zak's neck.

Zak watched disorientated as Sid leapt into its path.

Their swords met with a *clang*.

The Mothman leader swiped at Sid, who ducked the blade. The Mothman attacked again. This time, Sid anticipated the attack and in a swift movement ran him through.

To Zak's astonishment, the Mothman evaporated in a cloud of dust.

The kitchen door burst off its hinges and two more Mothmen flew in.

Irene raced to Sid's side, her Magnasword raised. A Mothman attacked her, but her reflexes were lightning fast. She cut him down with one blow. More dust filled the air.

Another Mothman set on Sid, who swung his Magnasword high and sliced off its head. More dust.

'Irene,' Sid yelled. 'Take Zak.'

'I'm not leaving you.'

'But there are too many of them…'

'I don't care.'

Zak watched terrified as the Mothmen attacked the old couple. Rage welled in his stomach. Looking for a weapon, he scooped up the cake tray as a Mothman hurtled towards Sid. He swung the tray, smashing the creature full in the face, sending it crashing to the floor. Then he spied a discarded sword. He dropped the tray and picked it up.

From his right, Zak glimpsed a blade targeting his chest. Without hesitating, he pivoted left, dodging the strike, turned and sank his sword into the belly of a

Mothman, who vanished to powder before his eyes.

Zak was about to join Sid and Irene when he felt fingers grasp his throat, squeezing hard, choking the life from him.

Clawing for breath, Zak's legs buckled. He fell to his knees. Then, to his astonishment, the Mothman's hands *crumbled* to dust.

Sucking air into his lungs, Zak looked up. To his astonishment, someone else had joined them in the kitchen – a handsome man with a face he found vaguely familiar stood over him.

About forty years of age, the man had cropped black hair, piercing blue eyes and a long scar on his cheek visible beneath a layer of stubble. He was holding a Magnasword, which gleamed brightly beneath the kitchen lights.

'Are you hurt, kid?' the man said.

'No.'

'Good.' The man turned back to the fight, his eyes alive with a controlled fury. Then, with astonishing speed, he tore into the remaining Mothmen like a ferocious ballet-dancer, his every movement graceful, measured and lethal. In seconds, the kitchen was filled with dust.

The Mothmen were dead.

'John.' Irene flung herself into the man's arms. 'Thank God.'

'Hello, Irene,' the man replied in a tender voice.

'John Kurnan,' Sid said in a thankful voice. 'You took yer time, didn't ya?' He extended his hand and the two men shook.

'Good to see you again, Sid,' Kurnan said.

'How is my old novice?'

'I'm well.' There was genuine warmth in Kurnan's voice. 'Aren't you a bit long in the tooth to be fighting Mothmen, old man?'

'You're never too old to squash Mozzies,' Sid replied with a grin.

Kurnan smiled back. Then his face turned grave. 'I must get Zak to Avernon at once. And you must leave. More will come. Maybe something worse than Mothmen.'

Sid nodded sadly. 'Aye. You're right.'

Zak stood there, dazed. 'What's happening? What were … those things?'

'Those things are called Mothmen, Zak,' Sid replied.

'What on earth are Mothmen?'

'They ain't from earth, that's the problem,' Sid replied. 'But this is John Kurnan. He's a good friend. He'll tell you more 'bout that later.' His voice cracked. 'You have to go with him now. He'll take you somewhere safe.'

'I don't want to go anywhere,' Zak replied. 'I want to stay with you.'

Tears were streaming down Irene's cheeks now. 'And we want that, Zak. More than anything… but you can't. I wish things could be different.'

'I – I don't understand,' Zak said.

'But you will, son … you will,' Sid replied miserably. 'Just know this … the time we have spent with you has been the very best of our lives.'

Her body trembling, Irene pulled Zak close. 'We love you so much, Zak.'

'And I love you,' Zak replied. 'Please say I don't have to go.'

'We can't,' Sid said. 'Because you do.' He moved

toward Zak and Irene, and wrapped his arms around them both.

The three of them remained in a soundless embrace until Kurnan's hand found Sid's shoulder.

'I'm sorry, Sid,' Kurnan said. 'I have to take him now. It's still dangerous.'

'I know, John,' Sid replied. 'And what about the others?'

'The Order of the Rose are rounding them up now. Hopefully we've got to them all in time.'

Zak's head was swimming. *"Hopefully we've got to them all in time?"* What did that mean?

'I'm sorry about Alex,' Sid said. 'I know you two were close.'

'He was a good knight and a better friend,' Kurnan said. 'And we can mourn him later. For now, I gotta get Zak as far away from here as I can.'

'Of course,' Sid replied.

'Look after him, John,' Irene exhaled. 'He's everything we thought he would be... everything and more.'

'I will, Irene,' Kurnan replied.

Zak fought back the tears as his eyes met Sid's. He had no idea what was going on, but he trusted his foster parents completely. 'Will I see you again?'

Sid managed a smile. 'Of course you will. One day. When the time is right.'

Irene stared at Zak, tears spilling onto her dress. 'Just remember, Zak. We will always be there for you. No matter what. You have the power to do so many things. You don't know it yet, but all will become clear. You really are the most special boy in the world...'

- Chapter 4 -
Leaving Addlebury

Zak didn't even have time to change out of his school uniform when Kurnan whisked him down the front path to a jet-black Bentley parked chaotically out front.

Walking in a daze, Zak heard Irene sobbing uncontrollably behind him. He glanced at Kurnan who kept constant vigil, clasping his Magnasword tightly, his eyes scanning the mouth of Halfpenny Lane as if danger could appear at any given moment.

As they reached the car, Irene pulled Zak back. 'Good luck, darling,' she said, struggling to keep it together. 'If you ever need us, *they* will let you contact us.'

'Who's "*they?*"' Zak asked. 'And what's this Avernon place?'

'It's somewhere Sid and I know very well. In fact, it's where I met him. You'll be safe there… you'll be guarded by the very best.'

Zak was at a loss for words. 'But why am I in danger?'

'You'll understand soon enough.'

Staring into her enflamed eyes, a deep ache filled Zak. 'Tell me I have to go, Irene. Tell me there's no other way.'

Irene took a heavy breath. 'You do. There is no other way.'

'We love you, son,' Sid said, stroking Zak's cheek with his thumb. 'Now go with John. And I'll tell Mrs Potsworth she slipped on an Eccles cake and banged her head.'

Zak forced a smile.

Kurnan looked at Sid. 'And you take Irene and get as far away from here as you can, old man. At least for a short while.'

'Aye.' Sid turned to Zak. 'And God be with you, Zak. I know he will be.'

'I'll see you soon, Sid,' Zak said. Unable to look at Sid anymore, he climbed into the car and took one last look at Fumbletree Cottage. Then he faced front, unable to bear the crippling pain of all he was about to lose.

'Take care of him, John,' Sid said. 'You know what he means to us.'

Kurnan nodded. 'I know what he means to *all* of us...'

*

For the next half hour, Zak didn't say a thing. His mind struggled to process all that had happened: Mothmen, Magnaswords, being ripped away from the closest thing he'd ever had to a home.

As he stared out of the speeding car, fragmented images crashed through his head: of Sid and Irene, of his friends at Saint Quentin's, of the happy times in Addlebury.

Why was he being taken away?

Although it didn't come naturally, Kurnan made some effort at small talk, but Zak didn't feel like joining in. For some reason, he felt this was Kurnan's fault. He knew it was unreasonable, irrational even, that if anything Kurnan had saved all their lives, but he couldn't shake that feeling. Eventually, when his frustration settled he accepted he was being unfair.

'So where are you taking me?' Zak said.

Kurnan glanced up at the grey sky to see the North Star had appeared, luring the eye like a diamond. 'We're heading to a safe-house for the night. But first thing tomorrow morning, we're driving to Avernon Monastery in Cornwall.'

'Cornwall? But that's like the other end of the country.'

'That's why we'll need food and rest.'

'And why a monastery?'

'You'll understand soon enough.'

Zak fell silent again. 'Will I see Sid and Irene again?'

'Sure. At some point you'll see all your foster parents again.'

'All my foster parents?' Zak said. You know about them?'

'I'm the one who's set you up with them, coordinated every one of your moves ever since you were a baby. I've overseen everything... making sure you were placed in the right family to teach you the necessary skills.'

'What do you mean necessary skills?'

'Special skills that you might need in later life.'

Zak felt frustrated. Each given answer presented further questions. 'But why? Why do I need *"special skills*"? What's so different about me?'

Kurnan's voice softened. 'Everything's different about you. You must know that. You must've realised you're not a normal kid. Think about it... you've never been sick, you've never cut yourself climbing a tree, you've never even bruised your shin playing football. You can outrun other kids your age, your senses are superior, you learn quicker and you possess an amazing memory. I know you've never bragged about it... if anything you've played it down - letting others beat you on school sports day, allowing bullies to pick on you rather than fight because you knew you could really hurt them if you fought back - but you are different. That's just the way it is.'

Zak swallowed hard. He wanted to contradict Kurnan, to offer a reasonable argument. But he couldn't: *Kurnan was right.*

He'd always tried to conceal the fact he was faster, smarter, stronger than his friends, always preferring to shy away from the limelight and any unwanted attention.

Zak spoke in a quiet voice, 'But why am I different?'

Kurnan shifted awkwardly on his seat. 'I'm gonna leave Pottsy to tell you about that.'

'Who's Pottsy?'

'Ichabod Potts. He's Chief Knight at Avernon. He's got a better way of putting things than I have.'

'So are you a monk?'

Kurnan laughed. 'Far from it.'

'Are you in the army? Is that how you know Sid?'

'Not an army you're familiar with.'

'Then what kind of army?'

'Let's get to the safe-house, and then I'll tell you

about me, about my world... about *your* world.'

*

As darkness descended, the lush green countryside morphed into wide stretches of scrubland, barren and hostile. The lamp-lit roads gave way to dark, dusty trails as they climbed in altitude to a misty mountain range, many miles from civilisation.

Throughout, Zak remained silent, pondering the many questions he would ask when the opportunity arose: How were Sid and Irene involved in all of this? What were Magnaswords? Where did Mothmen come from? What did Kurnan mean by *"your"* world?

Through the heavy mist, Zak spied an ancient structure ahead, framed by a huge mountain to its rear. Fashioned from grey stone, the church's ornate exterior was dominated by flying buttresses, a pyramidal spire on a south-facing tower and stained glass windows, their colours brightened from the light within.

'This is Saint Catherine's Chapel,' Kurnan said. 'It's as good a place to stay the night as anywhere.'

As Kurnan pulled the car to a halt, an old man wearing a cassock and surplice emerged from the front door. Most of his face was hidden behind an unruly silver beard and his fingers were clenched around a large cross that hung from his neck.

Kurnan climbed out of the car, quickly followed by Zak.

With long strides, Kurnan approached the priest. 'Evening, Father Edward.'

To Zak's surprise, Father Edward was trembling from head to toe; not once did he make eye contact with Kurnan. Instead, his eyes were locked on Zak.

'G-good to see you again, John,' Father Edward

replied nervously.

'You ain't seen me once yet,' Kurnan replied. 'I'm over here.'

Father Edward snapped from his trance and looked at Kurnan. 'I am sorry.'

'No sweat. Anyway, thanks for letting us stay. I promise we won't be a burden and we'll be gone first thing in the morning.'

Unconsciously, Father Edward's eyes returned to Zak. 'I-it's an honour,' he stammered. 'An absolute honour.'

'Zak, this is Father Edward Flaherty,' Kurnan said. 'He's a bit of an oddball, but bearable most of the time. Me and him go back a long way.'

Zak smiled at Father Edward. 'Hi.'

'Father Edward,' Kurnan said. 'This is Zak Fisher.'

Leaning forward, Zak went to shake the priest's hand, but as he did the most unexpected thing happened.

Father Edward sank to his knees and began to sob. 'I-it's a miracle,' he blubbered. 'A true miracle...'

- Chapter 5 -
The Knight at Night

'Now, now, Father,' Kurnan said irritably, heaving the priest to his feet. 'We don't want any of that. You'll make Zak feel uncomfortable.'

'I'm sorry,' Father Edward replied. 'It's just – it's just I've never seen an -'

Kurnan interrupted before he could finish his sentence. '- I know, but keep it to yourself, eh? Zak's had a crappy day and the last thing he needs is any fuss. If you could just show us where we're gonna sleep that'll be fine.'

'Of course,' Father Edward said. 'I apologise, Zak. I don't know what came over me.'

'Err, that's okay,' Zak said.

But in reality it was far from okay. Frustration welled inside him. Why did Father Edward react like that? What was a miracle?

Father Edward opened the door. 'Please, follow me...'

Stepping inside, Zak had never seen anywhere quite like it. The hazy glow of candlelight illuminated walls and pillars that were covered top to bottom in strange and unusual carvings - of crosses, sword wielding knights, angels, dragons and hundreds of other symbols he'd never seen before.

Father Edward noted the astonishment on Zak's face. 'It's a remarkable place, isn't it?' he said, pride in his voice. 'Saint Catherine's Chapel is over seven hundred years old and has barely changed in all that time.'

'What do the symbols mean?' Zak said.

Father Edward glanced at Kurnan, who gave an almost imperceptible shake of his head, making it clear certain matters should not be discussed.

'They mean many things,' Father Edward replied. 'And many of them to this day have yet to be accurately deciphered. Actually, it's the blend of symbology, religious, folkloric and cultural, I find particularly interesting. In terms of their origins, we have Moorish, Christian, Atenistic, Pagan, Norse, Islamic, Mithraist, even Roman. I've spent a lifetime studying them and shall never come close to unravelling all of their secrets.'

Zak's eyes were drawn to a statue of a medieval knight; flawlessly sculpted in white marble, the knight wore a helmet, chain mail, and a tunic and cape both adorned with a large cross. The knight's head was bowed downward as if in prayer, his hand clasping a tear-shaped shield with what looked like a brilliant sun carved into its centre.

Zak walked over and stopped to study it.

'The Effigy of the Lost Knight,' Father Edward said, appearing at Zak's shoulder. 'It's a beautiful sculpture, isn't it?'

'It is,' Zak agreed. 'Who is he?'

'No one knows,' Father Edward replied. 'But it's dated at 1304AD, which is around the time Saint

Catherine's was built. I like to think he was the first object placed in the chapel and that he guards it at all times.'

Zak's gaze found the statue's base where he saw a stone plaque bearing the words: *Facilis Descensus Averno – Virgil*.

Zak searched his memory. 'Virgil was a poet, wasn't he?' he said. 'A Roman poet.'

'Very good, Zak. He was indeed a poet, perhaps Rome's finest.'

'What do the words mean?'

'The descent to Hell is easy,' Father Edward replied simply. 'And truer words were never written. It's choosing the more difficult path to Heaven that takes courage and effort.'

Zak was led through a wide arch and down a central aisle passing a few dozen wooden pews that looked like they hadn't been used in forever.

'Father Edward,' Zak said. 'How far is the nearest town or village?'

'That would be the hamlet of Fledgwick. It's about ten miles away.'

'Then do people actually come here?'

'Not really,' Father Edward replied glumly. 'In fact, not at all. I always think it's a wonder I haven't gone stir crazy with all the time I spend on my own. Come to think of it, perhaps I have.'

'So how can you afford to keep it going - pay the bills and stuff?'

'Money's not exactly an issue,' Father Edward said.

'Why not?'

Father Edward looked awkwardly at Kurnan, who knew it was his turn to say something.

'Because Saint Catherine's and many others like it are bankrolled by another organisation,' Kurnan said. 'My organisation. And we're rich.'

Zak was intrigued now. 'What organisation?'

'The one we'll be talking about later.'

Kurnan said these words in such a way it was clear he had no intention to having this conversation now.

Father Edward turned, picked up a candelabrum from a side table and approached a stone door to the right of a lead font, adorned like everything else with bizarre markings. He opened the door and they all walked back outside into the biting cold.

Scanning the grounds, Zak saw endless rows of gravestones, age-old and weather-beaten, beyond which a ramshackle stone cottage merged into a mountain behind. Streams of silvery smoke spiralled upward from its chimney.

Father Edward directed the candelabrum at a mossy path ahead and said, 'This way.' Within seconds, they had entered the cottage.

Inside, Zak was taken aback at how homely everything was. Large vases filled with flowers of periwinkle blue sent a honeyed fragrance all around.

They passed through a narrow hallway lined with oil canvases depicting biblical scenes and, rather surprisingly, crudely painted pictures of a fridge and a sandwich toaster. Zak suspected these had been painted either by a very young child or a very drunk Father Edward in one of his stir-crazy moments. He favoured the latter.

'I'm afraid there are only two bedrooms,' Father Edward said, 'so you'll have to share.'

'That's fine,' Kurnan replied.

'Good,' Father Edward said. 'I've been slaving away in the kitchen since you rang, John, so I do hope you're both hungry.'

'It's safe to say *we* are.'

But Zak had stopped feeling hungry some time ago. The only hunger he felt was for answers, and he knew they wouldn't be forthcoming until John Kurnan was good and ready. There was no doubt about that.

*

Dinner was a pleasant affair, and Zak found himself warming to Father Edward a great deal. Although an excellent cook, the old priest was certainly very odd. He had a somewhat unusual obsession with household appliances and spent the main course regaling Zak with his knowledge of vacuum cleaners. However, although Zak enjoyed the evening he was desperate to retire so he could talk to Kurnan.

It was nearing ten when Zak and Kurnan went to bed. Their room was small with a low beamed ceiling, a mahogany writing bureau placed upon which was a leather bound bible, and two single beds, each with a bath towel folded neatly on a single pillow.

Kurnan had brought a silver goblet and a half a bottle of wine with him, and Zak couldn't help but wonder if he needed the drink to help him through the impending conversation.

Kurnan looped his long black coat over the door hook and removed his holstered Magnasword, sliding it beneath his pillow. Then he filled the goblet and sat down. 'Okay, Zak,' he said. 'I suppose it's time you knew a few things. Have you heard of the Knights Templar?'

Zak's eyes widened. 'Are you a Templar?'

'Yes,' Kurnan replied. 'Now just how much do you know about the Templars?'

Zak searched his mind. Immediately, he remembered his history classes at Saint Quentin's. His teacher, Mister Wilbert, a man many thought had picked the wrong profession because of his indisputably square head and terrible stutter, had been obsessed with the subject and would, on countless occasions, dismiss the required syllabus and talk for hours about the Templars.

'I know quite a bit. The crusades and all that stuff. I had a teacher who was crazy about the subject.'

'Yeah, well whatever you think you know about the Templars is mostly wrong.'

'Err, okay,' Zak replied. 'So they weren't involved in the crusades?'

'I guess they were,' Kurnan replied. 'But not quite as the history books tell it. You see, the popular myth, the one your teacher knows all about, the one in those history books, states a French nobleman, Hugues de Payens, formed the Knights Templar in 1119AD, shortly after the First Crusade to protect pilgrims visiting the Holy Land. Now that did happen, but the reality is the Knights Templar were set up over two thousand years before then… in Israel, around the time of King Saul.'

'You're saying they've been around for three thousand years?'

'Yeah,' Kurnan replied. 'As an organisation we predate the Iron Age.'

Zak was flabbergasted. 'And why doesn't anyone know this? Why do all the history books say they started in medieval times?'

'Because that's exactly what we wanted everyone to think. Hugues de Payens was a high-ranking Templar, and it was his job to propagate the myth the Templars started then and were merely defenders of the Christian faith. He did a pretty bang up job, actually.'

'But why?'

'Because it was considered essential to hide the Templar's true purpose from the world.'

'What purpose?'

'We were protectors, but it had nothing to do with just protecting any single faith – it was to do with protecting the Earth.'

'From what?'

Struggling to find the words, Kurnan sat back, drained his cup and said in a slow, steady voice, '*Hell exists....*'

Zak's mouth fell open.

'Not the Hell as most people know it,' Kurnan continued. 'Not a place with fire and brimstone where bad people go when they've kicked the bucket – that might exist, I don't know – but what I'm talking about is a Hell that's as real as Earth, a Hell that exists in an alternate dimension, an actual world that operates alongside our own.'

'Like a parallel universe?'

'That's right,' Kurnan replied. 'And there are portals … they're called *Stargates*, that means we can get there, and Hell Demons or *Hellians* – well, they can get here.'

Zak's forehead creased. 'You are kidding me?'

'Where do you think Mothmen come from - Blackpool?'

Zak couldn't find a reply.

'Like Earth,' Kurnan continued, 'Hell is inhabited with all kinds of creatures, the good and the bad. As a matter of fact, for thousands of years Hell and Earth existed together in harmony. And to be fair, back then some of them were much more advanced than we were. It was because of the Hellians we acquired all kinds of knowledge, about every aspect of society - construction, astronomy, science, mathematics, medicine. We were still coming out of the caves and they were building machines.'

'Really?'

'Yeah. In fact, some of the most famous human achievements were created using their technology and expertise.'

'Like what?' Zak asked.

Kurnan thought for a moment. 'The Great Pyramids at Giza.'

Zak looked shocked.

'You didn't think humans did that without help, did you?'

'I never thought about it,' Zak replied. 'What else?'

'The Puma Punku stones at Tiwanaku; The Megalithic Temples at Malta; The Trilithon at Baalbek... and loads more.'

'Stonehenge?'

'Nah. That was summat different. But let's face it, it's not like mankind hasn't been left major clues we'd been getting help from someone not from these parts.'

'What kind of clues?'

'You must've seen the ancient Egyptian hieroglyphs depicting flying aircraft found at the Temple of Seti I on YouTube? The Abydos Helicopter has got like a million hits or something. I thought that's how teenagers spent most of their time nowadays when they should be outside playing footie?'

'I don't go on YouTube much.'

'Good for you,' Kurnan replied. 'Anyway, it's because of findings like the Abydos Helicopter that some people generated all kinds of Ancient Alien theories and broadcast them all over the net. When I say "people" I mean fluffy bearded nerds, mostly -'

'*Ancient Alien Theories*?'

'Yeah, the idea that thousands of years ago earth was once visited by aliens, and they helped advance humanity – well the reality is those nerds got it right. Luckily, the truth about the Templars and the existence of the actual Hell has never got out. Thank God.'

Zak took a few seconds to process all of it. 'This is amazing. I mean, really mind-blowing.'

'I guess.'

'So what happened?'

'With what?'

'You said Hell and Earth coexisted in harmony – why'd that come to an end?'

'Just over three thousand years ago there was a great war in Hell,' Kurnan said. 'It tore their world apart. The honourable powers that once ruled were defeated and replaced by a dark power, a real evil bunch headed by a creature called *Gilliath*, the first Hell King. Gilliath didn't see Earth as a neighbour … he saw it as a feasting ground and a place to be pillaged. And that's when mankind decided to fight back. And therein lays the true origins of the Knights Templar. That's why we were formed – to fight back against Gilliath and his cronies. The first thing these early Templars did was destroy the Stargates … and they did, but some still exist. And although Gilliath was killed in a –'

He stopped himself as if he had something more to say but wasn't quite ready to say it.

'- in battle,' he continued. 'Hell has been ruled by a series of Hell Kings each worse than the next. The one at the moment – his name's Morloch – well, he's as bad as there's ever been.'

Zak paused again. 'And Sid and Irene were Templars?'

'Yeah. Sid was a First Knight of the Order of the Rose – my Order - and he was my mentor when I was a novice. There are dozens of Orders across the world, not to mention those stationed on Hell.'

'And what about Father Edward?'

'Does he look like a Templar Knight?'

Zak laughed. 'Not really.'

'That's because he isn't. The Templars have all kinds of help from civilians.' Kurnan sighed heavily. 'Unfortunately, so do the other side.'

Zak looked shocked. 'Who on earth would help them?'

'You'd be surprised. But that's another story for another day.'

'So … what have I got to do with all this? The Mothmen were after me. How am I involved?'

'That's the one question I won't answer, I'm afraid. That's what Pottsy will discuss with you tomorrow. He wants you *all* there when he explains it.'

Zak's ears pricked up. 'What do you mean "all"?'

Kurnan gave a heavy sigh. 'You're not the only kid in this situation. And that's all I'm gonna say.'

And with that he made it clear the time for questions had ended.

- Chapter 6 -
The Hellfire Club

Dawn had barely broken when Zak woke with a start. For the briefest of moments, he thought he was back in Fumbletree Cottage until the revelations of the day before crashed over him. In the last twenty-four hours the life he knew had gone forever, replaced by one that barely made sense, even after all he'd seen.

He turned over to see Kurnan's bed empty, his coat gone. Judging by the state of the sheets and the fact his towel was still folded on the pillow, Zak wasn't certain Kurnan had slept at all.

Zak climbed out of bed and put on his clothes, wishing he had something other than his school uniform to wear. Kurnan had promised him new ones when they arrived at Avernon.

Barely able to contemplate what the day had in store, he left the room and descended the stairs. Reaching the bottom step, he heard low voices coming from the kitchen.

'I don't wanna talk about it,' Kurnan said.

'But you need to talk about it, John,' Father Edward

pressed. 'I mean, seeing Zak, spending time with him might open some of those old wounds... and you don't want that.'

'I don't *need* to do anything,' Kurnan growled. 'I know you mean well, Father, but just keep outta this. This ain't none of your business.'

'But I can't keep out of it, John,' Father Edward replied. 'How could I? I remember what you were like. I remember what happened at Benidan Towers, and I know what it did to you... to your soul.'

'I know you know, Father,' Kurnan snapped back. 'And I appreciate all you did. But it won't happen again. I'm fine. Nothing like that's gonna happen again.'

A floorboard creaked under Zak's foot.

In a single lightning fast movement, Kurnan drew his Magnasword and squeezed its grip. By the time the blade had extended, Kurnan was in a full battle stance. His eyes locked on Zak like lasers.

'Err, sorry,' Zak said, 'it's just me.'

Embarrassed, Kurnan lowered the Magnasword. 'I thought you were an intruder.'

'Yeah. I can see that,' Zak said.

Father Edward stepped into the hallway. He was wearing a tartan dressing gown, pink pyjamas and had a hairnet looped over his beard. 'Good morning, Zak.'

'Morning,' Zak said. 'I'm sorry. I didn't mean to interrupt. I wasn't earwigging or anything.'

'Of course you weren't,' Father Edward replied.

'You ain't interrupted a thing,' Kurnan said. 'Now are you ready to get going? We've gotta long journey ahead of us.'

'Sure,' Zak replied. 'Thanks for letting me stay, Father Edward.'

'Not at all. It's been my pleasure, Zak. I've packed some cheese sandwiches for your journey, which I pray is an untroubled one.'

'Thank you,' Zak said.

'Let's go then.' Kurnan moved toward the front door. He turned to Father Edward, his expression mellowing. 'Thanks again, Father. Much appreciated.'

Compassion lined Father Edward's face. 'You're welcome here anytime, John. I hope you know that.' He smiled at Zak. 'And you too, Zak.'

'Cheers,' Zak said. 'Thanks for everything.'

'The honour has truly been mine,' Father Edward said. Then he gave a deep bow. 'Good luck, Zak Fisher... with all that follows.'

Zak wasn't exactly sure what he meant by this, but wasn't about to question further. After all, he'd grown quite used to understanding only *some* of what people said to him nowadays.

*

A muted sun peeked over the mountains as the Bentley powered away.

Zak glanced back and watched the tiny chapel fade into the distance, before sitting forward and staring at the road ahead. The previous day had been so life-changing he couldn't help but wonder what astonishing revelations this one had in store.

As the minutes passed, it became clear Kurnan had no intention of addressing any of it. In fact, he seemed more than happy to maintain his silence for the entire journey.

Zak, however, wasn't about to let that happen. 'Mister Kurnan?'

'It's just Kurnan.'

'Kurnan, you said last night some civilians help the Hell King… you said it was a story for another today. Today's another day.'

For the first time since the altercation with Father Edward, a smile curled on Kurnan's mouth. 'Why? Because Morloch's stinkin' rich. On Hell, gold is more common than here – there's even a region we call The Gilded Peaks, a mountain range where gold is literally everywhere… thick streams of it. And the fact is, plenty of humans would willingly sell their mothers for the right price, so Morloch has no problem recruiting his little helpers. We call the humans that help him *'Assists'*, and sadly some of them have risen to positions of great influence in our world. In fact, the sleazeballs have infiltrated every part of society: governments, the armed forces, businesses, banks, even the media.'

'That's bad. Really bad.'

'It ain't great,' Kurnan replied. 'And the Assists are given their orders by an organisation made up of some of the top human scumbags to have ever goose-stepped the earth… they're known as *The Hellfire Club*.'

Zak searched his memory. 'I've heard of the Hellfire Club.'

'Yeah, well whatever you think you know isn't true. Like the Templars, the Hellfire Club created their own myth about how and when they started. Most people believe they were formed in the 18th Century as a kind of extreme Gentlemen's club, but the reality is they were formed five hundred years ago to aid Hell demons on earth.'

'Help them how?'

'Originally their main function was to find safe houses on earth for the Hellians – let's face it most of them don't look like your average earth dweller, but recently their mandate has changed a bit.'

'How's it changed?'

'Because now they're putting things in place to pave the way for Morloch's arrival on Earth.'

A chill scaled Zak's spine. 'His arrival?'

'Yeah,' Kurnan replied. 'He's coming... and soon. He wants the earth for himself, you see. And the way things are goin' he's gonna get it. The Hellfire Club are intent on makin' that happen.'

'But if the Templars know about the Hellfire Club then why don't you just stop them?'

'We don't know all of its members. They're a shadowy bunch of creeps at the best of times. Furthermore, to expose them we'd have to expose ourselves. We'd have to reveal to the world that Hell exists, and the war between us and Morloch is very real.'

'But that's a good thing, right?' Zak said. 'I mean, then more people would join you. Surely, as a planet, we can defend ourselves?'

Kurnan shook his head. 'The war needs to remain an underground one. At least for now.'

'But why? People should know.'

'I used to think that,' Kurnan replied. 'But in order to understand why we can't make the war public, you have to understand the different species of demon that Morloch's got on his side. Not all of them are like Mothmen...'

When Zak looked puzzled, Kurnan continued, 'Mothmen only have one form... butt ugly and scary as hell. They're obviously not of this world. However, some species are different – some even look quite human. There's even one that has the ability to transform its appearance at will.'

Immediately, Zak thoughts turned to his dentist, Dr Alexander *'The Butcher'* Kutchner, a man who fitted the demon as human theory perfectly.

'Really?' Zak said, aghast.

'Yeah,' Kurnan replied grimly. 'They're called *Morpheans* but we call them *Shapers*. They're rare. We haven't seen one for over fifty years, in fact we think they're extinct, but they did exist. And it was the very existence of creatures like Morpheans that made the Templars keep the war with Hell secret from the rest of the world. Just imagine if Joe-public heard there are demons out there that can appear human - well, just think of the chaos. Suddenly, anyone that did anything bad or who was a bit different would be accused of being one - the annoying neighbour, the teacher that sets too much homework. Before you know it we'd turn on ourselves – *total anarchy*. And that would suit Morloch just fine. He'd just enter our world after we've slaughtered each other and take what's left.'

'So what other species are there?'

'There are Aqualids, Reptilaks, Strimmers, Molaks, Secters, Terraxors, Serpans, Arachnoids… and loads more. But all species answer to one creature, Morloch's right hand man on earth: *The Hell Lord*.'

'The Hell Lord?'

'That's what they call him. And recently there's been a new one. We've only just found out about him. His name's Lord Ballivan, and from what little we know about him from a very reliable source is he's amongst the worst we've ever had to face … and believe me that's saying something.'

Zak sat back. The one question he was most

desperate to ask was the one he felt certain wouldn't gain an answer. 'But what's any of this got to do with me?'

Kurnan's eyes stared fixedly on the road ahead. 'That's summat I'm leaving for Pottsy to tell you about. He's better at that sort've thing than me.'

'Then will you tell me about the other kids?' Zak asked. 'You said I wasn't the only one in this situation.'

'No,' Kurnan replied. 'You ain't. And all I can say about them is that you'll get to meet them soon enough.' His mouth pressed into a hard line. 'That's if they're all still alive...'

- Chapter 7 -
The End of the Road

Although Zak had countless more questions, there was something about Kurnan's expression that suggested he'd already done more talking in the last twenty-four hours than in the last year.

Zak decided to leave him alone for now.

It was almost midday when they crossed the Devonshire border into Cornwall. Zak had only visited Cornwall once before but remembered being impressed by its rolling countryside, desolate moors, rugged cliffs and unforgiving shoreline.

After about an hour, it struck him there had been no signs of civilisation for some time - no towns or villages, no traffic or people.

'So how far are we away from Avernon?' Zak asked.

'Not far,' Kurnan replied. 'All this land is owned by the Templars.'

'Really?' Zak scanned the area. Looking at the granite tors, the marshes, and the flat grassland stippled with yellow gorse and heather, he didn't see anything that suggested anyone owned it at all. 'You haven't done much with it, have you?'

'What d'ya suggest we'd do with it - build a theme park?'

A tall, electrified fence appeared on the horizon. Capped with thick coils of barbed wire, it extended for miles like the boundary of an open prison.

'That's a lot of security for a monastery,' Zak said.

'Oh, this isn't for Avernon – that's still a distance away.'

'What's it for then?'

'We don't want your average rambler witnessing our comings and goings.'

'What do you mean?'

'You'll see…'

Kurnan pulled the Bentley to a halt before a tall gate. All at once, green and blue laser beams shot out from a tiny metallic box above, probing every inch of the car. A light bulb above the box flashed green and the gate opened.

Kurnan kicked the Bentley into life again and they set off along a flat path that tapered into the distance.

'So why again am I going to a monastery?' Zak asked.

'Actually, Avernon hasn't been a monastery for a very long time, that's just a cover story for the outside world.'

'What is it then?'

'It's an Academy - a place to train Templar novices.'

'You mean a school?' Zak said, surprised.

'I guess. But we transferred the kids and most of the staff to Perigorn Castle in Wales about six months ago, to prepare for –' Kurnan hesitated.

'Prepare for what?'

'Well… *you*,' Kurnan replied. 'And the others.'

But Zak had had enough. 'Listen, you'd better start telling me –'

A loud bleep cut him down. A scarlet light blinked madly on the dashboard.

'Damn!' Kurnan growled under his breath.

'What's happening?' Zak asked. 'What is it?'

Kurnan didn't answer. His eyes had locked on the wing mirror.

His heart in his mouth, Zak whipped round. In the distance, he saw a flock of birds spiralling in formation. 'What's going on?'

Kurnan slammed his foot on the accelerator. 'We've got company.'

The Bentley shot off like a bullet.

'What company?' Zak shouted over the engine.

Kurnan ignored him. 'Pass me what's under your seat.'

Bewildered, Zak reached down. For a moment, his hands clutched at nothing, before his fingers curled round a tubular object. He gasped as he pulled it into the light. It was a futuristic looking pistol with a circular magazine stocked with short metal arrows.

Zak glowered at Kurnan and repeated, 'WHAT COMPANY?'

'*Grippers*!' Kurnan said bluntly.

Zak looked back again. To his horror, it wasn't a flock of birds at all. Instead, twenty gigantic creatures were soaring toward them. With huge wings set into their feathered torsos, the Grippers had muscular limbs, with oversized hands and feet tipped with sickle-like talons; their heads were dominated by elongated beaks and dull, black eyes.

Zak thrust the arrow gun into Kurnan's hand as a

pair of claws tore through the canvas roof.

Kurnan didn't hesitate. Pointing the arrow gun upward, he fired.

Zak heard a shriek and found himself covered in dust. Glancing up, he saw more Grippers circling above them, their hideous screeches drowning out the engine's roar.

Another Gripper swooped down.

Kurnan swung the Bentley a sharp right, at the same time raising the gun to his left and taking aim. He fired again. This time, the arrow missed Zak's face by an inch as it shattered the passenger window and pierced the Gripper's skull. In a dust cloud, it evaporated.

'I hear you're good at clay pigeon shooting.' Kurnan spun the wheel left, before throwing the gun to Zak, who caught it. 'Imagine they're bloody big pigeons!'

Three more Grippers attacked.

Zak fired the arrow gun once … twice … three times.

Each time, his arrow hit its mark.

As more Grippers swooped down, Zak heard Kurnan say in a thankful voice, 'Hello, boys and girls!'

Zak whipped his head forward. Ahead, he saw five Bentleys parked against the road, beside which were a succession of men and women, each dressed in an identical black coat to Kurnan, each clasping an arrow rifle.

Templars.

The next instant, arrows fogged the air. A moment later, frenzied screams echoed as the remaining Grippers dissolved to dust.

Speeding past the blockade to safety, Zak gave a relieved sigh. He was, however, surprised to see Kurnan had no intention of decelerating. If anything, they were gaining pace.

'The attack's over,' Zak said. 'Aren't you going to slow down?'

'Can't,' Kurnan replied. 'We need a good run up.'

'A run up to what?' Intrigued, Zak stared at the road ahead. To his dismay, it appeared to just stop. Panic filled him. They were approaching a high cliff, hundreds of feet above the rough seas below. 'WHAT ARE YOU DOING?'

'Avernon isn't on the mainland,' Kurnan said simply. He leaned over and pressed a button on his steering wheel.

Instantly, Zak felt his seatbelt tighten even further, cutting into his shoulder blade, pinning him to the seat.

Kurnan forced the Bentley to maximum speed. 'You might wanna close your eyes...'

And with that, he drove them over the cliff's edge.

- Chapter 8 -
The Freak Club

His face pummelled by the wind, Zak couldn't breathe. Blurred colours and shapes passed before his eyes, but nothing would focus, not even the rapidly approaching ocean.

Zak knew they were dead. The water would smash them to pieces in a heartbeat.

As he braced for impact, he glanced at Kurnan, but saw no semblance of fear on his face as he calmly flicked a green switch on the dashboard.

Immediately, the car's undercarriage churned, angling the car forward. Strange whirring sounds came from the chassis.

And then an amazing thing happened.

The instant before metal struck water, a great power surge launched them forward, like the sudden rush of an aeroplane on take-off.

Zak felt a hefty jolt. His seatbelt threatened to sever his shoulder.

But they didn't crash into the water. Instead, the Bentley was suddenly skimming the ocean lightly like a speedboat.

Relief flooding him, Zak looked at Kurnan, who wore a mischievous grin.

'That was fun, eh?' Kurnan said.

'What kind of car is this?' Zak gasped.

'It's an Aquacar,' Kurnan said. 'Great gadget, eh? It's pure James Bond.' He chuckled. 'You should've seen your face.'

But Zak didn't find it funny at all. 'And you didn't think of warning me?'

'That would've ruined the surprise. We don't usually do the cliff drop anymore in case we're spotted – there's an underwater tunnel that connects the mainland to Avernon so we normally take that - but I figured I'd make it a trip to remember.'

'And you didn't think a Gripper attack had already done that?'

'I wasn't planning on that. Anyway, why don't you just sit back and enjoy the view? I mean… we've even got a chaperone.' He nodded to his right.

Zak looked over. A dolphin leapt in and out of the water beside them. Straightaway, his anger faded. As a smile settled on his mouth, he inhaled deeply and let the salt air fill his lungs. 'So where did you get an Aquacar?'

'We have our sources,' Kurnan replied. 'Plus, we have some of the world's best scientists, engineers, architects and inventors on our payroll. In actual fact, the Aquacar was invented by a friend of the Templars and the best inventor in the country: Percy Halifax. You might even know him… he's a mate of Sid's and lives in a big house near Addlebury, Bowen Hall.'

'I've heard Sid mention him,' Zak said. 'But I've never met him.'

As the words left his mouth, he froze. In the distance, rising out of the water like a tiered wedding cake was a large island. On its southwest corner, atop a sheer granite cliff stood an imposing stone structure, as ancient as time, *Avernon Monastery.*

Kurnan steered them toward a crescent shaped alcove, where a submerged wooden ramp emerged from the water, crossing the beach and vanishing into a large cave.

Zak sat enthralled as the car connected with the ramp, drove over the sand and entered a tunnel lit by thin strip lights. Seconds later, they emerged into a subterranean car park with dozens of bays, both empty and occupied by other Aquacars.

Kurnan pulled into a bay and switched off the engine. 'Here we are,' he said. He switched off the engine and got out.

As Zak did the same he heard the clatter of heavy footsteps echo from his right.

'Looks like someone's eager to meet you,' Kurnan said.

Zak turned and saw a short round man emerge into the light. He was old with a bearded face and wore an impressive snow-white robe with a scarlet cross in its centre. He would have looked quite regal, except for a novelty baseball cap that sat crookedly on his head with a stuffed cigar protruding from its crown, below which were the words, '*Don't mess wit da BOSS!*'

The moment the old man saw Zak his face split with a smile.

'GREETINGS!' he roared in a strong Welsh accent. He skipped over with the lightness of a much younger man and gave a deep bow. 'Please, Zak, let me introduce myself – I'm Ichabod Potts, but feel free to call me Pottsy, and I should formally like to welcome you once again to Avernon Monastery.'

The words struck a chord with Zak.

'Hello, Mister Potts,' he said. 'What do you mean *again*?'

'You came here as a baby. Actually, you weren't even a baby. Your mother came here when you were growing inside her.'

Zak was stunned to silence. He'd never known anything about his mother. 'S-she did?' he stuttered.

'Yes. And you'll find out about that soon enough.'

But Zak had no intention of waiting. 'I'd like to find out now, please.'

'Let's get you settled in first,' Pottsy replied. 'After that, I'll tell you all I know. I trust Kurnan has mentioned you're not the only new arrival at Avernon.'

Zak gave a distracted nod. 'Yeah.'

'And how are the others?' Kurnan asked.

'They're here and they're safe,' Pottsy replied. 'The Mothmen attack at Addlebury and your Gripper encounter were the only ones we've had. Now, what say we get you out of that school uniform, Zak, and settled into your room?' He wheeled round and approached the stairwell.

Zak and Kurnan followed close behind. They negotiated a set of spiralling stone steps, barely wider than their shoulders, and reached a heavy oak door, which Pottsy pushed open with a loud creak.

A moment later, Zak found himself in a magnificent cloister bolstered by dozens of archways, which flanked a rectangular grass lawn with a towering statue of a Templar Knight in its centre. A high wall extended into the distance, bordering the many buildings within the complex, including dormitories, a stone chapel, a Chapter House, a Fraterhouse, and many other buildings of various types. Templar Knights, both male and female, their long coats bulging from concealed weapons, patrolled the high walls, which were dotted with sentry boxes at fifty-metre intervals.

Zak took it all in. 'It's like an open prison.'

Kurnan laughed. 'That's one way of lookin' at it. We prefer to think of it as a fortress. It might look pretty lo-fi but trust me it boasts some of the most advanced security systems on the market and a few that ain't even there yet. I promise you, kid, your welfare is our priority and we ain't taking that for granted. You'll be safe here.'

With Pottsy leading the way, they traversed an arched footpath and entered a two-story building Zak assumed was a dormitory. Once inside, they walked down a dimly lit corridor lined with doors on either side.

Pottsy approached a door, secured to which was an engraved bronze plaque that read: **Zak Fisher**. 'I think this should suit your needs. Now I'm going to leave you to gather your thoughts, get changed and have a bite to eat. I'll be down to collect you soon for that chat.'

Zak nodded. 'Okay.'

Kurnan placed his hand gently on Zak's shoulder. 'I know this is all a lot to take in, kid. But if you ever need to talk I hope you'll turn to me. I'll answer whatever question you've got. You see, I'm gonna be your mentor from now on. Is that okay with you, kid?'

'Yes, Mister Kurnan.'

Kurnan smiled warmly. 'It's still just Kurnan.'

As Kurnan and Pottsy walked away, Zak opened the door. Stepping inside, his eyes widened. It was identical to his room at Fumbletree Cottage – his Liverpool FC poster was there, his books, films, even his television and games console... everything. Astonished, he walked over to the wardrobe. He opened it to see all his clothes hanging beside ones he didn't recognise: a black hooded rain poncho, a ceremonial Templar robe, and an assortment of T shirts and sweatshirts in various colours, all of them sporting the Templar symbol – the scarlet cross pattée within a white circle – on the left breast. He also found a map of the buildings and grounds in his dressing table drawer.

Changing into a pair of jeans and shirt, he washed in the sink in the corner of his room, sat down on the bed, picked up the plate of sandwiches left on the side table and began to eat. The moment he'd swallowed his last mouthful, a knock rattled the door. Before he had the chance to respond it opened and a tall, athletic black teenager entered.

'Hey up, mate,' the boy said. 'Glad you finally made it.'

'Err, hi,' Zak replied.

'You've got naff taste in footie teams, haven't ya? Liverpool – they're rubbish! I'm a Stoke fan, myself. Anyway, I'm Andrew Duncan, but everyone calls me Dunk.'

'I'm Zak... Zak Fisher.'

'I know. Read it on your door. I'm clever like that.' Dunk grinned.

'Oh, right.'

Dunk studied Zak's face and gave a satisfied nod. 'Yep. You've got it, too.'

'Got what?' Zak replied.

'The crazy eyes.' Dunk pointed at his own eyes.

'One blue, one brown. Looks like that makes something else we've all got in common.'

It was then Zak saw Dunk wasn't alone. Standing in the corridor were two girls. One was short and petite with dark brown shoulder length hair and olive skin; the other was of mixed race, tall, pretty and wore rather too much make up.

The tall girl marched in. 'Hi. I'm Leah Emerson. Do you know anything about what's going on? I mean, has anyone told you why we're here?'

'No,' Zak replied honestly.

'Damn,' Leah said. 'You were our last hope.'

Dunk leaned sideways and nodded at the other girl. 'Come in, Sar.'

Sheepishly, the brunette girl walked in. Her eyes found Zak's and she said in a quiet voice, 'Hello. I'm Sarah Miller.'

'Hi… Zak Fisher.'

'Sarah's a bit shy at first,' Dunk said. 'She's sound though, ain't you, Sar?'

'Thanks, Dunk,' Sarah replied.

'And she's clever,' Dunk added. 'You wanna see her room. It's got books from floor to ceiling. And it's not a pose, either. She's actually read them.'

'I like books,' Sarah replied, sounding almost guilty.

'Makes no difference to me, Sar,' Dunk replied. 'Reading's good. As long as I don't have to do it.' He flopped down on the bed and turned to Zak. His face grew serious. 'Did your Templar tell you 'bout this supposed war between Earth and Hell, about a Hell King and demons and all that mad stuff?'

'Yep. Crazy, eh?'

'And do you believe it?'

Zak didn't hesitate. 'I do… yeah.'

'Don't you think it's all a bit a bit far-fetched?'

Zak didn't feel like sharing his encounters with Mothmen and Grippers at the moment. 'Just because it's far-fetched doesn't mean it's not true.'

Dunk shook his head. 'Well even if it is, I don't see what it's got to do with us.'

'That I don't know,' Zak replied. 'When did you all get here?'

'Last night,' Leah said. 'I'd just got back from school and was off out to buy a new phone when I was bundled in a car and basically kidnapped by some woman claiming to be Templar Knight. It was so embarrassing. I'm just glad no one saw it.'

'And I had tickets for the Stoke game,' Dunk said, 'but didn't get to go coz this massive Templar called Big Al shoved me into a Bentley before driving me all the way here at two hundred miles an hour. Don't get me wrong - it was a sweet ride, but I'd rather have gone to the game. Stoke battered Everton three nil. Anyway, Zak, if you're here then I'm guessin' you've got the same freaky background as the rest of us.'

Zak looked puzzled.

'Oh, your Templar didn't tell you about any of that?'

'Told me what?'

Dunk glanced at Leah and Sarah. 'Well, pretty much the only thing we've figured out is the three of us have actually got loads in common. And I don't just mean the crazy eyes. How does this sound? You're an orphan, your birthday is on New Year's Day when you'll be fifteen, you've never been sick, you're faster and stronger than any other kid you know, you learn quicker, and you've lived all over the country with loads of different foster parents who've taught you tonnes of weird stuff, much of it to do with beating other people up. Sound familiar?'

Zak's mouth fell open. It took him seconds to respond. 'Err, yeah.'

Dunk pointed at Leah, then Sarah, then himself. 'Join the *freak club*, mate... '

- Chapter 9 -
The Angel Prophecy

Another voice joined the conversation. 'How nice to see you all getting acquainted.' Pottsy stood at the door. 'So is your room to your liking, Zak?'

'It's fine.'

'These are not actually your belongings,' Pottsy said. 'Just a duplicate of everything you own at Fumbletree Cottage. We've been planning your arrival for some time and wanted you to feel as comfortable as possible when you came. So, to put your mind at ease, your room is still there at the Shufflebottom's and intact for when you next visit.'

'And when will that be?' Zak asked quickly.

'I'm not sure yet.'

'How are Sid and Irene?'

'They're safe,' Pottsy said. 'Obviously very sad you're being relocated here for the time being, but they knew this day would come.'

Zak hesitated. He opened his mouth to pursue this further when Dunk's angry voice cut him down.

'Well we're very sad at not being told anything, Pottsy. So are you finally gonna spill the beans?'

Pottsy smiled at Dunk. 'The beans are indeed about to be spilt.'

'Good,' Dunk said. 'Coz you'd better have a good excuse for all of this. You could get banged up for kidnapping four teenagers.'

'As I've told you before, Mister Duncan, you've not been kidnapped… you've been brought here for your own safety.'

'By people calling themselves knights pretending to fight a war against goblins. You do know how mad this all sounds?'

'I'm aware of that,' Pottsy replied. 'And it will for the moment. Perhaps after our chat it won't seem quite so irregular.'

Dunk folded his arms. 'Then get talking.'

'Excellent idea,' Pottsy replied. 'Please follow me to the Chapter House where I'll tell you everything.'

'Lead the way,' Dunk said, nearly knocking Zak over as he marched out.

A minute later, Pottsy led the group over a cobbled path that curved right into another courtyard, bordered by a small chapel and more dormitories.

They entered a timber building with a pointed roof and stopped at a heavy door. Heaving it open, Pottsy ushered them into a hexagonal room with dozens of hangings that covered every inch of wall space. A large candelabrum shed light over a circular table that dominated the room, seated at which were Kurnan and three other Templars, one man and two women, each wearing the same ceremonial robes as Pottsy.

'Please, Zak, Dunk, Leah and Sarah … sit down.' Pottsy pointed at four empty chairs, before sitting down himself.

As Zak drew a chair, he noticed another man sitting in the far left hand corner of the room. Almost completely in shadow, he wore a floor length velvet cloak, its black hood pulled up, concealing his face entirely.

Pottsy cleared his throat. 'Now I know you've had an emotional twenty-four hours. Still, circumstances dictated we extracted you from your foster homes when we did. You'll understand why when you have the full picture. Let me just say you are very, very special boys and girls...' His eyes scanned each one of them in turn. 'So let's start with what you perhaps already know: You're all orphans... you all share the same birthday... and you are all gifted in ways other young people are not. I'm not sure what your mentors have told you but I'm going to start where I see fit. You see, I knew all of your mothers...'

Shocked gasps filled the room.

'You knew our mums?' Dunk said.

'I did,' Pottsy said. 'They each came from different parts of the country to Avernon Monastery three months before they gave birth. I don't know why they came here, they didn't know, but something drew them here. Furthermore, each of the women had two things in common: there was no father to their baby and they too were orphans. Anyway, after you were born the Templars took charge of your upbringing. You were under threat for reasons that will become clear. That's why we moved you around the country so much to live with various foster families. Now, your mentors should have told you about the true origins of the Templars -'

'- Hang on,' Leah interrupted. 'Tell us more about our mums - what happened to them?'

Pottsy's face grew cheerless. 'Now is not the appropriate time, Miss Emerson. I'll talk to you about that later on an individual basis. It's a tender subject and I'm sure you would all prefer some privacy when it's discussed. Is that acceptable?'

Leah looked at the others, before mumbling, 'I s'pose so.'

'Then allow me to continue,' Pottsy said. 'You know of the war between Hell and Earth, what you will not know is what part you play in that war.' He swallowed a deep breath. 'You see, there is an ancient prophecy found in a lost book of the Bible by a prophet called Samuel the Seer and, to a large degree, everything it foretold has come true. It predicted that over three thousand years ago the doorways between Hell and Earth would open and that a Hell King would attempt to gain power on Earth and bring about what Samuel called 'The End of Days.' It was also said he would be defeated by a Watcher -' he paused, 'a being more commonly known as an *Angel*...'

Dunk sniggered. 'An Angel?'

'Yes, Mister Duncan, an Angel,' Pottsy replied. 'And the prophecy came true. A Hell King did enter our world. He did make a bid for power... and he was defeated by an Angel - you even know the names of both parties: The Hell King was called *Gilliath*... the angel was named *David*. The story of David and Goliath was basically true. Just not how the Bible tells it.'

Zak shot an incredulous glance at the others.

Pottsy continued. 'Anyway, the prophecy states that every thousand years the Earth would be tested by another Hell King. The last time was nearly a thousand years ago. Again, the Hell King was defeated. Anyway, we are rapidly approaching the end of the next thousand years. Subsequently, the current Hell King, *Morloch*, is readying his armies and planning his assault on our world. And, as has happened before, more angels have been sent amongst us to fight him.'

Pottsy hesitated. '*You are those Angels*. It is your destiny to battle the Hell King and prevent the End of Days.' He gave a weak smile. 'Now does anyone fancy a cup of tea?'

Zak, Sarah, Dunk and Leah stared at each other with disbelief. Moments passed, each of them waiting for another to speak.

Finally, it was Leah who broke the silence. 'Just to clarify... you're saying we're Angels? Us four... *Angels*?'

'We can call you Watchers if you'd prefer ... but yes, I am.'

'That we've been sent here, to earth, to save mankind?'

'Yes.'

Leah sat back in her chair, took a few moments to process this, and started to giggle. 'Oh, please....' The giggle soon became a belly laugh.

Moments later, Dunk was laughing, too.

Only Sarah and Zak remained stone-faced.

'What a crock!' Dunk said. 'Seriously, Pottsy, you're one hell of a comedian. You should be on the telly.'

Pottsy smiled politely. 'Although I do consider myself quite the humourist, Mister Duncan, I'm afraid every word I've spoken is true.'

'Mister Potts,' Sarah said, her voice low but steady. 'Why do you believe we're Angels?'

'Because he's a nut job!' Dunk fired out.

Pottsy stood firm. 'Because it's all there in Samuel's

prophecy... everything... about your mothers coming bearing fatherless children, about your birthdays, about how you are different from others. And, although I may well be a nut job, Mister Duncan, that doesn't deny the fact you are *all* Angels.'

'Just because we're a bit different from other teens doesn't make us The Avengers.' Leah said. She pointed at Dunk. 'And he's certainly not Thor!'

'I'm sure he's not,' Pottsy replied. 'But what I would say is your full transformation hasn't happened yet.'

'What d'you mean?' Zak asked.

'According to Samuel's prophecy, at the stroke of midnight on your fifteenth birthdays you shall change – an event that has come to be known as *The Renaissance...* the rebirth.'

'We're being reborn?' Leah said.

Dunk grinned. 'That's gonna be pretty painful for some poor woman.'

'And really messy for us,' Leah said.

'I don't think he meant that kind of rebirth,' Pottsy replied. 'It just means you'll be given certain abilities.'

'What kind of abilities?' Leah asked.

'I don't know,' Pottsy replied.

'If we're Angels shouldn't we get wings?' Dunk said.

'Perhaps,' Pottsy replied calmly. 'We really don't know.'

'Great,' Dunk said flippantly. 'We're all having wings for our birthday! Damn... and I wanted a bike.'

Leah feigned a look of horror. 'And I can't possibly have wings! How will I ever get my dresses to fit?'

'If that's what is to pass then so be it,' Pottsy replied. 'We can still get you a bike, Mister Duncan. And we can modify your dresses, Miss Emerson.'

'Come on, Pottsy,' Dunk said with a dismissive flick of his hand. 'We might be kids, but we ain't daft. Have you heard yourself: Wings? Hell Kings? Demons? I mean, you lot are off your rockers... and I for one am tired of it. I want you to take me home right now. If not, I'm calling the cops...' He pulled out his mobile phone and slammed it on the table.

'I know all of this is difficult to comprehend,' Pottsy replied. 'But everything I've said is the truth. Anyway, you don't have to take my word – do you believe demons exist, Zak?'

Zak felt all eyes fall on him. 'Yes. I know they do.'

Momentarily stunned, Dunk's said, 'Then he's as loopy as you.'

Pottsy gave a wry smile. 'It just so happens I prepared for a certain amount of scepticism, which is why I invited Mister Gudrak to join us today.'

He turned toward the cloaked man in the corner, who had remained so still Zak wasn't convinced the others had noticed him.

'Mister Gudrak. Can I ask you to show our guests why you teach Demon-lore at Avernon?'

'You may, Ichabod,' the man replied in a deep, soulful voice.

Mister Gudrak stood up and stepped into the light. Slowly, he removed his hood, before letting his cloak tumble to the floor.

The breath snagged in Zak's throat.

At over seven feet tall and as wide as a barn door, Mister Gudrak was unlike anything any of them had seen before. With leathery yolk-yellow skin and a curved horn that sprouted from his forehead, he had a single eye as big as a dinner plate. 'Good afternoon, everyone. I am Nathanaryn Gudrak,' he said graciously. 'It is an honour to meet you all.'

Amidst Leah's shrieks and his own pounding heart, Zak's eyes confirmed a Hell Demon worked at Avernon Monastery.

- Chapter 10 -
Mister Gudrak

In the minute it took Leah to stop screaming, Zak looked away only once from Mister Gudrak, when he glanced at Pottsy who looked particularly smug as if he hoped they'd be sceptical so he could enjoy his big reveal.

Mister Gudrak waited until a hush cloaked the room. 'Now is that out of your system, Leah?'

At hearing her name, Leah began to scream again, but this soon petered into a mild whimper and lots of heavy panting.

'I'm aware I may look somewhat alarming to you,' Mister Gudrak said, 'but in Hell I'll have you know I'm considered quite the - what is it you teenagers say - the *hottie.*'

Pottsy clapped his hands with delight. 'I'm sure you are, Mister Gudrak.'

'W – What are you?' Dunk spluttered.

'I'm a Cycloid, Mister Duncan.'

'You've – you've got a horn!' Leah gasped.

'Ah, you noticed?' Mister Gudrak curled his thick fingers over his horn. 'Do you like it? My kind believes the character of a Cycloid can be measured by the length and quality of their horn. I'm very proud of mine.'

'It is a most impressive horn, Mister Gudrak,' Pottsy said, clearly enjoying himself. 'Most impressive indeed.'

'Thank you, Ichabod,' Mister Gudrak said. 'The first thing you must understand is that not everyone in Hell is evil. It is not the place you have been warned about in your places of worship. No one is saying that place does not exist, it may well do - but certainly the Hell I know is not as your works of art imply. It is a beautiful world with locations to rival Earth's finest. However, for far too long it has been governed by the bad, and that's why I chose to bring my family to your planet and offer my services to the Templars.'

Mister Gudrak gave a heavy sigh.

'I wish my world to be free of wickedness, but that is easier said than done. One day, however, I hope it can be the goodly place I know it can be, and it is then I shall return and breathe once more the sweet air of the Pellion Fields and watch the setting of the three moons. I believe in my heart that day shall come... and it shall be because of you.'

His large eye found each one of them in turn.

'So believe me young ones, everything Ichabod says is true. And I hope, in time, you shall feel as extraordinary as we know you are. To be an Angel is a heavy burden to bear, but I hope you can see your calling fulfils a higher purpose for us all. On a personal note, I hope you'll join me and my wife, Mrs Gudrak, in my hovel for a spot of Herbuggle Tea and a slice of Jamble cake. Thank you for listening. You may now scream again should you wish.'

Mister Gudrak picked up his cloak and returned to

his seat.

'Thank you, Mister Gudrak,' Pottsy said. 'I must suggest you take up the offer of a slice of Mrs Gudrak's Jamble cake. It's a genuine treat for the senses. Anyway, on that note of generosity perhaps we should end these proceedings. Any questions?'

No one said a thing. They were all still looking at Mister Gudrak who stared wistfully at the ceiling.

'Very well then,' Pottsy continued. 'I shall visit you shortly on an individual basis to discuss your mothers. Thank you...'

As Zak left the room, he knew making sense of any of it was an impossible task. However, it wasn't seeing Mister Gudrak or even the idea of his being an Angel that blew his mind – he would worry about that madness later - no, it was the fact Pottsy had known his mother.

For some reason, Zak had always felt he wasn't so much born into the world as appeared in it one day, like a pimple. He had always been told his mother died in childbirth, and it was the finality of this, alongside the deep guilt this made him somehow responsible for her death that made him hesitant to even think about her. And the fact he loved Sid and Irene so much, prevented him from dwelling on a past he could never reconcile.

Leaving the Chapter House, Dunk spoke in a voice that for once lacked all of its customary bravado.

'What d'you think about this?' Dunk said. 'I mean it's bonkers, ain't it?'

'Completely,' Zak replied.

'I mean, Hell obviously does exist,' Dunk said, 'but that doesn't make us Angels, does it? I mean, don't get me wrong I've always felt, you know, a bit different to my mates, but... an Angel? And what was all that about a Renaissance? I mean it's gotta be a load of rubbish, hasn't it?'

Zak sighed. 'I don't know anything anymore.'

'How come Pottsy knew you believed in Hell demons?'

'Because I've been attacked twice by them,' Zak replied. 'The first time was at my foster parents' house by these things called Mothmen, and then by these flying creatures called Grippers. It was freaky stuff.'

'Oh, right,' Dunk replied quietly. 'So d'you think we're Angels then?'

'I've no idea.'

And he really didn't. It seemed like all he knew had been cast aside, that his former life had gone forever, a distant memory never to be retrieved. And it was clear the others felt the same way. Reaching the dormitory, they each scurried to their separate rooms, heads bowed and silent, each needing the space to reflect on all of this.

Zak entered his room and lay on his bed. He curled his pillow around his head and closed his eyes. The moment he did, however, a heavy knock rattled the door. Fully expecting it to be Pottsy, he leapt off the bed and opened it.

Disappointment lined his face when he saw John Kurnan standing there.

Kurnan noticed. 'Sorry, were you expecting someone else?'

'Err, no,' Zak said. 'I was just hoping that –'

'– That it was Pottsy coming to chat about your mum?'

'Yes.'

Kurnan returned a gentle smile. 'He asked me to do

it. I knew her, too.'

Zak's heart leapt. 'You did?'

'I did.' Kurnan approached the window and stared out at the dulling sun.

The seconds it took for Kurnan to speak were the longest of Zak's life.

'Your mother's name was Lisa Fisher,' Kurnan said. 'She was twenty-two when I met her. Like you, she was an orphan and had been brought up by foster parents in Shrewsbury. Anyway, one day she found herself pregnant... but the astonishing thing was there was no father.'

Zak's head reeled. 'I didn't have a father?'

'Not in the normal sense. Anyway, Lisa was six months pregnant when she just upped and left Shrewsbury and travelled to Avernon. She didn't know what made her come... she didn't know what to expect when she got here... but she came, nevertheless. Something drew her here, to the Templars. And perhaps even more remarkably, she wasn't alone. On the day your mother arrived so did three other women, all from different parts of the country and from different backgrounds, but they were all in identical situations to your mum's - they were all six months pregnant with no father to their unborn child. It was during your mum's time here I got to know her.'

Zak could barely bring himself to ask the next question. 'And what was she like?'

'She was the most remarkable woman on the face of the planet. Beautiful in every way. There was only good in her.'

Feeling tears welling in his eyes, Zak turned away. 'So was I born here?'

'No,' Kurnan replied. 'All four women were taken to Saint Bernard's Hospital, a Templar facility in Kent. You were born there.' He hesitated as if it caused him physical pain to continue. 'And it was as a complication of childbirth that she ... she passed away.'

'Were you with her?'

'No,' Kurnan replied bitterly. 'They wouldn't let me travel to Kent. I should've gone... I should've been there through everything, and I'll regret that until the day I die.'

'And what about the other mothers?'

'They died in childbirth, too.'

Zak couldn't believe it. 'All of them?'

'Yes.'

'But how's that possible?' I mean... the odds of four women dying like that are astronomical.'

'I don't know,' Kurnan replied. 'I've asked myself that same question a thousand times. But that's what happened. All four women are buried in the grounds of Saint Bernard's. I'll take you there one day.' He exhaled. 'Just know that you were born to a woman unlike any other, better than any other.' Slowly, he withdrew a letter, sealed with a wax stamp. 'I've looked after this for a long time. It's yours now.' He passed it over.

Looking down, Zak's heart pounded as he read the four words written in an elegant script on the envelope:

'To my darling Zak.'

- Chapter 11 -
The Past in the Present

Zak grasped the letter tightly. He didn't even notice Kurnan leave the room. Lightly, he traced his fingers across the words and then opened it. He began to read.

Dearest Zak,

I just wanted to write a few words before I leave for Kent where I pray you will be delivered to me safely.

Just to think that next year you will be almost one. It truly amazes me. I intend to spoil you rotten.

Today is Boxing Day. The snow is thick outside and I'm sitting in my bedroom at a place called Avernon Monastery. I can't imagine a more idyllic part of the world and a bit of me is sad I can't give birth to you right here. But I am taking the advice of the Chief Knight, Wilbur Combermere, who's a very nice and wise man, and he thinks that I, and the three other ladies in my situation, should be transferred to a Templar hospital in Kent for the birth.

Still, Avernon would be a wonderful place to be born, I think.

I suppose by the time you read this you'll already be aware of the miraculous way you'll have entered the world. You will also be aware of the Knights Templar and of the war between Hell and Earth. Even now (and I've known about it for a few months) it blows my mind. They've also told me that an ancient prophecy says you'll play a part in this conflict, but they refuse to go into any detail. I'm pretty sure it's because I would never want you to be involved in any kind of war, and they'd be right. I just want you safe and healthy and completely protected from any of that.

I suppose I just want to tell you before I actually meet you how much I love you. From the moment I discovered I was pregnant – and believe me that was a shock - I was dizzy with joy. Pure joy. I have watched you grow inside me and every time you move or kick, it sends waves of delight through me. Some parents worry how their child will turn out, but I don't. Somehow, I know you'll become the miracle you already are.

Anyway, a lovely (not to mention handsome) man called John has promised to take me for a going away dinner tonight in a nearby town called Beridian, so I suppose I'd better stop writing and get ready. Not that I'll be even vaguely attractive – I'm roughly the size of a small moon.

Anyway, just know this: I am so deeply proud to be the one who brings you into the world. Even before we meet, I love you so much it hurts.

You have made my life worthwhile, Zak. I just hope I can make you as proud of me as I already am of you. I'll see you very soon and I promise to give you the best life a mother could ever give a son.

All my love forever,

Your mummy.

xxx

By the time he'd finished, Zak's face was raw with tears. He did nothing for the next two hours except revisit the letter again and again. Just reading his mother's letter, knowing fourteen years ago she too was at Avernon composing such tender words, made him feel closer to her than ever. He didn't need to know what she looked like. He could picture her exactly.

And more than anything, he wanted to talk to John Kurnan.

Kurnan had accompanied his mother on her last evening at Avernon. He wanted to know what she ate, what she wore, what they talked about. He wanted to know every last detail.

Still, he knew that could wait.

For the first time in his life, he had contact from his mum. And it made him happy. Deliriously happy.

Finally, he returned the letter to its envelope and slipped it carefully beneath his pillow. Tonight, when he slept he wanted to be as close to her as possible. As he did there was a *knock* on his door.

Quickly, Zak checked himself in his mirror to see his eyes weren't still red and said, 'Come in.'

The door opened and Dunk ambled in, his entire body devoid of any of its earlier gusto. It was clear from his eyes he'd been crying, too. 'Y'alright?' he mumbled.

'I'm fine,' Zak said. 'How about you?'

'I'm okay,' Dunk replied unconvincingly. 'Has Pottsy been?

'No. It was John Kurnan.'

'Did he know your mum then?'

'Apparently so.'

'Have you had a letter from her?'

'Yes.'

'Me too,' Dunk replied. 'How'd you feel about it?'

'I don't know,' Zak replied. 'Sad. Happy. I'm not

sure.'

'Me neither,' Dunk said. 'But it's all true, isn't it? I mean, we *are* Angels.'

'Is that what your letter said?'

'She thought so, yes,' Dunk replied. 'Plus everything else they've told us is true. Why would they lie about that?'

'I guess so.'

'So do you think we're Angels?'

'I think we are…yes.'

'So what're we gonna do about it?' Dunk asked. 'I mean… we're kids.'

'What can we do?'

'We could run away? Go back to our old lives.'

'I don't think our old lives exist anymore,' Zak replied. Sadness filled him as he remembered Sid and Irene. 'These Hellians know who we are… that means we're not safe, but more importantly neither are the people we care about if we're near them.' He sighed. 'We make them walking targets.'

Dunk's body deflated. 'You're right. I suppose we just have to wait and see what happens on New Year's Day. If we don't sprout wings I guess we're off the hook. Someone else can save the planet.'

'I guess.'

At that moment, Dunk remembered something. 'Oh, Pottsy asked me to give you this.' He passed over a sheet of paper. 'I guess it is a school after all. Classes start tomorrow.'

Zak looked down at a timetable. On one hand it resembled his timetable from Saint Quentin's – with two-hour blocks for English, Maths, Geography, Literature and Science. However, these were set alongside a number of subjects they certainly didn't teach at his old school: Demon-lore, Weaponry and Combat, Templar History, Hand to Hand Combat and *Flower Arranging*.

Zak looked up, bemused. 'Flower arranging?'

'Weird, isn't it?' Dunk replied. 'Pottsy teaches it. I don't know much about flowers, but he's certainly off his tree.'

'I'm surprised they want us learning those normal subjects, too.'

'Pottsy reckons it's important we get a fully rounded education,' Dunk replied. 'I'm not sure why. Let's face it, knowing differential calculus is hardly gonna help us batter a Hell King and his evil minions though, is it?'

Zak couldn't help but agree.

*

They had been told their evening meal would be served at six thirty, so Zak, Dunk, Leah and Sarah made their way through the pounding rain to the refectory hall with five minutes to spare.

Entering the hall, Zak's nostrils were assaulted by the most amazing smells coming from the adjoining kitchens. He looked round and saw rows and rows of oak tables, enough for a few hundred people, although the vast majority were empty. Ancient paintings of Templars adorned the walls, some of them portraits, others depicting Templars engaged in ferocious battles with a variety of monstrous looking creatures.

Zak's gaze found Kurnan, who was sitting at the head table talking to a heavy-set Templar with bushy ginger hair and a thick beard. Pottsy was sitting next to them, and beside him a severe faced man with thick steel rimmed glasses drank from a metal goblet. Others at the table included a short, elderly man with an agreeable face and an infectious smile, and two female Templars, one blonde, the other brunette, both in their late twenties.

At seeing Zak and the others, Pottsy leapt from his chair and dashed over to them. 'Good evening everyone,' he said.

'Evening,' Leah said, her eyes scanning the dining hall. 'Cool room.'

'It's lovely, isn't it?' Pottsy replied. 'Normally it would be busier than this by now but we've asked most of the Templars to dine out tonight so as not to overwhelm you. Still, the *Fraterhouse* is nearly seven hundred years old, and it's been accommodating hungry monks, knights and novices for all that time. So are you peckish?'

'Pottsy, I could eat you,' Dunk replied.

'That shouldn't be necessary, Mister Duncan,' Pottsy said. 'We have excellent catering at Avernon.' He grasped his belly in both hands and gave it a jiggle. 'As I'm sure my ample paunch can confirm.' He led them over to a nearby table. 'Now if you'd care to sit and I'm -'

From over his shoulder, a booming female voice cut him off.

'You tryin' to do my job fer me, Pothole?'

A wide-hipped woman with dyed blonde hair scraped into a bun marched over to them. Deep into middle age, she wore heavy make-up and her thick purple lipstick made it look like she'd just eaten beetroot.

'Absolutely not, my dear,' Pottsy replied. 'I would never presume -'

'- Good. Now why don't you skedaddle back to your table like a good little boy? I've got business with these kids.'

'As you wish, M'lady,' Pottsy said.

'Now that's more like it,' the woman said. 'Now shoo.'

Pottsy bowed. 'Shooing, M'lady.'

As he left the woman blew him a kiss, before approaching Zak, Dunk, Leah and Sarah.

'I love the old goat, really,' she said. 'Anyhow, good evenin', me dearies. I'm Mabel Gubbins – head cook an' bottle washer round 'ere. And it's lovely to see y'all. Now I've heard all 'bout ya – everybody has - but I won't be givin' ya any preferential treatment. It's my job ter keep you fed, and I'll be doing with that with a heart fulla pride, so all ya 'ave to do is approach the counters over there.' She pointed at two long tables buckling under the weight of platters of food. 'And fill your plates as often as yer wish. You're all growing kids so I expect ya to load those plates high. In fact, the higher ya load 'em, the wider me smile will be.'

'I like you, Mabel,' Dunk said.

'Thank you,' Leah and Sarah said simultaneously.

'Yeah, thanks,' Zak said.

'My pleasure, me dearies.' Flashing them a broad smile, Mabel waddled back to the food court.

Dunk turned to the others. 'Well, if we're gonna be saviours of the earth we owe it to the planet to keep our energy levels up. Let's eat!'

Zak had the steak and kidney pudding, the recipe of which Mabel assured him was a family secret and had been passed down through seven generations of Gubbins ladies. He also found himself astonished by the sheer quantity Dunk could eat.

Dunk had piled his plate twice as high as the others, with two meat and potato pies, four fish fingers, two lamb chops, a mountain of chips and a full boat of onion gravy, and it was clear from the offset he had every intention of finishing the lot. As he shovelled food onto his fork, he nudged Zak and gestured over at the gigantic red-haired man talking to Kurnan.

'That's Big Al. He's the Templar that brought me here. He's my mentor. He's also teaching us hand-to-hand combat, which should be fun because - well, look him... he looks like a ginger Hulk. Is that your mentor with him?'

'Yeah,' Zak replied. 'His name's Kurnan. He doesn't smile much but he's cool. And you want to see him with a Magnasword? He's fast. Really fast.'

'What's a Magnasword?' Dunk asked.

The question was barely out there when a door crashed open to their right, the noise of which made the walls tremble. Standing in the doorway was a tall, slim figure in a rain drenched Templar poncho, their face masked by an upturned hood. Without warning, the figure collapsed, a distinctive ivory coloured bone-handled Magnasword clattering to the floor beside them.

In a flash, Kurnan had leapt from his seat and raced over. Big Al and Pottsy followed. Reaching the figure, Kurnan sank to his knees. The figure's hood had fallen away to reveal a young woman's pretty face, swollen with bumps and bruises, her shoulder length golden hair discoloured by blood.

'Kelly?' he breathed.

The woman forced her eyes open. 'John? Thank God it's you.'

'DOCTOR PUDGBURY... OVER HERE!' Kurnan shouted over to the head table, where the short, elderly man was already scurrying over.

The doctor reached Kurnan. He knelt down and reached out to examine the woman's injuries when she pushed his hand away with all the strength she could muster. Her eyes found Kurnan's.

'Kurnan, I know what Ballivan's searching for…' She swallowed the deepest breath she could. 'It's the Seal. He's after the Seal…' Then her head slumped backward and she lost consciousness.

- Chapter 12 -
King Solomon's Ring

Zak stared with disbelief at the woman, her last words echoing in his skull.

I know what Ballivan's searching for... It's the Seal.

In that moment his conversation with Kurnan returned to him, and more specifically a name: Lord Ballivan, the new *Hell Lord*.

But why was Ballivan searching for a seal? That didn't make any sense.

'What should we do?' Sarah asked Zak.

Before Zak could answer, Pottsy approached the table with a calm authority. 'I'm sorry you had to witness this,' he said. 'But can I suggest you go to the novice social room whilst we take care of Kelly. It's highlighted on the map I left in your rooms.'

'Forget social rooms,' Dunk said. 'How's the lady?'

'Would you like me to look at her?' Sarah said. 'I've always been pretty good at... well, healing things... animals, people.'

'I'm sure you have, Miss Miller,' Pottsy replied. 'And thank you for your concern Mister Duncan, but I can assure you Kelly will be just fine. Doctor Pudgbury is one of the finest physicians in the country so she's in excellent hands. Please, all of you go to the social room and I'll come and see you shortly… I promise.'

*

Moments later Zak and the others walked in silence along the eastward path to the novice social room. It was pitch black and an hour of ceaseless rain had turned the ground to paste. Beyond the high perimeter walls, the roaring ocean sounded like a discordant orchestra. They entered the social room to find themselves welcomed by a raging coal fire, the heat from which thickened the air.

Looking round, Zak could see the room was a treasure trove of old and new objects and paraphernalia collected over the decades by novices who had gathered here, each generation adding something of their own, without taking away the vestiges of the previous novices.

There was a kitchen area with a sink, sofas, armchairs, a pool table, four retro arcade machines and a 90" U-HDTV screen attached to a Gamebox 3 console. The walls were covered with posters of film stars and bands and sportsmen and women, some discoloured with age, some looking like they had only been put up that day. Almost every spare inch of wall was covered.

It seemed, however, Zak was the only one to notice any of it.

Instead, Sarah and Dunk had slumped onto leather armchairs and were staring blankly at the fire.

Leah paced up and down impatiently, covering the large floor area in seconds flat. 'This place is dangerous,' she said. 'We shouldn't be here.'

'Too right,' Dunk agreed.

But Leah wasn't inviting a response. 'I mean, how

dare they?' she continued, her voice rising. 'They bring us here against our will, tear us from our homes, our families and friends, our favourite shops, dump us in a glorified prison on a rock in the middle of the sea and tell us some crazy story about us being Angels here to save the planet. I'm not saying this war isn't real, I don't know what to think about any of that, but what do they expect us to do about it?'

No one offered an answer.

'Do you think Kelly will be all right?' Sarah said.

'I'm sure she will," Zak replied.

'What was it she said before she conked out?' Dunk asked. 'Was it summat about seals?'

'Yeah,' Leah added. 'And a Lord Baboon.'

'Lord Ballivan,' Zak corrected her. 'Kurnan, my mentor, told me about him. Apparently, he's the new Hell Lord.'

Zak suddenly found all eyes upon him once again.

'What's a Hell Lord?' Leah asked.

'He's like the Hell King's number one guy on earth - his representative or something. Kurnan killed the last one, Lord Venogant, but from what he told me Ballivan's even worse.'

'Terrific,' Dunk muttered.

'Then what does Lord Ballivan want with a seal?' Leah asked.

'Maybe he wants to learn how to honk for fish?' Dunk said.

A blast of cold air caused the fire to flicker as the door opened. Everyone turned to see Pottsy standing there, his face weary. 'Kelly's going to be fine,' he said. 'We've moved her to the infirmary and Doctor Pudgbury has examined her thoroughly. She's awake and in good spirits... so that's one less thing we all have to worry about.'

'Good,' Leah said. Before she knew it the following question tumbled from her mouth. 'Why is Lord Ballivan looking for a *seal*?'

Pottsy sighed. 'Let's worry about that tomorrow, shall we?'

'Let's worry about it now,' Dunk said. 'I mean, you've thrown us smack in the middle of this mess. We've gotta right to know what's going on.'

Pottsy gave a reluctant nod. 'Very well,' he replied. He took a few seconds to gather his thoughts. 'Have any of you heard of King Solomon?'

'Yes,' Sarah said. 'He was a King of Israel a thousand years or so before Jesus Christ. He supposedly built the first Temple in Jerusalem.'

Zak looked at Sarah, impressed.

'That's correct, Miss Miller. The very temple from which the Templars took their name. So can I assume you can recall the name of Solomon's father?'

Sarah didn't waver. 'David.'

'Correct again, Miss Miller,' Pottsy replied. 'And as you now know David was like you... an Angel. Apparently, when David killed Gilliath he took an object from him... a powerful object.'

'What kind of object?' Zak asked.

'A ring,' Pottsy said. 'A ring he eventually passed on to one of his sons: Solomon. From then on, the ring became known as the *Seal of Solomon*.'

Leah thrust her left hand forward, presenting a gold ring on her index finger. 'As in this kind of ring?'

'Yes,' Pottsy replied. 'Only you can't buy it from just any shop.'

Indignation flared on Leah's face. 'I did not buy this from just *any* shop,' she said as if the recipient of an insult. 'I'll have you know that it's from - '

Pottsy gave an apologetic bow. '- I'm sorry, Miss Emerson,' he interrupted. 'I didn't mean to offend. It is a beautiful ring. Most stylish. I just meant The Seal of Solomon is not merely a decorative item. It is purported to have great supernatural power.'

'What kind of power?' Zak asked.

'Well, amongst other things it's allegedly a portal between our two worlds – Earth and Hell. A portable Stargate if you will.'

'So the Seal is a doorway?' Zak asked.

'Of sorts,' Pottsy replied. 'And because of its portable nature it's a doorway we cannot protect or defend. That makes it a very dangerous artifact indeed.'

'So where is it now?' Zak asked.

'That's the thing – no one knows,' Pottsy replied. 'Some time after King Solomon's death, the Seal came into our possession and remained with us for thousands of years, hidden far away from the clutches of the Hellians or their supporters. However, hundreds of years ago it disappeared, and hasn't been seen since.'

'What happened to it?' Dunk asked.

'The answer to that has been lost to history,' Pottsy replied. 'The story goes the last person to have it was an English Templar named Sir Robin Guppingham – a respected scholar and engineer, who was the Templar Grandmaster from 1285 until his death in 1307.'

'What's a Templar Grandmaster?' Zak asked.

'The Head Templar, the Knight of Knights, the leader of the Orders across both worlds. Yes, he was a fascinating man was Robin Guppingham, a great knight, a sculptor, a cunning diplomat and it just so happens a quite brilliant architect. As a matter of fact, Avernon was one of his many constructions across Britain, Italy and France. Anyway, if the Seal of Solomon did come to him he never passed it on.'

'Why not?' Dunk asked.

'He simply didn't know who to trust.'

'So what did he do with it?' Zak asked.

'Your guess is as good as mine. The fact is that nobody knows. The most popular myth claims that it is hidden here, buried somewhere at Avernon, concealed perhaps in one of the many thousands of caves and tunnels beneath our feet. Some even believe Guppingham left markers as to its location.'

Zak's ears pricked up. *Markers?*

'What kind of markers?' Dunk asked keenly.

'Clues... visual signs that are supposed to lead to it,' Pottsy replied. 'But to my knowledge no marker has ever been found. I'm afraid, although it is a most fanciful tale - a schoolboy's adventure yarn filled with mystery and intrigue – there is absolutely no proof to any of it.'

'But if Lord Ballivan does get the seal then Morloch can enter our world whenever and wherever he wants?' Sarah said.

'That's the long and short of it,' Pottsy replied. His next words had an apprehensive edge. 'And there's something else...' He paused.

'What?' Dunk asked eagerly.

'It is said the holder of the Seal will be victorious in the impending End of Days War. It is said its power is such it makes the holder invincible.'

'It didn't do that for Gilliath,' Leah said.

'I'm just saying that's how the story goes.'

Dunk's face blazed with purpose. 'Then we need it,' he said. 'We've gotta find it before Ballivan gets his grubby paws on it.'

Pottsy sighed. 'Mister Duncan, there are countless stories about the Seal, and most of them are just that: stories. As I said there's no evidence as to its location, or, to be honest, any tangible proof it even existed in the first place.'

The rain hammered the roof like firecrackers as Pottsy approached the door. 'And on that note I shall bid you a good night. Please don't stay up too late. You really do need your sleep. It is, after all, a school night.'

- Chapter 13 -
WAC

Despite Pottsy's words, the four of them stayed up well into the early hours, talking about everything that had happened. As the time passed everyone seemed more willing to accept all they'd been told. And as the conversation weaved from one topic to the next, the subject they returned to again and again was the Seal of Solomon. Did it exist? Did Sir Robin Guppingham bury it at Avernon? Did he leave markers leading to its location? If so, what and where were they?

'I'm gonna start looking for it tomorrow,' Dunk said.

'Err, why?' Leah replied with a scornful edge.

'Because it'll be a laugh.'

'You're going to search an enormous monastery with God knows how many buildings, not to mention thousands of caves beneath it for an ancient ring the size of a cornflake that may or may not exist? Good luck with that!'

Dunk didn't appear to care. 'A man's gotta have a hobby.'

'But you're not a man,' Leah replied. 'You're a little boy with a big mouth.'

'I'm all man if you ever wanna find out, baby.' Dunk winked at her.

Leah pretended to vomit.

Thinking it best to intervene before things got out of control, Zak said to Dunk, 'Where would you start looking?'

'Dunno yet,' Dunk replied. 'Maybe there's summat in the library. Big Al told me there are books in there that date back thousands of years.'

'A library?' Leah said. 'I'm surprised you know what one of those is.'

'There was one in Stoke. Never went, but it was next to a great kebab shop.'

'Can you even read?' Leah said.

Dunk flashed her a sarcastic smile. 'D'you even know what your face looks like under all that make-up?'

Zak had heard enough. 'Pack it in, will you?' he said irritably. 'We do have to live together.'

Leah shot Dunk a cutting glare, before saying, 'Okay.'

'Fine,' Dunk said. 'So what d'you reckon, Zak? Do you wanna come to the library tomorrow and help me look for it? I mean, if there is gonna be a war we need it if we're gonna beat Lord Ballimory.'

'Sure.'

'Good man,' Dunk replied. 'It'll be like a treasure hunt.'

'A treasure hunt with zero chance of finding any treasure,' Leah said. 'Yay!'

'You just can't help yourself, can you?' Dunk said. 'Anyway, ignore her, Zak, we're going on a quest for an ancient relic.'

It was then Sarah entered the conversation. 'Of

course, this ancient relic, if real, could bring about the end of the world. Have you considered that?'

Even Dunk had no reply to that.

*

That night Zak tossed and turned in his bed, his mind restless. He was also excited about their first class: *Weaponry and Combat*. John Kurnan was to be their tutor and he hoped for the opportunity to discuss his mum's letter.

The next morning a dazzling golden sun took the edge of what was a bitterly cold day. The group made their way to the refectory for breakfast where, unlike the previous night, they found the hall packed with Templars, every single one of them, Zak presumed, under clear instructions not to stare at Avernon's four newest residents.

The group received word the class would be held in the Training Yard, so after breakfast they walked to the most westerly point of the grounds, adjacent to a high cliff that plunged into the ocean, where they saw a stone amphitheatre, its circular arena flanked by dozens of stone benches, flag poles and four tall floodlights.

Kurnan was standing beside a table, set upon which were what looked like four *Magnaswords*.

'Good Morning,' Kurnan said, as they filed in line before him. 'My name's John Kurnan. You will call me Kurnan - not Sir or Mister Kurnan or John. Kurnan is fine. In time, you'll probably call me plenty of other things but you'd better not let me hear them or I shall *kill* you... Angels or not!'

The group swapped nervous glances.

Kurnan hesitated, before saying, 'I am joking.'

Each of them forced a weak laugh.

Quite simply, Kurnan radiated power.

'Now although this is the first time we've formally met,' Kurnan said. 'I know more about you than you're aware. I was the one who coordinated your movements from birth. I've kept in close contact with your foster families and therefore know precisely at what stage your training is at. In short, I know what you're good at, and what you need to improve upon. For instance, Miss Emerson, I know you excel at martial arts, gymnastics, and you're an expert with the throwing knife, possibly the best in the world.'

Leah beamed back at him. 'Thank you.'

'And Miss Miller,' Kurnan continued. 'I know you're highly accomplished in Shaolin Kung Fu, archery and a truly exceptional markswoman.'

'Thank you, sir.'

'No, 'sir'. It's still just Kurnan.'

'Thank you, Kurnan,' Sarah said.

Dunk could barely wait his turn. 'And what about me?'

'Well for one thing, Mister Duncan, I hear you're an outstanding ballet dancer. Good for you.'

Leah laughed.

A look of horror crossed Dunk's face. 'And fighting,' he mumbled. 'I'm good at fighting.'

'I know precisely what you're good at,' Kurnan replied. 'How's this – you're an expert in Brazillian Capoeira, kickboxing, Tae kwon do and Korean Hankido. I also know you're an excellent pilot of small aircraft.'

Dunk's chest swelled. 'Any vehicle, really: car, motorbike, speedboat, helicopter. You name it... I can handle it like a pro.' He shrugged. 'I'm gifted... what can

I say?'

'That inflated ego of yours will get you killed quicker than any demon could,' Kurnan said firmly, 'so keep it in check.'

Dunk's grin vanished in a flash.

Kurnan turned to the others. 'Anyway, all these disciplines and techniques will help you with what's to come. You've already received the best training you can have. You just weren't aware of it. Now -'

'- Hang on … what 'bout Zak?' Dunk said. 'What's he good at?'

Kurnan's eyes met Zak's. 'There's very little he doesn't excel at. Plus, he's got the potential to be the best swordsman on the planet.'

Zak could scarcely believe his ears. *After all, he'd seen Kurnan in action.*

'But the fact is you're all outstanding swordfighters,' Kurnan continued. 'And every foster family you've lived with has ensured swordsmanship has been at the heart of your training… that's because the Magnasword is the primary weapon of the Templar Knight.'

Kurnan pulled his Magnasword from a leather holster strapped to his thigh. 'This is the Magnasword.'

'Watch this…' Zak whispered to Dunk.

Kurnan gave the handle a firm squeeze and a shimmering blade shot out, much to the astonishment of his audience. He turned the sword and its reflection gleamed in his eyes.

'It's like a giant flick knife,' Leah said.

'Or a Lightsabre with a real blade,' Dunk said.

Kurnan frowned as though he'd heard this a thousand times before. 'The Magnasword's been around a lot longer than any fictional space weapon.'

'Why's it designed like that?' Zak asked.

'Simple… *concealment*,' Kurnan replied. 'We have to operate in the same world as everyone else. The fact the blade retracts into the grip makes it easier to hide, and therefore never raises questions with the police or at airports or in a variety of other scenarios. Plus… *it's damn cool.*'

Everyone smiled.

'Why do you still use swords?' Dunk asked. 'I mean… it's a bit King Arthur, innit? Why not get a Glock 20 and blow the heads off the demons?'

'Guns make it too easy to kill,' Kurnan replied. 'They take self-accountability out of the act. And that needs to be there. Shoot someone from a mile away and you've taken a life, but you may as well have shot a tin can. You don't see the consequences of your actions… you don't *feel* those consequences.' He paused. 'The sword makes you feel everything… and if you're going to take a life you should feel it. It's the least you can do…'

In the silence that followed, Zak noticed an unusual but distinctive purplish tinge to the blade. 'What kind of metal is it made from?'

'*Magnathian*,' Kurnan replied.

'Never heard of it,' Dunk said.

'You wouldn't have,' Kurnan replied. 'It can only be found on Hell. It's much stronger than any metal we have on earth, yet weighs considerably less.' He moved over to the table. 'Anyway, enough of the talk… these are training weapons.' His hand fanned over the four Magnaswords. 'They're blunt, so you don't do each other any harm. Here…' He threw each one of them a Magnasword.

Zak caught his comfortably. It felt weightless in his hands. He squeezed the grip and the blade shot out.

Kurnan stepped away from the table, and led them through some basic moves. In that moment, Zak recalled the many hours of Kendo training with Irene Shufflebottom. Of course, at the time he thought she was a quirky old lady with a curious hobby and not a veteran Templar Knight.

They practised for two hours, and Zak was impressed with each and every one of them. Dunk was considerably faster than he looked. Leah was excellent at defensive moves and Sarah was a first-rate reader of her opponent.

After the class ended it was clear Kurnan was delighted with their efforts. He bade each of them farewell with an encouraging pat on the back and a friendly smile.

As they picked up their coats, Dunk said to Zak, 'I can't see Pottsy's flower arranging class being as good as that, can you?'

'The best class I've ever had,' Zak replied.

'And you really are summat special with a Magnasword.'

'Cheers,' Zak replied. 'But everyone was pretty good.'

'Good, yeah,' Dunk said. 'But you were incredible. It's like an extension of your arm.'

Leah and Sarah approached them.

'Are you two coming to the refectory before Geography?' Leah asked.

'Sure are,' Dunk replied.

But Zak had something he wanted to do first. 'I'll catch you up in a few minutes,' he said. 'I just want to have a little chat with Kurnan.'

'Creepin' up to teach, already?' Leah grinned.

'Not exactly,' Zak replied. He watched the others leave, and then walked over Kurnan, who was returning the Magnaswords to his kitbag.

'Sir,' Zak said.

Kurnan didn't look up. 'It's still just Kurnan.'

'Can I have a word...Kurnan?'

'Sure, kid,' Kurnan said. 'You were great today by the way.'

Usually Kurnan's approval would have thrilled Zak, but at this moment he had something far more important on his mind. 'Thanks.'

'What d'you wanna talk about?'

Zak swallowed a deep breath. 'My mum.'

Kurnan didn't respond immediately. 'What about her?'

'The letter she left,' Zak said. 'The one you gave me. It mentioned you were taking her for dinner on her last night at Avernon.'

'So?'

'So I was hoping you might tell me about it?'

'What do you want to know?'

'I don't know. Where did you go? What did she eat? What did she wear?'

Kurnan exhaled slowly. 'I took her to Beridian - it's a town on the other side of the island, about four miles from here. We went for dinner at a small seafood restaurant called Hops. She had scallops and asparagus, and she wore a scarlet beret, a lace cardigan and the prettiest yellow dress I've ever seen. She was self-conscious about her size, but I didn't care – I'd never seen a more stunning woman in my life.'

'What did you talk about?'

Kurnan looked away.

Zak knew he was prying but he couldn't stop himself. 'I don't mean to be nosey,' he said. 'And if you don't want to talk about it then –'

'– I asked her to marry me...' Kurnan said bluntly.

Zak opened his mouth to speak, but nothing came. 'And what did she say?'

Kurnan inhaled deeply. 'She said we'd discuss it when she returned from hospital. She wanted you to be with her when she gave her answer. I never saw her again...'

- Chapter 14 -
Anne

'*I asked her to marry me...*' Those six simple words shook Zak to his core.

John Kurnan could have been his father.

At once, he saw flashes of how his life could have been - with two parents and maybe even brothers and sisters. *A real family.* A cold resentment rose inside. Why did his mother have to die? He glanced at Kurnan who looked as if this very admission had drained him of all energy.

Zak dearly wanted to find words to console him, but no words came. 'I am sorry,' he said eventually.

'Don't be,' Kurnan replied. 'It's you who lost a mother. At least I got to know her, and I consider myself lucky for that. You didn't.' His dark eyes found Zak's. 'I'll never say I feel sorry for you, kid... but I don't always say what I feel, anyway.'

Zak didn't join the others in the refectory but did attend that afternoon's Geography class, which was taught by a squat, tubby Templar with a strange habit of shoving his chalk up his left nostril when he wasn't using it. When the class finished, Zak declined a game of football with Dunk and went searching for Pottsy. He found him in the gardens and asked for permission to leave the grounds to go for a walk. He guessed Kurnan had already talked to him, because Pottsy sounded sympathetic and agreed at once.

Fierce sunlight blinded Zak as he tracked the winding path beside the cliff's edge. He watched the gulls swoop overhead, their shrieks jarring to his ears. He'd been walking for an hour when he spied a town fashioned into a horseshoe-like bay. Made up of narrow cobbled streets, snaking alleys and rickety stone cottages painted in blues, greens and yellows it had the picturesque charm of a child's painting. Countless boats rocked back and forth on the busy harbour, and a small ferry approached the dock delivering tourists from the mainland.

For a moment it gave him comfort. There was still a world unaware of hell kings, demons and ancient prophecies. He considered walking into Beridian to find Hops, the restaurant Kurnan and his mother visited all those years ago, but now he was here he couldn't bring himself to do it.

He faced the ocean. Waves crashed against rocks and spray spotted the air like pellets. Then, out of the corner of his eye, he saw a girl sitting on a protruding mass of rock; her long golden hair fluttered wildly, her face flushed from the sea breeze. She looked so peaceful, serene even, as if she hadn't a care in the world.

Zak turned about and set off for Avernon. He'd taken two steps when his eyes were drawn to an abnormally high wave that hammered the shore. His eyes flicked back to the girl, but she'd vanished.

The bare rock was soaked.

Alarmed, Zak searched the ocean. He saw arms flailing in panic. Without hesitation, he threw off his coat and set off at speed.

The path turned into dry sand, which softened as he approached the water. Charging into the ocean, he felt the waves around his ankles, then waist. He launched into a dive.

'HELLLLP!!' the girl screamed before being swallowed by water.

His arms pumping the water like pistons, Zak swam at an incredible speed, barely feeling the cold. Then he filled his lungs with air and threw himself beneath the surface, into the marine world, its deathly silence threatening to crush his skull.

He stared ahead, but it was as black as tar.

He couldn't see the girl anywhere.

He couldn't see a thing.

It was then the strangest thing happened; the darkness brightened, as if someone had switched on a soft bedside lamp. He could see things much clearer than before - the endless seabed strewn with rocks and debris, the clusters of seaweed waving to and fro, all became visible like the bizarre landscape of an alien planet.

Then, about five metres away, he saw the girl's body sinking further into the murky depths. He powered over to her and grasped her wrist. His fingers tightened and he pulled her close.

Propelling himself upward, he aimed for the light above. Seconds later, they broke the surface. He looked at her, but she wasn't breathing, her face as grey as stone.

Pulling her horizontal, Zak rounded toward the shore and swam as fast as he could. Moments later, he lowered her onto the sand. His years of first aid training kicked in – *he knew exactly what to do.*

Tilting her head, he clasped her nose and breathed into her mouth. He pressed down on her chest three times then repeated the action.

With a tremendous shudder, water exploded from the girl's mouth, showering Zak's face. Her eyes shot open and she scratched for air.

Zak waited for her breathing to normalise, before saying, 'Are you okay?'

The girl coughed again, finally clearing her lungs. 'Y – Yes.' She looked at him, scared, confused and bewildered.

Zak smiled at her. ''You're okay now. Just relax.'

Now the colour was returning to her cheeks, he could see she was a pretty girl about his age with flawless ivory skin and sapphire blue eyes.

'You saved my life,' the girl said.

'It's nothing. I was just passing by.'

The girl face creased with shock as if suddenly grasping what had just happened. She flung her arms around Zak's shoulders and began to cry. 'Thank you. Thank you.'

'That's all right,' Zak replied. 'Anyone would have done it.'

The girl pulled away, shivering madly. 'I'm An – Anne. Anne Dixon.'

'Zak Fisher. Hang on.' He raced over to his jacket, scooped it up and ran back, coiling it tightly around Anne's shoulders.

'T-thanks,' Anne said, teeth chattering. She shot Zak a puzzled look. 'Why aren't you shivering?' She leaned over and stroked his face. 'You're warm. How is that possible?'

It occurred to Zak he'd never shivered in his life.

'I don't know,' he said. 'Anyway –'

Anne was about to press the issue when her fingers patted her neckline. 'Oh, no...' she said, horror-struck. 'Please, no.'

'What is it?'

'My necklace. I must have lost it.' Anne began to cry again, this time even more violently than before.

'Maybe you can get another?'

'I-it's not that,' Anne gasped in between spluttering breaths. 'It was the last ... the last thing my dad gave to me before he died a month ago.'

'Oh, I'm sorry,' Zak said. 'I really am.'

'It's not your fault,' Anne sniffed. 'I'm being silly. You've just saved my life and here's me crying over a silly piece of jewellery.'

'It's not silly.' Zak's thoughts turned to the letter he'd recently received from his mother. 'Not silly at all.'

They sat there in silence for what seemed like an age, letting the afternoon sun tender whatever warmth it could. It struck Zak his troubles were trivial compared to hers. She had just lost her father - her pain was raw, brutally so. He'd never even known his mother. And as he looked at Anne he recalled something Sid once said to him: *"The dead need the living to live."*

After five minutes or so, Anne mopped her eyes a final time and stood up. 'I'd better be getting home.'

'Okay.'

Zak and Anne left the beach and headed to Beridian.

'Are you on holiday here?' Anne asked.

'No,' Zak replied. 'I'm staying at Avernon Monastery.'

'Oh,' Anne said, finally managing a grin. 'You're one of *them*, are you?'

'What do you mean?'

'Well up until six months ago there were loads of kids that lived there. It's a private school, isn't it?'

'I guess,' Zak replied. 'I only arrived yesterday.'

'So have all the kids come back?'

'What d'you mean?'

'I work at O' Reilly's Diner - it's where the local kids hang out. We used to get loads coming in from Avernon, but then they just stopped. I'd heard the school moved to Wales or something. Has it reopened?'

'I guess so. But there are only four of us.'

Anne looked stunned. 'A school with only four kids in it?'

'Yeah.'

'I wouldn't fancy that,' Anne replied. 'You all must be pretty special.'

Zak smiled. 'Or so much trouble they can't have us round other kids.'

'I doubt that's true,' Anne replied. 'Besides, you can't be trouble... you're *my hero*. Anyway, I hope you'll come to O' Reilly's and bring your friends if you want. The burgers are great.' She flashed him a smile. 'And I'm buying... whatever you want. It's the least I can do.'

Although he really wanted to say yes, Zak didn't have a clue what the rules would be for him at Avernon. 'I don't know. Maybe.'

'I won't take no for an answer,' Anne said.

'Then I'd better try,' Zak said.

Reaching the fringes of the town, Zak stopped and said, 'Listen I'd better be getting back.'

'Okay.' Anne looped Zak's coat from her shoulders

and handed it over.

'No… keep it,' Zak said. 'You're still wet.'

'So are you, and I'm nearly home.'

'Seriously… take it,' Zak insisted. 'You can give it me back if I come to O' Reilly's.'

'You mean *when*.'

'Okay, when.'

'And make it soon.' Anne threw on the jacket, leaned over and kissed Zak's cheek. 'Thanks again, Zak.'

Zak watched her leave, before turning and breaking into a run, only too aware everyone at Avernon would be getting worried. However, when he reached the spot he'd first met Anne he stopped, pulled off his jumper, trousers and shoes, and raced back into the ocean. Some time later he emerged with a jubilant smile on his face.

He was holding a silver necklace.

- Chapter 15 -
Demon-lore

As Zak sprinted back to Avernon, he found he thought about Anne constantly. He'd never been that comfortable around girls but she didn't seem as irritating as some and he thought her face looked quite nice.

On his return he felt compelled to apologise to Pottsy for being longer than intended and felt a pang of guilt at seeing Pottsy's anxious expression, although he tried to justify it by claiming his fairy primroses had reacted badly to a new plant food.

Zak returned to his dorm where he bumped into Dunk in the corridor.

'Why are you wet?' Dunk asked.

'It's a long story,' Zak replied.

'D' you think I've actually got anywhere to be?'

'I saved a girl from drowning.'

'Oh, right,' Dunk said casually. 'Was she fit?'

'Err, well, she was all right. She works at a diner in the town.'

'There's a diner?' Dunk replied. 'And where's this town?'

'About four miles away. It's called Beridian.'

'They kept that quiet,' Dunk replied. 'Excellent. If

you saved her life she owes you a slap up meal then.'

'That's what she said.'

'I like this girl,' Dunk nodded. 'Let's see if Pottsy will let us go this weekend?'

'Okay.' Zak entered his bedroom.

Dunk followed him in. 'I'm goin' down the library before dinner to check out that Guppingham bloke. You wanna come?'

Making sure Dunk didn't see, Zak slipped Anne's necklace into his bedside drawer. 'Sure. Give me a few minutes to get changed.'

Ten minutes later, Zak and Dunk entered the library to find it considerably larger than any other building they'd come across so far. It was also deserted. A distinct smell of mould lingered on the air and a single flickering light bulb cast dancing shadows on the thousands of musty books and gnarled parchments packed tightly on to dozens of timber bookshelves. To their surprise and relief, they also found a large computer room populated with a large number of high-spec workstations.

They searched the Internet for information on Sir Robin Guppingham but found little other than he was considered the most accomplished Templar architect of the fourteenth century, a lauded military strategist, a sculptor and a poet. They did, however, find plenty of information on The Seal of Solomon, but none of it had to do with its true purpose as a gateway to another dimension. They rifled through a number of books but found some of the language, particularly in the older volumes, difficult to understand. At the end of a very frustrating two hours, they accepted they were none the wiser and gave up.

'This is useless,' Dunk said.

'Looks that way,' Zak said.

'Do you want to explore those caves? Maybe we'll find something there?'

Zak had come to the conclusion they really were searching for a very small needle in a planet-sized haystack. 'Or maybe Leah's right and this pointless?'

Dunk scowled. 'Don't join her side.'

'I'm not joining any side.'

'Well you should... *mine*!'

'What is it between you two?'

'I don't think she likes me very much.'

'You don't act like you like her very much, either.'

'She's all right. She's got an ego the size of Wales but she's all right.'

The words 'Pot', 'Kettle' and 'Black' entered Zak's head.

A short while later, the two of them headed to the fraterhouse for dinner, where they met up with Sarah and Leah.

'So you didn't find anything?' Leah said.

'Nowt,' Dunk replied, thrusting a fat slice of quiche into his mouth. 'But if you think about it why would we: if Guppingham hid the fact he'd been given the Seal then why would there be anything in a book? There's got to be summat somewhere, though.'

'I still think it's a waste of time,' Leah said.

'And you're entitled to your opinion as long as I don't have to hear it,' Dunk replied. 'I did find out summat else though.'

'Go on.'

'Zak's got a girlfriend.'

'What?' Sarah said.

Everyone stared at Zak, whose eyes were suddenly

locked on his baked potato.

'He's got a girlfriend,' Dunk repeated.

'I have not.'

Leah looked impressed. 'When did this happen?'

'He saved some bird's life this afternoon,' Dunk said, 'and she's invited him on a date.'

'It's not a date,' Zak said. 'She just wants to buy me a burger to say thanks.'

'Sounds like a date to me,' Leah said, arching her eyebrows.

'Well it isn't,' Zak replied.

'What's her name?' Leah asked.

'Anne.'

'Zak and Anne,' Dunk said. 'That's got a nice ring to it.'

'Oh, shut up,' Zak said irritably.

'What happened?' Sarah asked.

'A wave swept her into the sea. She was drowning. I jumped in and got her out. What else was I supposed to do?'

'But you could've drowned, too,' Sarah said. 'The Irish Sea is brutal this time of year. What were you thinking?'

'I was fine,' Zak said. 'I'm a good swimmer.'

'Of course he was fine,' Leah grinned. 'He's the big tough hero. No wonder Anne's fallen in love with you.'

'No one's fallen in love with anyone,' Zak growled. 'Now can we just forget about it?'

But Leah had no intention of complying. 'I don't know, Zak Fisher, I reckon you're a sly one.' She nudged Sarah. 'What do you think, Sar? He comes over like butter wouldn't melt in his mouth, but I reckon he's a bit of a player, don't you?'

'Maybe,' Sarah replied.

'I'm not,' Zak said.

'Personally, I think he's a right dog,' Dunk smirked. 'He acts like the angel he's s'posed to be, but really he's the devil in disguise.' He laughed.

It took all Zak's resolve not to shove Dunk's big fat quiche in his big fat face like a big fat custard pie.

*

The next morning, the four of them gathered in the Cellarium for their first Demon-lore class. Apprehension filled each of them.

What on earth would it be like being taught by a Hell Demon?

The Cellarium was a wide, draughty room beneath the refectory that Zak assumed used to be a storeroom. As he looked round he saw tables and chairs and a raised platform at the far end with a computer, projector, and a stack of old and very thick leather bound books. They each sat down when, from behind, the rear door creaked open and a cloaked Mister Gudrak walked past them to the platform. He carried a metal cage swathed in a thick black cloth.

'Good morning,' Mister Gudrak said. 'Or as we would say in Cycloidese: *Yaraka Mahh.* He placed the cage down on the floor. 'Welcome to your first Demon-lore class. You will get an insight into another world. However, much as I would dearly love to teach you about the fascinating flora and fauna, or indeed give you an insight into the gentle animals and kindly humanoids that flourish in Hell, my priority has to be with the dreadful species that have found their way to your planet.'

Mister Gudrak scooped up the stack of books and

distributed them to the group.

'Here is your copy of *'Demons and Demonilla'* by Arrytk Grapspoon. Mister Grapspoon, a fellow Cycloid, was amongst the first Hellians to work closely with the Templars in the nineteenth century and has written a most fascinating tome. Everything you need to comprehend about Hell's inhabitants is in there. I suggest you absorb it from cover to cover. It could save your life. So let us begin with some of what I believe are the most noteworthy demons at the Hell Lord's command.'

Mister Gudrak keyed in a button and the computer wakened as if from slumber. Four light beams shot out from the projector, but instead of sending an image onto a screen, the beams came together as one, forming a life-sized three-dimensional holographic image … a terrifying image.

And one that Zak knew only too well.

'This is a Mothman,' Mister Gudrak said, as Leah panted with disgust. 'Zak, I believe you've come into contact with a number of these.'

'Yes, sir.'

'Then you were fortunate to survive,' Mister Gudrak replied. 'Mothmen are foot soldiers to the Hell Lord. They are cruel, cunning and can fly but not for long periods of time. They are moderately intelligent and stronger than the average human. They are also accomplished swordsmen.'

Zak could see both Sarah and Leah looked visibly shaken. This didn't help when Mister Gudrak flicked to the next holographic image - a thin, skeletal creature with eight limbs and a pasty humanoid face.

'Oh my God,' Leah gasped. 'How revolting is that?'

'Indeed, Miss Emerson.' Mister Gudrak said. 'Even on Hell, the *Arachnoid* is considered a most unsightly creature. Arachnoids are subterranean beasts and hate light. As you can see they have eight limbs and can use them to move at great speeds. What they lack in intellect, they make up for in sheer ferociousness. They are, make no mistake, deadly in the extreme.'

A third image appeared on the screen. Zak felt his stomach churn. It was a reptilian creature with green leathery skin, beady yellow eyes and an extended jaw with twisted teeth.

'Now these are some of the most dangerous creatures at the Hell Lord's disposal,' Mister Gudrak said. 'These are *Reptilaks*. They are strong, cunning, incredibly agile and can leap great distances.'

Mister Gudrak went on to explain about Grippers, which Zak had already encountered; Aqualids - a marine based shark-like humanoid; Secters –a giant insect-like creature with poisonous antennae, and Scorpoids - a grotesque invertebrate that walked on all fours and had a curled poisonous tail.

However, it was Dunk who asked the question on the tip of everyone's lips. 'And what kind of demon is Lord Ballivan?'

For an instant, rage flashed in Mister Gudrak's eyes before he composed himself.

'Ballivan is a *Terroset*, a very rare beast indeed. And a hugely powerful one. He has a range of abilities. He can fly, he's telekinetic which means he can move objects at will, and he is as strong as two human men. His tongue can elongate to great lengths and - '

'- Elongate?' Dunk said, scrunching up his face.

'Yes… up to two metres.'

'That's disgusting,' Dunk said.

'Indeed,' Mister Gudrak said. 'Furthermore, that same tongue splits into two parts and can suck memories from his victims, giving him access to great knowledge. Yes, Lord Ballivan is a truly loathsome and deadly adversary. Even on Hell, his name is uttered in the most hushed of tones.'

Zak stared at Mister Gudrak and was surprised to hear the following words spill from his mouth. 'So how do we beat him?'

'For all his powers, Ballivan bleeds like any other creature,' Mister Gudrak replied. 'Anyway, enough of such unsavoury talk. For today, and today only, we shall cut the class short. Mrs Gudrak requests the pleasure of your company and I dare not disappoint her. She is truly the most powerful Hellian of all. So does everyone fancy a beverage and perhaps a bite to eat?'

Everyone was too dazed to show any enthusiasm, but nodded anyway.

'Excellent,' Mister Gudrak said. 'And to prove not all Hell creatures are as fearsome as those you've witnessed today.' He reached down and pulled the cloth off the cage. 'I would like you to meet Iccy and Izreal.'

Mister Gudrak opened the cage door and a creature with luminous blue fur, sausage-like legs and a stubby tail bounded out. Excitedly, it sped over to the north corner of the Cellarium. Then it ran up the wall and hung upside down from the ceiling, yapping merrily at everyone below.

'Please come down, Iccy, Izreal,' Mister Gudrak said as though scolding two small children. 'I know you're both excited but I'd like you to meet four special humans and you can't really do that from up there, can you?'

Both? Zak didn't understand.

Only one creature had left the cage. But then as he stared at the creature, astonishment filled him.

Iccy and Izreal were the same animal but with separate heads.

- Chapter 16 -
Meet the Gudraks

Mister Gudrak wafted two pieces of something that resembled chocolate in the air and Iccy and Izreal scampered down the wall, snatched the food from Mister Gudrak and were soon zigzagging around everyone's feet; in all their excitement, each head seemingly had a different opinion on which direction to take and they were crashing into things left, right and centre.

Mister Gudrak chuckled. 'Apparently, there's a human phrase that claims two heads are better than one, well this doesn't apply to Iccy and Izreal. They disagree over everything.'

Everyone watched as Iccy forced Izreal headfirst into a table leg.

'What are they?' Sarah said.

'They're *Hunklids*,' Mister Gudrak replied. 'A rare breed of Hell Hound.'

'They're dogs?' Leah asked.

'They certainly share many characteristics with earth dogs, and, as with dogs, there are many breeds of Hell Hound, some of which are very ferocious indeed. The Hunklid, however, is a particularly good natured breed.'

Mister Gudrak crouched down and tickled Iccy and Izreal's wrinkled chins. 'Anyway, if you would all care to follow me.'

Zak and the others trailed Mister Gudrak out of the room and through a long corridor at the end of which was a door. Mister Gudrak heaved it open and they found themselves in a winding tunnel, illuminated by torchlight, angling downward at a steep gradient. The damp, black walls were decked with hundreds of symbols, dating back hundreds of years.

Within the minute they had reached a crossroads. Each pathway was marked by a stone carving on the wall: north showed a Griffon; east showed a mother and baby; south showed an old man wearing a crown; and west showed the symbol of two knights on horseback.

'What do you know about all these symbols, Mister Gudrak?' Sarah asked.

'Very little,' Mister Gudrak replied. 'Most originate from your historic period known as the *medieval times*.'

Mister Gudrak turned left and the tunnel curved into a brightly lit cavern. Immediately, the tunnel's musty smell was replaced by the sweet smell of lavender as the group approached a wide opening in the cavern wall.

Iccy and Izreal scampered ahead, disappearing through the gap, each head yapping loudly as if trying to outdo the other.

'This is Gudrak Hovel,' Mister Gudrak said, ushering them through the gap. 'My earthen home.'

Entering, the group found themselves in an even larger cavern. Stalactites hung down from the ceiling like pointed teeth, some of which were so long they touched the surface of a crystal blue freshwater pool. Four smaller caves were set into the north wall, brightened from within by soft candlelight.

Just then, a stern female voice that boomed out from one of the caves, reverberating off the walls.

'Nathanaryn Gudrak!' the female voice snapped. 'You are late!'

Mister Gudrak's face creased with panic. 'I - I am sorry, my sweet. Iccy and Izreal were -'

'I'm teasing you, Mister Gudrak,' the voice said in a much gentler tone.

A female Cycloid wearing a flowery apron appeared from one of the caves. She was smaller than Mister Gudrak, with a less muscular torso and a jagged flat-edged stump instead of a horn. Her features were considerably softer than her husband's and her single eye much smaller and blue in colour. In her arms were two baby Cycloids who were fast asleep and snoring lightly in what seemed to be synchronised rhythmic breaths.

Mister Gudrak gave an uncomfortable chuckle. 'I knew that, Mrs Gudrak.'

'Did you now?' Mrs Gudrak replied with a smile. 'Now, husband of mine, you will introduce me to our four young guests.'

'Of course, dearest,' Mister Gudrak replied. 'Everyone, allow me to introduce my beautiful wife, Delleana Gudrak.'

'Welcome to our hovel,' Mrs Gudrak beamed. She raised the babies into the half-light. 'Garrick and Gibblon would like to welcome you, too.'

Gibblon blew tiny bubbles out of his crooked mouth and Garrick's pink tongue flicked in and out as if licking an invisible ice cream.

Leah moved in closer to get a better look.

'They're adorable,' Leah said.

'Thank you, ,' Mrs Gudrak replied. 'You are very kind. We are proud parents. As a matter of fact, Garrick and Gibblon are the first of our kind to have been born on Earth, which makes them very special indeed. Anyway, I'll just lay them in their cribs and serve refreshments. Please, everyone join me.'

Mrs Gudrak guided them into the largest of the four caves. Inside there were three leather armchairs with embroidered cushions and an ornately carved dining table and eight chairs. A number of framed portraits of the Gudrak family through the ages hung on the wall, but the most striking object was a huge golden double-headed axe fixed to the left wall. It had a shimmering blade crafted from Magnathian and a thick wooden haft.

As everyone was steered toward a seat, Zak found himself drawn to the axe. He walked over and studied it.

'Do you like my axe, Zak?' Mister Gudrak said.

'Yes, sir.'

'It is named *'Eppnyax'* and it is the Gudrak family axe,' Mister Gudrak said proudly. 'It was forged by my distant ancestor, Tryrannik Gudrak, and has been passed down for generations. One day it shall be passed to my sons for their guardianship. My people believes that providing the family axe remains with its clan folk, that family shall survive a thousand generations.'

'It's fantastic,' Zak said.

'To the Cycloidese, the family axe is considered the most precious of objects,' Mister Gudrak said. 'Not for its capacity for combat, you understand, but as a tool for construction, a symbol of home building. Of course, the axe does make for a formidable weapon, but fortunately

I have not had cause to swing it in nine years. Violence is not in my nature. Now, please, sit down.'

Zak joined the others at the table as Mrs Gudrak appeared carrying a large tray warping under the weight of a large teapot, cups, plates and a cake the size of a car tyre. She set down the tray.

'This is Herbuggle Tea,' Mrs Gudrak said, filling the cups. 'It might taste different from your tea, but it is popular in Hell. I think you may enjoy it.'

Zak picked up a cup and hesitantly took a sip. The liquid slid down his throat like warm honey. It was delicious.

'Do you like it, Zak?' Mrs Gudrak asked.

'Very much.'

Mrs Gudrak smiled. 'Good. And this is Jamble Cake - a popular indulgence on Hell. This particular recipe has been with my clan folk for many years.' She passed each of them a generous slice.

Biting into it, Zak felt his mouth erupt with flavours, most of which he couldn't identify. It was so different from anything he'd tasted before. He looked over at Dunk who had swallowed his in one bite, his eyes silently pleading with Mrs Gudrak for another piece.

Mrs Gudrak took the hint. She placed another slab of cake onto Dunk's plate. 'Now are you all enjoying your time at Avernon? I can't imagine the shock you felt when you heard about who you are and the destinies that are yours to be followed.'

'Yeah. It's all been a bit of a shock,' Leah replied.

'How long have you been here, Mrs Gudrak?' Sarah asked.

'Nine years. Enough time to master much of your language and many of your earthly customs. Ichabod says he thinks I sound like the chairwoman of a Townswomen's Guild, although I'm not sure what he means by that.'

'Why did you come here?' Dunk said. 'Earth, I mean.'

'Now that is a long story,' Mister Gudrak said in a cheerless tone. 'And perhaps one for another day.'

Mrs Gudrak didn't seem to agree. 'Things became rather difficult for us on Hell,' she said, 'so Mister Gudrak and I made the decision to leave. It really was the only way.'

'Why difficult?' Dunk asked.

Mrs Gudrak's eyes dimmed. 'I'm afraid Mister Gudrak would be in mortal danger on Hell. And although he does not care about such things, I do. It was because of me that we left.'

'Why mortal danger?' Zak asked. 'Because he works with the Templars?'

'Morloch wanted him dead long before he worked with the Templars.' Mrs Gudrak cast her husband a proud smile. 'You see, in his youth Mister Gudrak was one of the leaders of an underground movement who strived to usurp Morloch as King. Morloch is a force of pure evil, but even he is vulnerable. And Mister Gudrak's rebellion was gaining momentum all the time. From all parts of Hell, many species began to listen. Many wanted the end of the Monarchy that had ruled so cruelly for so very long. They wanted a new type of leader, and many wanted that leader to be Mister Gudrak. Regrettably, Morloch heard of this, and wanted him dead. Mister Gudrak was forced into hiding. My father was dying and I could not join him in his exile, so Mister Gudrak and I separated. It was then -'

She hesitated. Her eye dampened.

'That's enough, dear,' Mister Gudrak said gently. 'You've answered the question and don't need to say more.'

'No, my husband,' Mrs Gudrak replied. 'I think they should hear it. They should know what they are up against. They should know theirs is a higher purpose with a righteous cause, and not just for their world but for ours.' She hesitated. 'One of Morloch's henchmen tracked me down. He murdered my father, kidnapped me, and under the King's instructions, tortured me. He wanted to know where Mister Gudrak was hiding. But I wouldn't divulge his location. And so he did terrible things to me - things I'm not about to repeat, but I still wouldn't tell him anything. So ... he took my horn.' Her fingers brushed the stump on her forehead. 'I had a beautiful horn and he hacked it off like he was felling a *Yaraken* tree –'

Tears streamed down her face now.

Mister Gudrak placed his hand gently upon his wife's. 'Please, dear, don't...'

'But they need to know,' Mrs Gudrak replied. 'The torturer's name was ...' She spat out the name. '*Verekus Ballivan.* I believe you have heard of him.'

Silence filled the cave.

'Anyway, I was lucky. Mister Gudrak rescued me, we escaped and -' Mrs Gudrak's voice failed her.

Mister Gudrak continued.' - And it was then I chose to leave Hell,' he said. 'I could not bear the thought of anything further happening to my wife. So we came here and the Templars gave us sanctuary. They gave us a home.' He drew a weighty breath. 'But one day, I hope to return to my world, when the evil winds have turned.'

He looked at each one of them in turn. 'One day, Morloch will pay for what he has done to my wife, to my family, and to my world. And so will -' He hissed the next words. '- So will *Verekus Ballivan*. I intend to meet with him one glorious day, a day I desire to be sooner rather than later. And on that day I shall, with a willing heart, swing my axe again. And I shall not miss...'

Zak was about to say something when someone else's voice entered the conversation - a gentle but firm voice he never expected to hear.

'I think I can speak for all of us, Mister Gudrak,' Sarah said. 'We will do everything we can to help you, your family, your world and our own. If we are the Angels we're supposed to be, then we'll do whatever we can to make all of this right. I can promise you that.'

Staring at Sarah, Zak had never felt so proud of anyone in his life.

- Chapter 17 -
Kelly Barnes

For Zak, the rest of the day crawled by at a snail's pace. How could a two-hour maths class about geometry compare with learning about Scorpoid venom or the attack patterns of an Aqualid?

And even though he was trying to digest all Father Percival told them about Cartesian coordinates, he couldn't help but dwell on Mister and Mrs Gudrak's ordeal - how Lord Ballivan had disfigured Mrs Gudrak, how they had to flee their home for fear of being killed. It saddened him to think there were countries on earth where people were still forced to do the same thing.

Zak found himself wanting to help the Gudraks, but this seemed to magnify the same question in his mind: *How could he, Zak Fisher, be an Angel?* And if he was, then exactly what did that mean? He felt like an outcast most of the time anyway, how would he feel walking into a chip shop with a set of wings and a halo?

At dinner, Zak was disappointed to see Kurnan missing from his usual seat. Ever since yesterday, he'd felt an urge to apologise for walking away after Kurnan's admission about his mother. Instead, he saw Kurnan's seat occupied by Kelly Barnes, the female Templar who had discovered Lord Ballivan's desire to find the Seal of Solomon. She appeared to have made a good recovery and was in excellent spirits, talking animatedly with Big Al about something Zak couldn't hear.

During the meal, Zak, Sarah, Leah and Dunk spoke quietly about the different species of Hellian they had studied that day.

'I can't believe how ugly they all are?' Leah said, scrunching up her nose as if inhaling a nasty smell.

'They're demons,' Dunk snorted. 'What d'you expect? Boy band wannabees?'

A second later, a sprout exploded on his nose.

'Pack that in!' Dunk snapped at Leah, wiping sprout leaves from his face.

When the laughter faded, Sarah turned to Zak and said in a small voice, 'So what were Mothmen like in real life, Zak?'

'I don't remember much,' Zak replied. 'Thankfully, Kurnan got there and a few seconds later they were all dead. It's well strange. They don't just fall down and die. They disintegrate.'

'Disintegrate?' Leah said.

'Crumble to dust,' Zak said. 'By the time Kurnan had finished the kitchen was like a thick fog of dead Mothmen bits.'

'That's just gross,' Leah said.

'Weird,' Sarah said.

'So are they easy to kill then?' Dunk asked.

'I wouldn't say easy,' Zak replied. 'Kurnan was amazing. I've never seen anyone move so fast.'

'Yeah, well I'm no slouch either,' Dunk said. 'Personally, I can't wait to get at them. They'll call me

Dunk the Destroyer.'

Leah snorted. 'Who will exactly?'

'I dunno… *people.*'

'But who exactly'

'People who know about these things.'

'You're an idiot.'

Dunk ignored her. 'Eh, Zak, maybe you and me should have a competition? First to take out a dozen Mothmen wins a tenner.'

Sarah shot him an irritated look. 'It's not a game, Dunk!'

'Chill, Sarah. I'm only kidding.'

'I don't see anything to kid about,' Sarah replied. 'You're talking about killing things.'

'They're not kittens, Sar,' Dunk replied. 'You've seen what they look like, what they can and will do. You've heard what happened to Zak. They're monsters… and they're here to take our planet. I ain't standing for that. Besides, it was you that said you'd do anything to help the Gudraks.'

'And I meant it,' Sarah replied. 'It's just killing doesn't exactly sit well with me.' Her eyes scanned each of them in turn. 'I mean, ask yourself - do you think you can kill?'

'I have done,' Zak replied. 'I shot a few Grippers with an arrow gun when they attacked Kurnan and me on the way here. I also killed a Mothman with a sword at my foster parents' house.'

These words triggered silence in the others. Just then, they heard an unfamiliar female voice.

'Hiya, everyone...'

Zak looked up to a young woman standing before them. Although she wore a wide smile, her pretty face was swollen with bruising around her eyes and cuts on her cheeks that resembled scratch marks.

'I'm Kelly Barnes,' she said. 'It's great to have you at Avernon … this place could do with some young blood again.'

'How are you feeling, Kelly?' Sarah asked.

'I'm sound,' Kelly replied. 'It looks worse than it is. I've been checked over and Doc Pudgbury has given me the okay, so I'm ready for action again. I must've given you all such a fright last night. Soz 'bout that.'

'No sweat,' Dunk said.

'As long as you're okay,' Leah added.

'I am,' Kelly replied.

Zak's eyes flitted to Kurnan's empty seat. 'Where's Kurnan?'

'He's had to leave for a while,' Kelly said. 'Templar business. Top secret stuff! Kurnan's often sent to do the jobs no one else will do.'

'What kind of jobs?' Zak asked, intrigued.

'Oh, they don't tell me stuff like that,' Kelly replied. 'I'm well down the Templar pecking order in terms of being told anything juicy. In all fairness, I was only *accoladed* a year ago so I'm not doin' too bad.'

'What does 'accoladed' mean?' Leah asked.

'It's when they make you a full Templar Knight… until then you're just a novice. Mind if I join you?'

As there were no words of objection, she pulled out a chair and sat down.

'Anyway, with Kurnan gone, Pottsy has asked me to take over your WAC class. I can't wait. I've never done any teaching before, so I hope I do okay.'

'I'm sure you will,' Sarah said.

Kelly smiled. 'So how are you all settling – '

But Dunk wasn't interested in small talk. 'So how does Lord Ballivan intend to get the Seal of Solomon?'

Kelly looked surprised. She glanced furtively over at Pottsy, who was talking to Dr Pudgbury, who looked much less cheerful than the previous night. 'You know about the Seal, do you?' she asked in a whisper.

'We heard you mention it before you lost consciousness,' Leah said. 'Then we asked Pottsy about it.'

'Oh, right,' Kelly replied. 'And what did he say? He doesn't know where it is, does he?'

'I don't think so,' Zak said.

'And he didn't tell us much,' Dunk said. 'I mean, he's told us what it is, but he hasn't told us how Lord Ballivan intends to find it.'

Kelly nodded. 'The fact is we don't know. Did Pottsy mention Sir Robin Guppingham?'

'Yes,' Leah said. 'But that's about all.'

Kelly seemed disappointed. 'Oh, okay. I have to say I'd feel much better if we did know where it was. At least the Templars could protect it.'

'But isn't it best it's never found?' Sarah asked.

'Maybe,' Kelly replied. 'But the Hell Lords always seem to find a way to get what they want.'

'So how did you find out Ballivan was after it?' Zak asked.

Kelly hesitated as if accessing a painful memory. 'For the last few weeks I've been working undercover in London, trying to get closer to a bloke we suspect is an Assist, maybe even a member of the Hellfire Club. He's a top solicitor in London – a real slug of a bloke - so I pretended to be one of his clients and managed to place a *Tector* on him.'

'What's a Tector?' Dunk asked.

'It's a tiny tracking device, about the size of a pinhead. It records someone's movements. Anyway, I tailed him to a meeting in this posh house in Kensington with a Reptilak called Karnak, one of Lord Ballivan's top advisors. Well, they must've found the Tector because before I knew it, I'd been captured and taken to a Demon Den, just off Oxford Street, and -' her fingers unconsciously traced the cuts on her face, '- and they demanded I tell them everything I knew about the Seal... as if I knew anything about it! Anyway, they tied me up and tortured me for, I dunno, maybe a day, could've even been two. Fortunately, I had a *smoker* – a smoke bomb - hidden on me and managed to escape. I got real lucky... and they got slack. One way or another, I got out. Thank God.'

'And where do they think the Seal was?' Zak said.

'They're convinced it's here at Avernon,' Kelly replied. 'Somehow, Lord Ballivan has discovered a letter from Guppingham to another senior Templar, Sir Peter Morbury saying something like that. However, the letter states the Seal is impossible to find without some kind of marker.'

'What's the marker?' Zak asked.

'Haven't a clue,' Kelly replied. 'And I'm pretty sure Lord Ballivan doesn't know, either, so that's something I suppose.'

'Then that's good,' Sarah said. 'There's no way the Seal can be found even if it does exist.'

'Fair point,' Kelly replied. 'But Lord Ballivan's a smart cookie – real smart. And he has ways of finding out things that others don't.'

'You mean his ability to read minds?' Leah said.

'Yeah… amongst other things. I dunno - he's dangerous, and I think most of us would feel much better if the Templars got hold of the Seal. Maybe we can destroy it somehow?'

'Do you think it's here… at Avernon?' Zak asked.

'I really don't know,' Kelly replied. 'But the one thing I know is that as long as Lord Ballivan thinks it is then none of us are really safe. Plus, the one thing that's certain is that Avernon is chockfull of mysteries, so it wouldn't surprise me if something important was hidden here. You've seen how big it is… and there are miles and miles of caves beneath our feet, probably covering most of this island. This place has all kinds of secrets.' Her smile grew. 'Hey, maybe the four of you should look for the Seal? If you're Angels then maybe you'll have some divine luck or something?'

'We've already started,' Dunk said.

'Have you?' Kelly replied. 'Good for you lot. I hope you get somewhere. Still, if you have I'd say nothing to Pottsy about any of it if I were you.'

'Why?' Zak asked.

Kelly leaned in and her face fell into shadow from the light above. 'He's adamant nobody tries to - '

Before she could finish, Pottsy approached the table. 'Making your introductions, Kelly?'

Kelly bolted upright. 'Yes, sir.'

'You don't need to call me, sir,' Pottsy replied. 'You're a fully trained Templar Knight now and not a novice. We are equal in every way.'

'Soz,' Kelly said. 'I forgot. Old habits die hard and all that.'

'I understand.'

'Pottsy,' Dunk said. For a moment, it appeared he

was going to ask Pottsy about the Seal, but a sharp look from Kelly made him change his mind. 'Err, I was wondering if the four of us could go to Beridian on Saturday? Apparently there's a diner there that's pretty good.'

'Ah, you've heard about O' Reilly's. I didn't think it would take long. Well, I don't want you to think of Avernon as a prison. However, if I do agree I'll have to ask each of you to take a Lectroflare… just to be on the safe side.'

'What's a Lectroflare?' Leah asked.

'Oh, nothing too conspicuous – certainly nothing that would ruin an outfit – it actually looks like a small pen. However, it's a very powerful transmitter and if you encounter any trouble you can activate it and it tells us your precise location.'

'Don't worry, Pottsy,' Dunk said. 'We'll avoid anything with five heads and fangs. Besides, Zak's met a girl so we've got no choice but to go.'

Pottsy looked dumbfounded. 'A girl, eh?' he said so loudly Zak shrank in his seat. 'Now that is a turn up for the books.'

'Yeah,' Dunk said. 'It's basically a date.'

'It's not a date,' Zak said flatly.

'Really?' Pottsy replied. 'Then of course you must go - after all, who am I to stand in the way of true love?'

'It's not like that,' Zak said angrily.

Dunk nodded. 'It's exactly like that!'

'Then I want you all to enjoy yourselves. Particularly you, Zak.' Pottsy winked at Zak 'It may hard for you to believe but even I was young once.'

The table erupted into smiles, except for Zak, whose face had turned gherkin green and Sarah who looked faintly glum as if irritated she was the only one aware of the dangers of leaving the monastery grounds.

'Fantastic!' Dunk said.

But Zak didn't see what was so fantastic about it. He felt annoyed everyone was making such a big deal out of it and the last thing he wanted was an audience when he met Anne again. Still, he did want to return the necklace, so he sat back, took a deep breath and decided as long as Dunk stopped teasing him he wouldn't feel quite so compelled to throw him off the cliff.

- Chapter 18 -
O' Reilly's

That night Zak tossed and turned for hours, listening to the angry wind assault his bedroom window. His thoughts flitted from the looming weekend and the trip to Beridian to Sid and Irene. It had only been a few days since he'd seen the old couple but he missed them more than expected. He'd received daily phone texts and Skyped them twice, but it really wasn't the same. He was relieved the Templar High Assembly had approved their return to Fumbletree Cottage as, with Zak gone, it was thought they were under no immediate danger, but it made him miss his former life all the more.

As it turned out the week flew by. His classes (even the ones that didn't involve Magnaswords) were much more fun than those at Saint Quentin's.

The Hand-to-Hand combat class was a particular highlight.

Big Al, despite being the size of a small country, proved to be nimble on his feet and positively lethal. Furthermore, he was a great teacher and regaled them with countless accounts of fights he'd been involved in, from a bar brawl in Bradford to a knife fight in a mining town on Hell called Mariaphx.

And even though Big Al insisted on no full contact, when Dunk suggested boys could fight better than girls, Leah roundhouse kicked him so hard he barely said another word for the rest of the day.

On Saturday, Zak woke to hear Dunk bellowing 'Love is in the Air' as he banged on his bedroom door. His insides churned. He didn't want to go to Beridian anymore. He wanted to spend the day researching The Seal of Solomon or practising swordplay or anything that didn't involve him leaving Avernon.

By the time he emerged from his room he felt queasy; Anne's necklace felt distinctly heavy in his pocket.

Throughout breakfast, Zak said very little and found himself staring into space for long periods of time, Every now and again Dunk would address him as 'Lover Boy' or 'Romeo' until Zak grew so angry he emptied his breakfast down Dunk's back. Dunk was still pulling flecks of scrambled egg out of his clothes an hour later.

At eleven, Zak, Dunk, Lean and Sarah gathered by the front gates where they met Pottsy who gave each of them a Lectroflare and detailed instructions how to use it. Leah had put on her shortest skirt and wore so much make-up Zak wasn't sure if any of her actual skin was visible anymore. Sarah had made an effort too, albeit a less showy one than Leah, and sported a new T-shirt and gypsy skirt, her hair down instead of in its usual ponytail. As they left the monastery grounds he could tell from her expression she had grave reservations about the excursion.

He wasn't the only one to notice.

'What's the matter with you?' Dunk asked Sarah as

they followed the path to the beach road. 'You've got a face like a bag of spanners.'

'I haven't,' Sarah replied. 'I'm just not sure this is a good idea.'

'Why not?'

'Because as far as the Hellian populace goes we're enemy number one. And they know we're at Avernon so what other reason do I need exactly?'

'You're worrying over nothing, Sar,' Dunk replied. 'Besides, if summat does kick off I'll protect you.'

'Oh, that's right. You're Dunk the Destroyer. Of course, you weren't destroying much when Mister Gudrak revealed he was a Cycloid. In fact, if I remember correctly you were too busy screaming like a baby.'

Dunk looked mortified. 'I did not scream.'

'You're right,' Sarah replied. 'It was more of a prolonged squeak.'

Leah laughed. 'You go, Sar!'

Dunk huffed loudly but didn't reply.

It was then Zak decided to buy Sarah a gift at the first possible opportunity. After all, with just a few simple words she'd done more damage to Dunk's ego than Leah's roundhouse kick ever did.

*

As Beridian came into view, Zak found the squeals from the circling gulls a welcome distraction from his pounding heart.

'You feeling okay, mate?' Dunk asked. 'You're looking a bit peaky.'

'I'm fine,' Zak replied, hoping no one could hear the anxiety in his voice.

With Leah studying the map, they tracked the quayside, passing an ice cream parlour, a fish and chip shop, two souvenir shops and an amusement arcade.

It was then Zak saw a sign that read '**Hops Seafood Restaurant**' and an arrow pointing right. However, before he had a chance to search it out he heard Dunk's voice.

'There it is… *O' Reilly's.*'

At the end of the dock was a white-washed building with a slate roof and a red, blue and white painted sign - '**O' Reilly's American Diner**' - fixed above the doorway. Zak glanced through the window and saw dozens of tables, sitting at which were groups of teenagers, chatting and tucking into plates of food.

'Now this is what I'm talking about,' Dunk said. He pushed open the door and marched in, followed by Leah, Sarah and finally Zak.

Inside, the restaurant walls were covered with posters of very old films and various other forms of Americana. A large American flag loomed above the counter and an old style juke-box was being fed by a young couple that were holding hands.

'So where's this Anne girl then, Zak?' Dunk asked.

Before Zak could reply, he heard a shriek and a waitress raced over, her pony-tailed blonde hair swishing left and right.

'Zak… I'm so glad you came,' Anne said. 'I really hoped you would.'

'My pleasure,' Zak said, keeping his voice as steady as he could.

'He's been looking forward to it,' Dunk said. 'It's all he's talked about all week.'

'No it isn't,' Zak fired back.

Anne laughed. 'I'm sure. Has he told you he saved my life? He was amazing.'

'He is amazing, isn't he?' Dunk said. 'Of course, I'd have saved your life, too, if I'd have been there. Does that mean I can have free food?'

'I'm paying for my food,' Zak said firmly. 'And so are you.'

'You're not,' Anne replied. 'It's on me. I'm paying for all of you.'

Dunk beamed. 'I love you, Anne.'

'Dunk,' Zak repeated. 'We're paying for it. End of story.'

'But she said –'

' - Shut up, Dunk,' Leah cut in. 'We're paying for our own food. Zak, aren't you going to introduce us?'

'Yeah,' Zak said. 'Anne Dixon, this is Leah, Sarah and Dunk. They're mates of mine.'

'Hi, Anne,' Leah said.

Anne smiled broadly. 'Nice to meet you all. So you're staying at Avernon Monastery, are you?'

'Yeah,' Leah said.

'Great,' Anne said. 'Then I hope you'll become regulars. It's really the only place for kids to go round here.' She pulled four menus from the counter top, directed them to a table by the window and gave each of them a menu. 'You have a think about what you want to eat and I'll tell Fergus, the owner, you're here. Zak, he said he wants to meet you if that's okay?'

'Err, sure,' Zak replied.

Anne disappeared through a door that led to the kitchens.

Leah grinned at Zak. 'She's pretty.'

'Is she?' Zak said. 'I haven't noticed.'

'Rubbish,' Leah replied. 'Isn't she pretty, Sarah?'

'Very,' Sarah replied.

A moment later, the kitchen door opened again and Anne emerged, followed by a thin, elderly man in a white shirt with rolled up sleeves and an apron flecked with oil stains.

'Everyone, this is Fergus O' Reilly,' Anne said. She pointed at Zak. 'And Fergus, this is Zak Fisher.'

Fergus walked over to Zak. '*So...* you're the famous Zak Fisher, eh?' he said in a thick Irish brogue. His face cracked with a smile and he pulled Zak close in a bear-hug. 'Bless you, ma boy. Thank ya so much for savin' our darlin' Annie's life. She's 'ad the hardest time of late, so she has.' He looked at Anne, his eyes misting over. 'And I dunna know what I'd do without her...'

'Err, no problem,' Zak replied.

Fergus released Zak and cupped his cheeks in his hands. 'Yer an angel sent from heaven, so y'are.'

Dunk exchanged a grin with Sarah and Leah.

'I was just passing by,' Zak said. 'Anyone would have done it.'

'That ain't true, boy,' Fergus said. 'Yer a true hero. Them seas can be as rough as gums after a night on the black stuff. Anyway, me place be yours so whatever Zak Fisher and his friends want ter eat and drink is on me. Yer money ain't no good 'ere.'

Dunk beamed at Fergus. 'I like you, Fergus. I really do.'

'Then I like ya too, son,' Fergus replied. 'Now, if yeh'll excuse me, I've got some steaks ter fry up.' With a parting wave, he returned to the kitchens.

'What a great guy,' Dunk said.

'He actually is,' Anne said. 'So can I get you all something to drink?'

Zak could see that Dunk was keen to order, but felt

it best he gave Anne the necklace so he could relax and enjoy his meal. 'Anne, can I have a quick word... err, outside?'

Anne looked surprised. 'Sure.'

Leah shot Sarah an incredulous look. Her mouth silently formed a '*wow*'.

Avoiding eye contact with the others, Zak weaved his way to the door. He pushed it open and moved just beyond the view of the window, so no one could see him. He turned to face a confused Anne.

'This'll only take a second,' Zak said, 'and I didn't want to give it you in front of the others.' He rooted in his pocket and pulled out the silver necklace. 'I think this is yours.'

For a lingering moment Anne stared blankly at the necklace. Then her bottom lip quivered and tears pooled in her eyes. Hands trembling, she took the necklace. 'But h – how?'

Zak wasn't about to say he'd returned to the sea and his enhanced vision made it possible for him to see through the blackness. 'It was washed up on the beach. Stroke of luck, eh?'

Anne gave no indication she'd heard him. She coiled the chain between her fingers and her head tilted up slowly. As her eyes found his, her face changed. 'Your eyes - they're different colours. I never noticed that before.'

'I know. It's weird, isn't it?'

'It's fantastic. You're fantastic.'

'Oh, err, thanks.'

'No, thank you,' Anne said softly, looping the necklace over her head. 'Thank you so much.'

Before Zak knew anything else, she had curled her

arms round his neck and was kissing him full on the lips.

The kiss only lasted a second but left feeling Zak dazed.

From nowhere, an aggressive voice interrupted them. 'What the hell's goin' on here?'

Zak spun round to face six teenage boys, all of them older and much larger than him. The boy that spoke was the biggest of the group with gym-honed muscular shoulders, brown hair styled in a quiff, and charcoal eyes that seethed.

'Kyle?' Anne gasped, stepping away from Zak in shock.

Kyle ignored her, his massive hands clenching into fists. He glared at Zak. 'Oi… you little scrote! I'm talkin' to you – why are you snoggin' my girlfriend?'

- Chapter 19 -
Kyle Dobson

Zak's eyes flicked from the boy to Anne and back again. However, before he had time to respond, Anne's angry voice shot back.

'What are you talking about? I'm not your girlfriend. I never was and never will be. You should sort yourself out, Kyle Dobson. You're sixteen. Don't you think it's time you grew up?'

'I'm not talkin' ter you,' Kyle growled, aiming a finger at Zak. 'I asked you a question, mate, now gimme an answer!'

Although Kyle was as wide as a tank, Zak didn't feel remotely intimidated. 'I don't think it's any of your business.'

'Maybe I wanna make it my business.' Kyle raised his fist.

'Then make it your business,' Zak said. 'I couldn't care less.'

Anne stepped between the two of them. 'Stop it, Kyle. This has got nothing to do with Zak, so you can just leave him alone. And me, for that matter. You're banned from O' Reilly's so don't think you're coming in or I'll call the police.' She seized Zak's hand and pulled him into the restaurant.

Even with the door closed, they could hear Kyle bellowing threats from outside.

'I am so sorry about that,' Anne said, shaking. 'He's such a moron. I was never his girlfriend. I went on one date with him a few months ago. Anyway, what a shock… he turned out to be a total loser and he's been pestering me ever since.'

'Don't worry about it,' Zak said.

'Seriously,' Anne said. 'He's trouble. So just be careful when you leave.'

'He's just a bully, like any other. No big deal.'

Anne stared into Zak's eyes. 'You really are amazing, aren't you?'

'Me? Nah.'

'I think you are. And thanks again for this.' Anne teased the necklace between her thumb and finger. 'You have no idea how special it is to me.'

Zak recalled his mother's letter. 'I think I do.'

'I'll have to get back to work now, but -' Anne pulled out her order pad, scribbled down a number and passed it over. 'Here's my mobile number if you ever want to go out? I hope you do. I think we'd have fun.' She smiled at him before dashing into the kitchens.

Zak stood there, shell-shocked. He'd never had anything to do with girls, and here was one giving him her number. He glanced over at Dunk, Sarah and Leah, who stared at him, open mouthed, before quickly returning to their menus. He walked back to the table, slightly taller than before.

'What was that all about?' Dunk asked.

Zak scooped up a menu and focussed on it with an

unusual degree of interest. 'I had to give her something.'

'What?'

'Nothing much,' Zak replied. 'A necklace.'

Leah laughed. 'Zak, you are so smooth. Jewellery, already?'

'No... it was her necklace. She'd lost it. I was just returning it.'

'Why did you go outside to do it then?'

'It's a personal thing to her. I didn't want her to cry or anything.'

'I stand corrected,' Leah said. 'You are *very* smooth.'

'It wasn't like that - her father gave it to her before he died.'

'What was all that shouting outside?' Sarah asked, eyes narrowing.

'Some lad, an ex of hers saw us talking, and he wasn't happy about it and started mouthing off.'

'Did you smack him one?' Dunk asked.

'Of course I didn't.'

'Did he catch you doing something you shouldn't?' Leah grinned.

'No,' Zak said, feeling irritated now. 'He just assumed something was going on... which it wasn't.'

For the next five minutes Zak fielded a barrage of questions about Anne from Leah and Dunk, the only reprieve coming when the food finally arrived.

Throughout the meal, Zak found his mind spiralling with thoughts on what to do next. He did want to see her again, he knew that, but how should he go about it? Should he call her that night? What would she say? And there was another problem: he lived in an ancient monastery with dozens of Templar Knights, four Cycloids and a two-headed Hellhound. Not to mention he was allegedly an Angel sent to earth to battle a Hell King and prevent the End of Days. None of it would win him a boyfriend of the year award.

By the time it came to leave, the restaurant was heaving. Zak didn't say another word to Anne bar a brief goodbye as she was rushed off her feet, but as they passed the window he glanced inside and saw her mouth the words *'call me'*, to which he smiled and nodded.

An amber sun lit the way home as the group strolled along the beach path, casting pebbles into the sea and talking about what they would eat the next time they visited O' Reilly's.

As Avernon loomed on the horizon, Zak felt a stab of relief. He'd seen Anne, given her the necklace and received her phone number, which he was keen to use no matter how nervous he felt about it. He was about to ask the others if they wanted to watch a film in the social room when an ugly shout echoed from behind. Looking back, he saw six youths cycling in their direction.

Kyle Dobson led the way, his hood pulled up and a half-smoked cigarette hanging loosely from his bottom lip. Within seconds, the youths overtook them, jumped off their bikes which they let clatter to the ground, and gathered like a pack of hungry wolves, whispering amongst themselves and sniggering loudly.

Kyle Dobson flicked his cigarette aside and approached Zak. 'Well, well, fancy seein' you again? Zak, isn't it? We didn't have the chance ter finish our little chat before, did we?' He turned to a tall gangly youth to his left. 'Jake... this is Zak.'

'Hi, Zak,' Jake said. 'You look like a tosser.'

'Now, Jake,' Kyle said. 'I reckon he's one of them

freaks at the monastery, so you've gotta be polite. We don't want them thinkin' the locals are yobs, do we?'

Dunk stepped forward. 'We don't,' he said coolly. 'You lot are though.'

Kyle's jaw tightened. 'I'd keep out of this, mate, if you know what's good for you.'

'But I don't know what's good for me,' Dunk replied. 'I'm dumb like that.'

'Stop it, Dunk,' Leah said.

'Yeah, listen to your bird and *stop* it,' Kyle smirked. 'Besides, I ain't here to see you.' His eyes locked on Zak. 'It's me and you that needs to talk.'

'What do you want, Kyle?' Zak asked.

'I wanna see how brave y'are when there ain't a girl standin' between us? Coz I don't reckon you're brave at all.'

'I'd leave now if I were you,' Sarah said.

'Jeez,' Kyle said. 'If he ain't got one girl protecting him he's got another. Stay out of it, luv, or you might regret it.'

'I really wouldn't threaten her,' Zak said calmly.

Kyle squared up to Zak. 'And what're you gonna do about it if I do?'

Zak hesitated for a moment and then said, 'I think you should turn around and go back to town. You really don't want to do this. Believe me, it would be a mistake on your part.'

'A mistake on my part?' Kyle quivered like jelly before bursting into laughter. 'Ooh, you've got me trembling in my boots here. Eh, lads... I'm gettin' the feelin' Zak here thinks he's hard.'

Zak gave a heavy sigh. 'Okay. What exactly is it you want?'

'Err, let me think...'

'You want to fight?' Zak said.

'Why not?' Kyle sneered.

'Okay,' Zak said, removing his jacket and passing it to Dunk. 'Fair enough. If that's what you want.'

'Zak...You can't!' Sarah said, glancing at Leah, who looked unsure as to what to say.

'It's okay, Sarah,' Zak replied. 'I know what I'm doing. Let's get this straight, Kyle, you want to beat me up?'

'I do... yeah.' Kyle grinned. 'If that's alright with you?'

'That's fine with me,' Zak said. 'Okay then, I'll give you a shot. If you can knock me down with one punch, I'll never see Anne again.' He heard Sarah gasp loudly. 'If you can't, then you'll leave me, my friends and most importantly Anne alone from now on. Agreed?'

Kyle's face ignited with delight. 'You're givin' me a freebie?'

'That's right.'

'Just to knock down a little gimp like you?'

'Yes.'

'Listen, you chav gorilla,' Dunk said to Kyle. 'If you lay one finger on him I'll –'

'– You'll do nothing, Dunk,' Zak said. 'I just want to see if big tough Kyle here can do it... because I reckon he's not all that. I reckon he's all mouth.'

Fury in his eyes, Kyle drew back his massive fist and, throwing all his weight behind it, let fly a punch. His fist connected with Zak's jaw with a sickening *crack*.

Horrified, Sarah's hand shot to her mouth.

No one was in any doubt. *It was a flooring blow.*

An instant later, however, Kyle's expression turned

from deep satisfaction to bewilderment. *Zak was still standing.* A smear of blood in the corner of his mouth and a patch of red on his cheek were the only sign he'd been punched at all.

Dunk gave a whoop and started to clap. Sarah and Leah smiled.

Kyle's friends stood there, unable to process what had just happened.

Kyle clearly felt the same way. 'Wha - ?'

Zak wiped the blood from his mouth, before looking up at Kyle. His eyes locked on him like lasers. 'Right, Kyle... I'm still standing... and you failed. Now get lost...' He leaned in and whispered in Kyle's left ear. 'And remember, don't bother Anne anymore. If I hear you have, you and I will have issues. Believe me, you don't want that.'

Kyle couldn't find a reply. He inhaled and, in a desperate attempt to regain some dignity, puffed out his chest and said, 'Come on, lads, we've got better things to do.' He picked up his bike, threw his leg across the frame and cycled off at speed.

Moments later, Kyle's gang were following him back to Beridian, faster than before.

Dunk stared at Zak with astonishment. 'Why did you do that? I mean – you gave him a freebie?'

'I don't know,' Zak replied. 'I suppose I just wanted to see what I could take.'

'Well you can take a punch,' Leah said. 'That's for sure.'

'I guess so,' Zak replied. 'It did sting a bit, though.'

'Only a bit?' Leah replied. 'That would've floored a rhino.'

'I still say you should have battered him,' Dunk

said.

'No,' Zak replied firmly. 'We're different. We all know it. If, for whatever reason, we go around beating people up, even scumbags like Kyle, then we're as bad as they are, picking on people weaker than us... because that's what bullies do.'

Dunk shrugged. 'Yeah, well, bullies like him should be taught a lesson.'

'And he has been,' Zak said. 'He'll think twice before he picks on someone younger or smaller next time. Anyway, we'd best get back.'

As he turned back to the beach road, he caught sight of Sarah, only to see her gaze was fixed on something in the distance. Eyes narrowing, her expression changed from one of puzzlement to shock.

'Oh, no!' she breathed.

Zak tracked her eye line and saw what looked like a flock of birds soaring toward them. But as he focussed, his stomach turned.

'What is it, Sarah?' Leah asked, panic in her voice.

But it was Zak that returned the answer.

'Grippers! Everyone ... RUN!'

- Chapter 20 -
Attack

For a moment, no one moved a muscle.
Then they ran.

Zak's heart hammered in his chest as he gathered speed. His eyes fixed on Avernon, but it seemed miles away. Remembering the Lectroflare, he thrust his hand in his pocket and activated it. But he knew it was futile.

There wasn't enough time for a rescue.

Glancing round, he counted at least a dozen Grippers. His mind raced with thoughts on how to fight back when he heard an inhuman shriek. A Gripper swooped down and seized Leah's shoulders. She screamed. Hoisted into the air, she wriggled like a hooked worm.

Zak veered right. With every ounce of strength he could muster, he hurled himself onto the Gripper's legs, his weight forcing it to drop in height. A rancid stench filled his nostrils. He glimpsed its grotesque face, its curved beak snapped wildly. With a jerk, he twisted the Gripper's right leg and heard the bone snap.

The Gripper howled and released Leah, who fell to the ground, landing heavily on her back.

Zak let go and landed beside her. Heaving Leah to her feet, he saw Dunk and Sarah rush over and together they formed a circle, each of them taking a combat stance, ready to face the coming attack.

'Stay close,' Zak yelled. 'Keep the circle!'

The sound of shrieks tore the air as the Grippers circled above. Zak felt a wave of despair - they were out-numbered and unarmed.

Then, from his left, he heard a roaring sound and his mouth fell open. A black car speeded toward them from the direction of Beridian.

'Templars!' Dunk yelled.

The car screeched to a halt and Kelly Barnes leapt out, clasping a sheer black leather satchel.

The Grippers gathered in formation, their shrieks reaching deafening levels, as, one by one, each folded its wings, streamlined itself and plunged like giant arrows toward the group.

Kelly pulled a brace of Magnaswords from the bag. 'HERE!' she shouted, throwing one to each of them.

Zak caught his comfortably, squeezed the handle and glimpsed the silver blade. In a lightning fast movement, he cut the first Gripper down and watched it disintegrate to ashes. He glanced over to see Sarah strike swiftly and powerfully. Dunk and Leah attacked next, parrying and sidestepping, cutting down their attackers with an effortless but lethal grace.

Zak drew breath and leapt into the fray, spinning like a dervish through the onslaught, avoiding the others. His Magnasword met its target time after time, until the air was thick like a winter fog.

In seconds, the battle was over.

His head spinning, Zak turned to the others who

were panting heavily.

All of a sudden, Leah's composed battle face turned
to one of panic and she squealed, hopping up and down
as if her toes were on fire. 'Ewww!'

Sarah looked alarmed. 'What is it?'

'Look at me. Look at me,' Leah wailed. 'I'm covered
in … *them*!' Her arms were everywhere, brushing herself
as if covered in a swarm of invisible bees.

Sarah traced her fingers through her hair. Looking
down, she grimaced when she saw the Gripper dust that
coated her fingers. 'Yuk!'

Dunk, on the other hand, didn't seem to mind one
bit. 'COME ON!' he yelled at the empty sky. 'Bring it on,
bird boys… Let's have another flock!'

'Wow. You guys were amazing,' Kelly said. 'I didn't
even have time to join in the fun.'

A thunderous rumbling from the direction of
Avernon interrupted her words.

Five Aquacars powered toward them, pearl-white
smoke jetting from their exhausts.

In no time at all the cars had reached them.

Pottsy, Big Al and six other Templars jumped out
and raced over, Magnaswords raised.

'You hit the Lectroflare, Zak,' Pottsy said, a mixture
of relief and panic in his voice. 'Are you all right? What
was it?'

'Grippers,' Zak said. 'About twelve of them, but
we're fine … thanks to Kelly. We wouldn't have stood a
chance without these.' He gestured at his Magnasword.

'I didn't do anything,' Kelly shrugged, smiling back.
'Oh, you should have seen them, Pottsy. It was beautiful.
Poetry in motion. These four are remarkable. Better than
we could've hoped. Even Kurnan would've been blown

away.'

Pottsy nodded but didn't appear to hear a word she said. 'But I don't understand, Kelly,' he said, confused. 'Why are you here? I didn't ask you to accompany them.'

'I wasn't about to let them go into Beridian alone,' Kelly replied simply. She smiled at the group. 'I'm sorry guys, but as you've seen it can be dangerous beyond the monastery grounds.' Her gaze found Pottsy again. 'I took an Aquacar, grabbed a bag of Magnaswords and snuck out. I hope that was okay?'

'Okay?' Pottsy blustered. 'Of course it was okay. And thank God you did. The ramifications if you hadn't would have been unthinkable. Thank you.'

'Yeah, thanks, Kelly,' Sarah said. 'We'd be dead if it wasn't for you.'

'We deffo would,' Dunk said. 'Cheers.'

'My pleasure.'

Pottsy looked more confused than ever. 'But I don't understand this – what is Lord Ballivan doing? I mean… sending Grippers to the island in broad daylight? What is he thinking? And how did he know you'd be out of the grounds – unaccompanied and unarmed? I just don't get it.'

Big Al stepped forward, his eyes still on the skies. 'Who knows, Pot-plant? And who cares? Let's just get the kids back and we can debate Ballivan's tactics later.'

*

Ten minutes later, as Pottsy, Kelly, Big Al and the other Templars left to discuss the attack, Zak trailed Dunk, Sarah and Leah to the social room, where they each made themselves a drink and gravitated to chairs in different parts of the room. Throughout, no one said a thing.

And Zak could understand why. This was the first time they had been involved in an actual battle, seen the enemy up close and personal, felt their own lives hanging by a thread. The Gripper attack confirmed who they were and the very real danger they were in. *It was a lot to digest.*

As the minutes passed, however, Zak could sense a change in the others. They had fought their first battle alongside each other, protecting each other in a fight they could have easily lost. But they hadn't lost. They'd won.

It was Dunk who eventually broke the silence. 'I guess we do make a pretty good team, after all.'

'I guess we do,' Leah replied, smiling.

'And I s'pose it's official then –' Dunk continued, '– we're Angels... and we'd better start taking all this seriously because if not we're dead meat. Plus, a lot's riding on us... the fate of mankind, the survival of this planet... all that trivial stuff.'

'I agree,' Sarah replied quietly.

'Me, too,' Leah said. 'And I also think we should get Kelly a present the next time we're in Beridian. It's only because of her we're still alive.'

Sarah spoke up, satisfaction in her voice. 'Yeah, well I don't think that's going to be anytime soon.'

'What d'you mean?' Leah asked.

'They're not going to let us go into Beridian again, are they? I mean... it's just too dangerous outside of these walls. We were lucky this time.'

'You're probably right,' Leah replied miserably. She looked at Zak. 'What are you going to do about Anne?'

Zak felt a sinking feeling inside. Leah's question rang in his head like a bell. He wasn't about to show it to the others but he really did want to see Anne again, maybe even go out on his first ever date, but deep down he knew he couldn't. He was a walking target and just being near him was dangerous, for anyone – Templar or civilian.

No... the relationship with Anne, whatever it was or could grow to be, was over.

Before it had even begun.

- Chapter 21 -
The Dark Knight Returns

Over the next few days, Zak found himself increasingly conflicted. He never once took Anne's number out of his pocket wherever he went and whatever he was doing, but he knew he couldn't use it. He didn't even feel he could text her in case she pressured him to meet up.

By the second week of December, a heavy snowfall clung to the monastery, burying its spires, towers and rooftops beneath a mountain of shimmering whiteness. The wind moaned and wailed, the statues became ice sculptures and swathes of snow coated the frozen ponds.

As the Gripper attack blurred into memory, so the mood around Avernon lightened, spurred on by the fact Christmas was on its way.

To everyone's surprise, the Templars made something of a fuss over Christmas. They decorated the monastery's interior, particularly the refectory, from top to bottom and erected a huge tree in the Chapter House, covering it in golden baubles.

Zak couldn't help but feel it wasn't done out of any genuine festive spirit, but simply to give him, Dunk,

Leah and Sarah the most conventional Christmas they could, despite their bizarre circumstances.

What wasn't open to debate, however, was just how much Pottsy adored this time of year. He could be heard at all hours wandering the grounds singing Christmas Carols, was rarely seen without a half-eaten mince pie wedged in his mouth, and he even decorated the cigar on his baseball cap in a band of golden tinsel.

And Zak noticed something else, too. The recent attack had stirred a new attitude within the group. Dunk, Leah and Sarah took their training much more seriously than before. By mid-December every single one of them knew *'Demons and Demonilla'* off by heart and Kelly's WAC and Big Al's Hand to Hand combat classes were attended both diligently and with the kind of concentration reserved for those who knew the knowledge acquired could genuinely save their lives one day.

Through all of it, Zak couldn't stop thinking about Anne. He knew with each passing day of silence he appeared ever more uncaring and indifferent, even verging on the plain rude. And that was the last thing he wanted. It was with these thoughts in mind that he returned to his bedroom the following Saturday night with the sole intention of phoning her and explaining his situation, even if he knew he couldn't tell the whole truth.

She deserved that at least.

Switching on the light, he took out his mobile phone and dialled her number. As he raised the phone to his ear, his mouth went dry. He hadn't felt this nervous facing off against a flock of Grippers. Almost immediately, the dialling tone clicked off and a soft voice met his ears.

'Hello,' Anne said.

Zak hesitated. 'Hi, Anne. It's me... Zak.'

The phone went silent.

'Oh...' Anne replied. 'I was beginning to think you weren't going to call.'

'I know. I'm sorry,' Zak said. 'It's just – well, it's been strange around here lately.'

'Strange, how?'

'Err, it's hard to explain.'

Anne's voice softened. 'You can try.'

'I'm not sure I can. But how are you?'

'I'm fine. Listen, Zak, I want you to be honest with me.'

Zak paused. 'Okay.'

'Do you want to see me again?'

'Well... yes, but -'

' - But what?'

'But things are a bit.... complicated.'

'They are if you make them complicated.'

'No... they just are.'

'Then what's complicated?'

'I can't say.'

'Well you should try because I'd really like to know what's going on.'

'I know... and I'm sorry.'

'You don't need to be sorry,' Anne said exasperatedly. 'If you don't want to see me again then that's okay, but if –'

' - It's not that.'

'Then what is it?' Anne replied. 'Because I really want to see you again.'

Zak's palms were sweating now. His grip tightened

on the phone in case it slipped from his hand. 'I – I just can't.'

'What's stopping you?'

Zak didn't reply.

'Fine,' Anne replied, rather curtly. 'Well, there's nothing else to say then is there? It's a shame because I think we could've gone out and had a really great time.'

'So do I,' Zak replied quietly.

Anne went quiet. 'Is all this because of Kyle?'

'Of course not,' Zak replied, surprise in his voice.

'Are you sure?'

'He's the last thing I care about.'

'Okay then. Well I suppose there's nothing more to be said. I'm sorry that's it, but it sounds like your mind's made up. Have a good Christmas, Zak. Thanks for saving my life. If you ever change your mind about going out you know where I am.'

A click echoed, followed by silence. Anne had hung up.

Zak exhaled heavily and flopped onto his bed, as a knock rattled his door. He didn't respond. The last thing he wanted was company.

A few seconds later, an even sturdier knock shook the room.

Zak knew he didn't have a choice. 'Come in.'

The door opened and a tall man entered, stooping slightly to ensure his head didn't hit the ceiling. 'Hey, kid.'

Zak looked over with surprise at the beard that covered John Kurnan's face. Flecks of fresh snow coated his long black coat and his eyes looked dull, buttressed by dark, heavy bags as if he hadn't slept in some time. A leather shoulder bag was slung across his shoulder.

Zak was overjoyed to see him. 'Kurnan... You're back.'

'I am,' Kurnan replied. 'But just for tonight, then I'm leaving again. And I'll be gone for some time. I'll miss the Renaissance and I'm sorry about that.'

'Where have you been?'

'On Templar business, but that's over. Now I have to do something for me...'

Zak felt frustrated. 'But you're my mentor. Shouldn't you be here to – well, mentor me?'

'I know,' Kurnan replied, guilt in his voice. ' And I'm sorry 'bout it, you can always go to Big Al if you need anything... or Kelly. She's a great kid.'

'I guess, but that's not the point,' Zak replied. '*We* need you here. Have you heard about the Gripper attack?'

Kurnan's face darkened. 'Yeah. And I hear you all handled yourself pretty damn well.'

'We did okay,' Zak replied. 'But what if it happens again?'

'Listen, kid.' Kurnan's face became difficult to read. 'I wouldn't leave if I didn't think it was of the utmost importance for me... and *you* for that matter.'

'What do you mean *me*? It's got something to do with me?'

'It doesn't matter. Forget I said it.'

'I can't just do that.'

Kurnan shrugged. 'Well, that's all I'm saying on the matter.'

Zak fell silent. 'That's not fair.'

'Tough,' Kurnan replied.

'So why are you here now?'

'Because it's nearly Christmas and I wanted to give

you a present.' Kurnan reached into his satchel and pulled out a leather belt that resembled a cowboy holster. 'Here...' He threw it to Zak, who caught it and held it up.

'What is it?'

'It's a magnet-lined Magnasword holster. You'll need it to hold this.' Kurnan reached into his bag and withdrew a Magnasword. He passed it over.

Zak's eyes widened. 'I'm getting my own Magnasword?'

'Yeah. Dunk and the others are getting theirs on Christmas Day, but I wanted to be the one who gave you yours, and I won't be here then.'

'Thanks.'

'No problem,' Kurnan replied.

Zak squeezed the grip and the metal blade shot out. The blade shimmered in the lamplight.

'Just to warn you it's not like the training weapons you use in your WAC classes. This is the real deal, and it's sharp enough to cut diamonds... so be careful with it, won't ya?'

'I will.'

Kurnan smiled. 'You wanna try it out?'

'What do you mean?'

'You and me, one on one, in the Training Yard.'

'You're joking, right?'

Kurnan pointed at himself. 'Does this look like the face of a joker?'

Looking at Kurnan, Zak knew the answer was an unequivocal, '*no*'.

A short while later, Zak and Kurnan trudged up the steep path to the Training Yard, their breaths forming clouds that glittered in the moonlight.

Reaching the amphitheatre, Kurnan placed his hand in his pockets and pulled out a gadget. He pressed a button and four floodlights exploded with light, brightening the arena.

'Isn't the ground a bit slippy for a Magnasword fight?' Zak said.

Kurnan threw down his bag and pulled out his Magnasword. 'Live a little, kid. It's hardly a duel to the death.... Just a bit of fun.'

'That's good to know,' Zak mumbled. He drew his Magnasword and extended the blade.

As Kurnan extended his, Zak thought he'd take the opportunity to question him further. 'Kurnan... when I first got to my room at Avernon you said me you'd answer whatever questions I'd got.'

'Ah, you remember that?'

'I've got a good memory,' Zak said.

Kurnan couldn't help but smile. 'Go on then.'

'Where are you going when you leave here?'

'I can't say.'

'Why not?'

'Because I'm goin' off the radar. Even the Templar bigwigs ain't knowing 'bout this.'

Zak was intrigued. 'Why?'

Kurnan paused. 'I'm going to find a man called Wilbur Combermere.'

Zak knew he'd heard the name before. 'My mum mentioned him in my letter. He was the Chief Knight at Avernon when she was here.'

'Yeah,' Kurnan replied.

'So why do you need to find him?'

'None of your business.'

'But earlier you said you said it was of the utmost

importance for me. Surely that makes it my business.'

'No,' Kurnan said curtly. 'Now are we gonna fight or not?' At once, he swung his blade at Zak's head.

Although the blow was fast, Zak could tell Kurnan was exercising restraint. He blocked the shot and a satisfying ring echoed as the blades met.

Zak broke off, thrusting his sword at Kurnan, who pivoted right and blocked with a solid defensive move. Kurnan counteracted, angling his sword down, targeting Zak's midriff. With incredible speed, Zak blocked the strike.

Smiling, Kurnan stepped back and circled Zak like a panther. 'You are fast, kid. I'll give you that.'

'So are you.'

'I'm not as fast as you.'

'You're older,' Zak replied with a grin, studying Kurnan's body language.

'You ain't wrong there,' Kurnan said. 'But then there's a reason I've survived this long. Never forget, with age comes experience and that can't be taught in a classroom or on a training yard. Always respect your elders... because they've probably made all the mistakes you'll ever make and survived them.'

Kurnan pivoted and attacked again, swinging his blade low.

Zak's blade met Kurnan's. And as they battled deep into the night, neither of them exposing the full extent of their abilities for fear of injuring the other, Zak had no idea the next time they would meet would not be on earth.

And John Kurnan would be trying his best to kill him.

For real...

- Chapter 22 -
The Visitor

Zak woke with a jolt to the sound of three sharp *knocks* on his bedroom door. His eyes flicked over to his alarm clock: 10.00am. He'd overslept and missed breakfast. He and Kurnan had stayed up until the early hours talking about the coming weeks, in particular his fifteenth birthday and the so-called *Renaissance*.

Kurnan explained how it was a momentous occasion for the Templars, that they had been waiting a millennium since the last one and that all the most notable Templars from across the globe would be in attendance.

Zak didn't know what to think about it. How on earth was he and others to be reborn? Would he really receive powers?

And if so, what would they be?

He climbed out of bed and opened the door. Fully expecting Dunk to be there asking why he wasn't at breakfast, he was surprised to see Big Al's colossal frame filling the doorway, grinning from behind his bearded face.

'Mornin', sleepy head,' Big Al said. 'Has that buddy

o' mine been keepin' you up half the night?'

'Yes,' Zak replied.

'Has he gone again?'

'I think so.'

Big Al shrugged as if he'd heard it all before. 'He's a law unto himself is John Kurnan. Anyway, yeh'd best get your best clobber on coz there's a young lady here to see ya – a pretty one, too. We can't let her into the grounds for obvious reasons, so she's waitin' at the front gate. Anne's her name.'

Zak's couldn't believe it. Anne was here... *at Avernon* – a vast quasi-military complex filled with Templars and creatures from Hell.

This wasn't good.

In no time at all he had dressed and sprinted to the front gate, trying his best not to lose his footing on the slippery ground. Glancing up at the towering walls he couldn't begin to think what Anne would make of it all.

As he reached the gate, he saw Anne and a tall female Templar in conversation. This ended abruptly as he approached.

'Speak of the devil,' the Templar said with a wry grin.

'Hello,' Zak said.

'Hi,' Anne replied with a wave of her gloved hand.

Zak felt the Templar's eyes upon him. He tried his best to ignore it. 'How are you, Anne?'

'Not bad, Zak,' Anne replied awkwardly. 'And you?'

'I'm all right. How did you get here?'

'I walked,' Anne said, before adding, 'and I only slipped over three times.'

Zak forced a laugh. 'What do you want?'

'To see you. I was hoping we might be able to... err, have a chat.' In case that wasn't clear to the Templar, Anne added, 'in private...'

Zak looked at the Templar, who returned a kindly smile. 'Why don't you both go down to the beach?' she said.

'Cheers,' Zak said.

As Anne turned away, Zak felt the Templar slide something into his hand. He recognised it immediately as a Lectroflare and slipped it into his pocket.

'I can give you ten minutes,' the Templar whispered as Zak passed her.

Zak joined Anne and they walked on to the path that led to the shoreline.

After a few moments of uncomfortable silence, Anne glanced back at Avernon and said, 'Is it a borstal or something?' she asked. 'I've never seen anything quite like it.'

'It's not a borstal,' Zak replied. 'But there is some... *security*.'

'Why?'

'Long story.'

'It's a bit weird.'

'I guess,' Zak replied. 'You get used to it.'

'Are you the son of someone famous?'

Zak laughed. 'What?'

'I'm being serious,' Anne said. 'You feel like the son of someone famous – a big politician or something.'

'I'm not really the son of anyone. I'm an orphan.'

Anne's face dropped. 'Are you? You never told me.'

'It never came up.'

'So are you adopted?'

'Yeah. Kind of. But they're not famous.'

'Then they must be rich,' Anne said. 'Because that place seems like the most exclusive private school ever. I mean, there are only four of you at the school and you've got a guard on the gate.'

Zak didn't really know what to say. 'I suppose it is exclusive.'

'Then who are you?'

'I'm nobody.'

'You sure don't seem like nobody.'

'Well I am. Nobody at all.'

'And your foster parents... do they live here?'

'No. They're back in Cheshire.'

'Is that where you're from?'

'I'm from all over,' Zak replied. 'But yeah, I suppose that's where I consider my home.' Stepping onto the beach, he stared at the heavy layer of snow that cloaked the sand for miles like a glittering white carpet. 'Anne... Why have you come?'

'I wanted to see you,' Anne replied. 'And you *said* you wanted to see me.'

Zak couldn't help but smile. 'What I said was I can't see you.'

'Yeah, well as my mum always says, "*Can't never could do anything*".'

'And what does that mean?'

'It means if you say you can't do something you never will,' Anne replied. 'And I think you can do anything you want, provided you want to enough.' She smiled. 'And I wanted to see you.'

'You like to get your own way, don't you?'

'Who doesn't?'

Zak spent a moment pondering what to say. 'I don't expect you to understand any of this. Even I can barely get my head around it, but I really shouldn't see you.'

'Shouldn't or won't?'

'All right then *can't*?'

'What do you mean 'can't'?' Anne said, sounding hurt. 'Am I not good enough for you?'

The words wounded Zak. 'No... Far from it.'

'Then be honest with me.'

'I am... as much as I can.'

'Can I ask a question?'

Zak hesitated. 'Go on.'

'I heard a story last night after I talked to you on the phone,' Anne said. 'After you came to the diner that day... did - did Kyle hit you?'

Zak paused. 'Yes.'

'And did he hit you really hard and you just took it?' Anne said. 'You didn't fall down? You didn't cry out in pain? In fact, from what I heard it barely affected you at all, is that true?'

'The punch wasn't as hard as it looked.'

'That's not what his friends were saying. They said it should've knocked you out for a week.'

'People like to embellish stories.'

'Yeah, well, it got me *thinking* about something else - how you weren't even shivering after you'd jumped into the sea to save my life. I mean, the Irish Sea in November is as cold as ice, but you weren't even shivering.'

Zak was stuck for words. 'Okay... I can see how this all sounds very – well – ' He had no idea how to finish the sentence.

Anne, on the other hand, knew exactly what she wanted to say. 'It sounds like you're different... that you're special. It sounds like you're a superhero or something?'

'I'm not a superhero.'

'A mutant? A Government weapon? A superspy?'

'And it sounds like you've got an amazing imagination.'

'Maybe I have,' Anne replied. 'But now I've seen the security at the monastery, and something very weird is going on there.'

'I'm none of those things,' Zak said. All of a sudden, his eyes were drawn to a figure, entirely in shadow, emerging from one of the many caves in the cliff face, before dropping out of sight. His interest piqued, he looked again and saw Kelly Barnes waving over at him.

'Zak!' Kelly shouted cheerily.

Anne looked surprised. 'Who's that?'

'It's one of our teachers,' Zak replied, thankful Kelly's appearance had steered the conversation away from him. 'Her name's Kelly. She's really nice.'

Kelly jogged over to them.

As she stopped, Zak could see she was wearing a grey tracksuit with a Templar cross on its breast pocket.

'What's going on here then?' Kelly asked. 'I'm not interrupting anything, am I?'

'Not at all,' Zak said. 'Hi, Kelly. This is Anne. She's my friend from Beridian.'

'Hi, Anne,' Kelly said. 'What are you both doing here?' Her eyes scanned the beach and she added, 'And you're unaccompanied?'

'Yeah,' Zak replied.

A mischievous look crossed Anne's face. 'We were just discussing how he's a superhero?'

Kelly's face creased with surprise. 'Really?'

'So is he?' Anne asked bluntly.

'Not to my knowledge,' Kelly replied. 'Are you,

Zak?'

'You know I'm not.'

'But he is a good lad,' Kelly said.

'I know,' Anne said.

Once again, Zak felt a burning desire to change the subject. 'What were you doing in the cave?'

Kelly hesitated. 'Actually, it's a bit embarrassing,' she said. 'I was out for a run when I was caught short, if you know what I mean. I didn't exactly expect an audience when I came out.' She chuckled. 'Not very lady like, is it?'

'I won't tell anyone,' Zak said.

'I'm not much of a lady anyway,' Kelly said. 'Anyway, I best be getting back. I've got tonnes of work to do. Nice to meet you, Anne.'

'And you,' Anne replied.

And with that, Kelly turned and ran off in the direction of the monastery.

'She seems fun,' Anne said.

'Yeah. She's great.'

'What's with the Knights Templar symbol on her sweatshirt?'

Zak swallowed hard. 'The what?'

'The symbol on her sweatshirt. It's that of the Knights Templar.'

'Are you sure?'

'Every year mum and dad take me to La Rochelle in France – my Grandfather lives there – well, hundreds of years ago La Rochelle was a major Templar port. Anyway, you can't visit La Rochelle and not see that symbol – it's everywhere. Plus, my Grandfather's a bit of an armchair historian and is always telling me stories about them.'

'I don't know then,' Zak said, doing his best to remain calm. 'I didn't notice it. But I do know I'd better be getting back to the monastery.'

As he turned, Anne slipped her hand in his and pulled him close. 'You are a mystery to me, Zak Fisher. And whatever world you live in is as mysterious as you are. But what I do know is I'm not sure if I'll ever see you again. So just in case I don't then I want you to have this...' She leaned in, until their lips were millimetres apart.

They breathed in rhythm, shared the same air.

And then Zak felt her lips upon his, their bodies locking as one. The sound of the ocean, the stiff breeze all faded to nothingness, replaced by the singular sound of his thumping heart.

It was a kiss that lasted forever.

As they broke off, Anne smiled awkwardly. 'I'm sorry. I'm not usually that forward.'

'Don't be sorry. It's fine.'

Anne's smile grew. 'It was just fine?'

'I-it was great,' Zak replied, stumbling over his words. 'You're great.'

'Then you really should see me again,' Anne replied. 'Because I don't want that to be the last kiss we have. So you go away, have a think about it if that's what you have to do, and you know where I am if you change your mind. I really like you Zak, and I think we could be pretty good together.' She reached into her pocket and withdrew a scarlet envelope. 'Merry Christmas.'

Before Zak could reply, Anne had turned away and jogged along the beach in the direction of Beridian.

Zak watched her until she was no more than a dot on the horizon, his head spinning.

He had enjoyed his first proper kiss with the most beautiful girl he'd ever seen. He inhaled deeply as joy swept through him. His eyes found the envelope. He opened it slowly and pulled out a Christmas card, a smile arching on his mouth. Then he opened it and read the words inside.

Dear Zak,

I just wanted to thank you again for all you've done for me. I don't know what's going on with you but if there is any chance we could maybe go out some time I'd really like that. Either way, you've put a little bit of hope into what's been the worst year of my life and I can't thank you enough for that.

Merry Christmas and a Happy New Year.

Luv

Me

Xxx

Zak returned the card to the envelope. More than anything he wanted to see Anne again, but he couldn't shake the feeling to do so would put her in danger and he simply couldn't have that.

As he headed back to the monastery, a place filled with humans and Hellians that cared for him, he realised he'd never felt quite so alone in his life.

- Chapter 23 -
Hops, Hopes and Hardships

'She actually came here?' Sarah said with disbelief, standing in the kitchen in the social room and pouring herself a hot chocolate. 'To Avernon?'

'Yes,' Zak replied.

'And they let you out for a romantic stroll along the beach?'

'It wasn't romantic,' Zak replied.

Sarah huffed. 'Whether it was or wasn't, it was still unsupervised.'

'Why would it need to be supervised?'

'Because there are creatures outside these walls that want to kill you,' Sarah said. 'Can I remind you we were recently attacked by Grippers.'

Zak sighed. 'You don't need to remind me.'

'Really?' Sarah said. 'Because it seems to me someone should. And if the Templars aren't going to do it then it might as well be me.'

'Calm down, Sar,' Dunk said. 'He can look after himself.'

But Sarah wasn't listening. 'I bet you didn't even have a Magnasword with you, did you?'

'Of course not,' Zak replied.

'Sarah, he's fine,' Leah said. 'It was only for ten minutes or so.'

'I just think some of the Templars are being a bit irresponsible with our lives,' Sarah said. 'I mean, if we're so important to saving the planet, then what are they doing letting him out of the grounds?'

'She didn't give them much of a choice,' Zak said. 'Anne can be pretty stubborn when she wants to be.'

Sarah scowled. 'Bully for her.'

'I think we're all forgetting the important question.' Dunk said. 'Did you snog her?'

'And that's an important question?' Zak asked irritably.

'It is to me,' Dunk said.

'Dunk, it's none of your business,' Leah said, before grinning at Zak. 'But did you?'

'I'm not saying anything.'

'So you did?' Leah pressed.

'I never said that.'

'What do you think, Sar?' Leah asked Sarah.

'I don't care,' Sarah replied sniffily. 'I just don't want him – or *her*, for that matter - killed because of some poor decision making on behalf of the people who are supposed to be caring for our well-being. I think I'm going to have a few words with Pottsy. There need to be some changes around here.'

But there was no doubt about it: Sarah was the only one remotely concerned about the matter.

*

Over the next few days Zak, Dunk, Leah and Sarah

were escorted separately into Beridian by discreetly armed Templars to buy gifts for each other and to afford them a break from the ever more suffocating confines of the monastery.

Though he usually enjoyed Christmas, Zak found his mood taking a downbeat turn. And it wasn't just to do with Anne, either. Walking around Beridian, seeing the joyful faces of young and old revelling in the familiarity of it all, hearing the strains of Christmas music blaring from the shops, made him feel more isolated from the outside world than ever.

And so he awoke on Christmas morning without any of his usual enthusiasm. Pottsy had arranged for presents to be exchanged in the Chapter House after breakfast, but Zak couldn't get excited about any of it. He missed waking up at Fumbletree Cottage, frost coating his window like a glittering spider's web. He missed the annual ramble in the Bickerton Hills before a hefty Christmas Dinner. He even missed Mrs Potsworth's annual Boxing Day party, which only the previous year ended in spectacular fashion with Mister Potsworth, a nervous and browbeaten man that suffered gout, drinking one too many Hot Toddies and toppling into the Christmas Tree to the considerable horror of his wife.

But most of all Zak missed Sid and Irene.

As he lay there, he wondered what they were doing now. Did they miss him and much as he missed them? He didn't think that was possible.

Heavy snow fell all around as Zak, Sarah, Dunk and Leah made their way to the fraterhouse, each carrying a large sack filled with presents. As they walked their excited chatter filled the air, all except for Zak who barely said a word. Entering the refectory they found it deserted, but for Mabel Gubbins, who wore a set of plastic antlers and a scarlet ball on the end of her nose. She would have looked the picture of festive fun but her eyes were puffy and bloodshot as though she'd been crying.

Leah was the first to reach the servery. 'Are you all right, Mabel?'

'I'm fine, deary,' Mabel replied, struggling to keep her voice steady. 'Anyway Merry Christmas to you all.'

'Merry Christmas, Mabel,' everyone said.

Mabel piled each of their plates high with sausages, bacon, black pudding, and field mushrooms. 'And ain't it nice ter be waking up to a White Christmas?'

'It's lovely,' Sarah said.

'Absolutely beautiful,' Leah said.

'Great Rudolph costume, Mabel,' Dunk said.

Mabel forced a smile. 'I wanted ter be Santa but Pothole beat me to it.'

'You could've been Mrs Claus?' Dunk said.

Mabel feigned a look of disgust. 'But then I'd have ter pretend I was hitched ter that old dog, and I'm not 'bout to do that, even in jest. Now, let's get to the important stuff - I've left your presents in the Chapter House with all the others.'

'We've all got you presents, too,' Leah said. 'Do you want them now?'

'Oh, that's most kind of ya, but I'll be following yer over ter the Chapter House so you can give me them then.' Mabel forced a smile. 'I'll tell you what, though. You have all been as spoilt as new-borns this year. I'm not sure whether all yer presents are gonna fit into your dorm rooms.'

'That's because no one thinks we'll be alive next year,' Dunk quipped.

From Mabel's change of expression it was clear that Dunk had struck the same nerve she'd been trying to conceal from them. She swivelled round, her face blushing scarlet and mumbled something about checking the turkeys as she scurried through the rear kitchen door.

Dunk stood there, confused. 'What did I say?'

'I think you said precisely what she was thinking,' Zak said.

Fifteen minutes later, the group left the refectory and walked over to the Chapter House, where they were surprised to see it decorated top to bottom in an explosion of colour; lights flickered everywhere, garlands hung from the ceiling, and four enormous Christmas trees adorned with baubles dominated each corner of the room. The circular table in the centre of the room was decked out with four huge piles of presents. The moment they entered, they saw it was filled with Templars.

Voices sounded all around them in a chorus of Christmas wishes and a loud round of applause raised the roof.

Amongst the many Templar faces, Zak saw Big Al, Kelly, Doctor Pudgbury and Pottsy, who stood directly beside Mister Gudrak (wearing a rather impressive Santa hat) and Mrs Gudrak, who rocked a carved wooden pram, presumably constructed by her husband.

Pottsy ran over to them. 'Ah, the special guests have arrived. Merry Christmas one and all.' He shook Zak's hand.

'Merry Christmas, Pottsy,' Dunk said. 'Which are

my presents?'

Leah laughed. 'Typical you.' She could tell he was only half joking.

'I believe that's your pile there, Mister Duncan,' Pottsy said, pointing. 'Now this afternoon there will be a church service which I hope you'll attend, but for now let's concentrate on pressie opening...'

'Terrific idea, Pottsy,' Dunk said.

For the next half an hour Zak, Dunk, Leah and Sarah unwrapped their presents, until the discarded paper was approximately the size of a mountain. It seemed every Templar at Avernon had bought them something. Big Al gave them each a set of throwing knives and a new pair of boxing gloves. Pottsy gave them a baseball cap and a book entitled 'Cornish Winter Flowers' and Mabel Gubbins bought them all a new pair of trainers. Finally, a beaming Mrs Gudrak gave them each a hand knitted pullover, three sizes too big in every way.

By the end, Zak, Dunk, Sarah and Leah felt thoroughly spoilt. But it was when Pottsy produced three cylindrical objects wrapped in gold paper and passed them over to Dunk, Leah and Sarah their eyes truly ignited.

'Fantastic,' Dunk said, ripping open his Magnasword and extending the blade for all to see. 'Now that's what I'm talking about.'

'They're not toys, Mister Duncan,' Pottsy said.

'If they were, Toys R Us would be a right bloodbath,' Dunk said.

Pottsy didn't get the joke. 'I'm sure,' he replied. 'Now we also have another little surprise for you, and I think you'll agree we've saved the best until last...' He waved to a Templar at the side of the Hall, who opened a door and moved aside to allow four couples to enter the room.

Zak's heart leapt.

Leading the group were Sid and Irene Shufflebottom, who walked toward Zak at such pace they were nearly sprinting.

Zak leapt to his feet as Sid opened his arms and hugged him.

'Merry Christmas, son,' Sid said, beaming. 'It's good to see yer again.'

'And you, Sid,' Zak said. 'Merry Christmas.'

The moment he released Sid, Irene's arms enfolded him.

'Merry Christmas, Irene,' Zak said.

'Merry Christmas, Zak,' Irene said.

'I'm so happy to see you,' Zak said.

'And we're happy ter see you,' Sid said. 'How're you findin' Avernon?'

'It's good.'

'A bit more exciting than Addlebury, eh?'

'I'd take Addlebury any day of the week.'

Sid's smile grew. 'Then you'll have to pop back for a visit soon. I'll talk to Pottsy and we'll arrange security.'

'I'd like that,' Zak said sincerely. 'I'd like that a lot. How is Mrs Potsworth? Did you convince her she slipped on an Eccles cake or did she remember what really happened?'

'Old bat didn't remember a thing,' Sid said. 'I'm tempted to bash her one again now I know I can get away with it.'

'Sid!' Irene said firmly. 'Don't talk like that!'

'I'm joking, luv,' Sid replied, although the wink he cast Zak suggested otherwise. 'Anyway, Zak, I can see you've already had a fair few presents but I hope you won't mind a few more.' He raised a bag into the air.

Zak smiled. 'Oh, if you insist...'

*

Zak, Irene and Sid spent a wonderful morning together. They walked the length of the sea front, pitching rocks into the ocean, and then went on a tour of the Monastery grounds, exploring every nook and cranny, even discovering parts Zak had never found before. Throughout, Sid told him stories about his years as a novice, and how he first met Irene in his very first Weaponry class in the early nineteen sixties. He even showed Zak a timeworn poster pinned to the social room wall of a Beatles concert in Crewe he and Irene attended on their first date.

Zak was delighted to learn Sid and Irene would be staying at Avernon until after the New Year and he helped them unpack their suitcases into a dorm room just a few doors down from his own.

In the afternoon they attended a church service and then went to the fraterhouse for Christmas dinner. Zak guessed that more Templars had been arriving throughout the day because there was a sea of faces he didn't recognise, many of them casting him furtive glances when they thought he wasn't looking. By seven there must have been a hundred Templars present, not to mention the Gudraks, and together they ate, drank, talked and laughed until the early hours.

Zak enjoyed every minute of it. However, his biggest thrill was yet to come. As the night drew to a close, Sid told him he'd obtained permission from Pottsy to take him take him away the next night for evening dinner. He was even more excited to learn Sid's restaurant of choice was Hops, the restaurant Kurnan had taken his mum to exactly fifteen years ago to the day.

Zak couldn't wait. Just visiting Hops, knowing his mother had visited there so many years before, made his connection to her feel all the more real. Furthermore, Sid seemed to know all about his mother's date with Kurnan and Zak was hoping to grill him for any details Kurnan may have left out.

And so at six the following evening, Zak, Sid and Irene set off for Beridian.

Pottsy had begged Sid to take an Aquacar and be accompanied by a second car filled with Templars but he had refused. Sid wanted it to be as normal a night as possible and claimed the long walk and sea air would be good for his arthritis. He did, however, agree to take a Lectroflare with him and Zak felt certain both he and Irene had Magnaswords concealed somewhere on their persons.

By the time they arrived at Beridian, the snow had stopped and a velvety black sky, as smooth as glass, cloaked the frosted rooftops of the town.

As they turned onto the deserted quayside, Zak spied Hops in the distance. He exhaled a nervous breath.

Sid noticed. 'Are you okay, son?'

'Yeah,' Zak replied. 'I just – well, it's the mum thing and -'

Sid looped his arm around Zak's shoulder. 'I understand. But it'll be good for you.' He paused, before muttering, 'I hope.'

Entering the restaurant, Zak saw it simply exuded elegance. High mullioned windows were concealed behind velvet curtains, and a grand piano overlooked a dozen tables each veiled by a silk tablecloth. Diners were scattered around the room, conversing in whispers as if the sophisticated setting demanded a quiet reverence.

Immediately, a waitress greeted them, taking their coats and checking their names in a reservations book, before showing them to a window table.

Zak sat opposite Irene, who looked resplendent in a floral dress and cashmere cardigan. In contrast, Sid looked as out of place as you could get in an ill-fitting brown suit, a crumpled shirt and a crooked cherry-red tie.

And judging by the look on her face, Irene didn't approve at all. 'Sidney, you really could've made an effort!'

'I have,' Sid replied. 'I haven't worn a tie since we got married.'

'Well you look like a tramp.'

'Nonsense, woman, I'm a right Dapper Dan. Eh, Zak?'

'You look cool, Sid,' Zak said, but his mind was elsewhere. He surveyed the room, taking everything in. He couldn't believe his mother and Kurnan were here fifteen years to the day. It was then he felt Irene's hand take his.

'And how are you feeling, my dear?'

'I'm good,' Zak said. 'I'm really glad we've come.'

'Me, too,' Irene said.

'And here's another piece of interesting trivia for ya,' Sid said. 'This is exactly the same table as John and your mother had when they came here.'

'Really?'

'Aye,' Sid said. 'John told me which one it was, and I asked them to put us here when I phoned through the reservation.'

'Awesome.'

'Your mother really was a wonderful woman,' Irene said.'

'She was that,' Sid agreed.

Zak hesitated. 'Kurnan told me he asked her to marry him.'

Irene sighed. 'We know. I think they would've made a perfect couple.'

'John loved her very much,' Sid said. 'It broke him up in all kinds o' ways when she died. I've never seen a man go ter such dark places. He was -'

Irene sensed Sid was going to say something he might regret. ' - That's enough, Sid,' she interjected. 'Let's focus on the happier memories tonight.'

'Of course, luv,' Sid said. 'Sorry, Zak.'

'No, really, I don't mind,' Zak said. 'I want to know everything.'

With the conversation turning to Kurnan, Zak recalled the last time they met. 'Can I ask you something, Sid?'

'Sure.'

'The last time I saw Kurnan he said he was leaving to find a Templar called Wilbur Combermere, and that he'd be gone for some time and wouldn't be back for the Renaissance.'

Sid seemed shocked. 'John's gone looking for Wilbur?'

'And he's missing the Renaissance?' Irene said.

'Yeah,' Zak replied.

Sid tented his fingers on his chin. 'Wilbur Combermere, eh? I'm surprised the old goat's still breathing. He must be ninety if he's a day.'

'Do you know where he is?' Zak asked.

'Nope,' Sid replied. 'He dropped off the face of the planet years ago.'

'Ten years, I'd say,' Irene added.

'He was Chief Knight at Avernon, wasn't he?' Zak asked.

'Aye,' Sid said. 'He were a lovely man. Could've been Templar Grandmaster in his younger days... he was certainly respected enough. Do you know about the Grandmaster?'

'Yes,' Zak replied. 'He's the big Templar boss, isn't he?'

'Aye, and William Brockenhurst's the current one,' Sid said. 'As a matter of fact, he's comin' to Avernon for the Renaissance so yeh'll get to meet him soon.'

'The thing is,' Zak said. 'Kurnan said it was of the utmost importance *for him and me* that he finds Wilbur. Do you know what that could be about?'

Sid took a moment to process this. 'Haven't the foggiest,' he said. 'What do you think, luv?'

Irene shook her head. 'I wouldn't have a clue.'

Zak looked deflated.

Sid's eyes met Zak's. 'What I do know is John must have a bloody good reason fer wantin' ter find Wilbur,' he said sincerely. 'Because there ain't no way he'd miss the Renaissance otherwise.' His tone grew solemn. 'I know he never married yer mother - never had the chance to - but when he asked her ter marry him it wasn't just 'bout bein' a husband, it was 'bout bein' a father, too. Yer the son o' the woman he loved... yer the son that should've been his.'

Zak struggled to find a reply.

'That's why he wouldn't miss the Renaissance

unless it was significant,' Sid said. 'Damn, I don't reckon he'd miss it unless it was a matter of life or death… or maybe somethin' more important.'

- Chapter 24 -
The Doctor's Out

Although pleased to be at Hops, Zak found it impossible to enjoy the evening. He just couldn't get Kurnan's situation out of his head.

As he left the restaurant, he could make out O' Reilly's in the distance and it struck him how he hadn't seen or talked to Anne for some time. Was she in there now? Guilt flooded him. There and then, he made a decision to contact her when the Renaissance was over, if it even happened at all.

A carpet of stars brightened their way back to Avernon. Zak didn't say much, and Sid and Irene had clearly made a decision to allow him some time with his thoughts.

It was when they neared the monastery, however, that Zak remembered there was something else he wanted to ask Sid and Irene.

'After Kurnan took me from Fumbletree Cottage,' he said, 'I went to stay for the night at Saint Catherine's Chapel with a priest called Father Edward.'

'Ah, yes, how is the old nutter?' Sid asked, warmth in his voice. 'I've not seen that crackpot for years.' He chuckled.

'He's fine,' Zak said. 'Anyway, the day after I got there I overheard Kurnan talking to Father Edward and my name was mentioned. Father Edward said I could open up old wounds for Kurnan... and he mentioned a place called Benidan Towers. Do you know anything about that?'

Sid stopped dead in his tracks. He glanced at Irene whose face had suddenly hardened.

'What did they say about it?'

'Well, nothing really,' Zak said. 'That's why I'm asking you.'

Sid opened his mouth to speak when Irene cut him down.

'Sidney, I'm not sure that you –'

Sid silenced her with a raise of his hand. 'I'm gonna answer the boy. Perhaps he's got a right ter know.'

Irene didn't look convinced.

'Go on. Tell me,' Zak said.

Sid inhaled deeply before he spoke. 'After your mum died, John went into a depression.... a depression like I ain't ever seen before. He barricaded himself up in a room at Perigorn Castle, and shut himself away from anyone and everyone. He was in such deep pain I never thought he'd come out of it. In fact, all o' us who cared for him feared he'd just take his Magnasword and end it right there and then.'

Zak looked shocked. 'Really?'

'Aye,' Sid replied. 'But that ain't really John. Still, he was as messed up as anyone can be. I tried ter talk to him, so did Irene. We couldn't get through. William Brockenhurst, Pottsy, Big Al, they all tried, but John were 'aving none of it. Nothing could change this dark cloud that ate away at him...'

'So what happened?' Zak asked. 'I mean... he obviously came out of it.'

'One day, he just upped and left Perigorn,' Sid said. 'He didn't tell anyone he was leavin', he didn't tell anyone where he was goin'. He just vanished.'

'Where did he go?'

'Somehow, he'd got wind a major meetin' was goin' down between some demons and a few of the Hellfire Club at Benidan Towers in Edinburgh. Anyway, Kurnan went there. Their security was top notch but he neutralised it in seconds. When he got ter the meeting room he found ten demons and five members of the Hellfire Club.'

Sid hesitated.

'Kurnan burst in and killed every one of 'em – human and demon,' he said. 'He didn't spare a single one. And more than that, every one o' them was unarmed...'

Zak gulped.

'John don't kill lightly,' Sid continued. 'And before then he had never killed a human. You see, as Templars we take a solemn vow when we're *accoladed* not ter kill unless in self-defence. Our sworn duty is ter always take prisoners, no matter what species they are – if they surrender or are unarmed.'

'And what happens to the prisoners?'

'We have a facility off the coast of Australia, we call it *The Fort* - a high tech prison on Temple Island off the coast of Australia. And it's where we lock up all members of the Hellfire Club and demons. As you can imagine, it's a pretty dangerous place.'

'So if you're not allowed to kill what happened to Kurnan?'

Sid sighed. 'The Templars have very old, strict rules 'bout such things. There was a trial and he was found guilty... guilty of murder with diminished responsibility.'

'And what happened to him?'

'The High Assembly accepted his mental state caused the whole sorry affair but they couldn't just let it go. He was jailed fer a year on Temple Island, and then was released into the care of Father Edward at Saint Catherine's. In time, he got over it and returned to his Order, but I don't think he's ever been the same since. John was always a complex man, but yer mum's death, his breakdown and all that followed... well, I'm not sure yer ever truly come back from that.'

Zak stared out at the ocean. As black as pitch, it fused seamlessly with the sudden darkness that filled him. He felt conflicted. On one hand, he knew Kurnan had done something terrible, monstrous even. On the other, he had never felt the kind of pain that had triggered such a sequence of events. His life, although unconventional, had always been a happy one. The loss and subsequent grief Kurnan had suffered was something he had never experienced. How would be know how that kind of pain would affect him?

How could anyone?

Just then, a scream pierced the night. It slashed at his ears. His head snapped up. Through the dimness, he glimpsed movement on the cliff face.

A body was plummeting downward, arms flailing wildly.

The scream got louder.

Irene gasped with horror.

Unable to move, his every muscle froze like ice, Zak

watched the body smash on the rocks. A nauseating *thump* punctured the air.

It was the foulest sound Zak had ever heard.

And suddenly he found himself racing over, but it was instinct that powered his legs, not logic. Deep down he knew it was pointless: no one could survive that fall.

Zak's pace slowed as the body came into view, twisted, broken and bloody.

Seconds later, Sid came to a halt by his side. 'My God,' he panted, struggling for breath. 'Henry?'

But there was no reply.

Doctor Henry Pudgbury would never answer anyone ever again.

- Chapter 25 -
New Year's Eve

The news of Doctor Pudgbury's death spread through Avernon like wildfire. Investigations began immediately and a team was set up to search for clues and scrutinise the events leading to the doctor's final moments.

In the meantime, Zak was escorted back to the monastery, one question filling his mind: Was Doctor Pudgbury's death accidental or something more sinister?

He entered the social room to find Sarah, Leah and Dunk already there.

'Have you any idea what's going on?' Dunk asked, before Zak had even closed the door. 'This place has suddenly gone nuts with activity, but no one will tell us anything.'

'Doctor Pudgbury's dead,' Zak replied.

'Dead?' Dunk said. 'How?'

'He fell off the cliff. I was there.'

'You were there?' Sarah gasped. 'How come?'

'I was walking back from Beridian with Sid and Irene when I heard a scream and saw this body crash onto the rocks. He was dead on impact. There was nothing I could do.'

'That's terrible,' Leah said.

'Are you okay?' Sarah asked.

'I'm fine. He's not.'

'So what happened?' Dunk asked. 'Did he jump? Was he pushed? Was he sleeping walking and took a wrong turn?'

'I don't know.'

The door opened and Pottsy walked in, trailed by Kelly, Big Al, Sid and Irene, all of whom had faces the colour of marble.

'Good evening, everyone,' Pottsy said. Instantly, it dawned on him what he'd said. 'Well, of course, it's not a good evening. It's a terrible one. I'm sure by now Zak has told you about tonight's tragic incident?'

'Yeah,' Dunk said. 'Have you found out any more about the Doc?'

'We've found a note,' Pottsy said. 'A…a –' He couldn't finish his sentence so Sid did it for him.

' - A suicide note,' Sid said grimly. 'It was left on his dressing table. It contained just two words: *Goodbye, friends.* That was it… no explanation, no reasons… nowt.'

Irene's legs refused to support her anymore and she slumped into an armchair. 'I would never have guessed it of Henry,' she said. 'He was always such a jovial, upbeat man. He was always making jokes, always laughing...'

Sid curled his arm around his wife's shoulder. 'We all thought that, luv. But who knows what goes through a man's mind when the laughter stops?'

'And he has definitely changed lately,' Kelly said. 'Quite a few of us had noticed. Rumour has it he and his wife were having a few marital problems.'

Irene looked at Kelly with surprise. 'But Blanche and

Henry had a wonderful marriage, they always have had. Gosh, they've been happily married for over thirty years.' Her voice cracked. 'No, it just doesn't make sense Henry would do this. I mean, it's barely a year Emily gave birth to his first grandson and I've never seen a happier man than when little Kenneth was born.' She considered this for a moment. 'I just don't believe Henry Pudgbury is the kind of man to take his own life.'

'An hour ago I would've agreed with ya, luv,' Sid said miserably. 'But he did...and that's that.'

'And I must take the blame for it,' Pottsy exhaled. 'I noticed about a month ago he stopped being himself... his legendary smile seemed to vanish overnight. He suddenly walked around as if carrying the weight of the world on his shoulders. I asked him many times if there was something wrong but he just fobbed me off with platitudes and weak excuses. But perhaps most telling was he didn't even have any plans to visit his family for Christmas, which should've set alarm bells in my head. But I didn't even raise the matter. I've just been so busy with my own problems I wasn't there for my dear, dear friend.' He shook his head miserably. 'This is entirely my fault.'

'Yer can't do that ter yourself, Pottsy,' Sid said. 'It's no one's fault. Henry made his own decisions... and the rest of us have to deal with that. Now has Blanche been told?'

'Not yet,' Pottsy said. 'I'm going to see her in a few hours.'

'Then I'm comin' with ya,' Sid said. 'We'll break the news to her together.'

'Thank you, Sid,' Pottsy replied.

'No thanks necessary,' Sid said. 'Henry was a

crackin' fella, and he saved my neck loadsa times. I mean...literally.' He lowered his collar to reveal a deep scar encircling his throat. 'That man stitched my wounds up more times than I can count and kept the breath in my lungs. I just wish I'd had the chance ter do the same fer him...'

Over the next few days the mood around Avernon reflected the weather - dark, gloomy and grey. The Christmas decorations remained in place but it was clear Doctor Pudgbury's death prompted the end of all celebrations. It was evident he'd been well liked by everyone, and any discussion amongst the Templars about what motivated his death were confined to low whispers by small groups, far away from the general populace.

The funeral was to be held at Saint Laurence's church in the small village of Little Herrington. And on that bitterly cold day Templars left the monastery in droves to attend, leaving Zak and others with the bare minimum of guards.

Although sad for Doctor Pudgbury's family and friends, Zak had something else pressing on his mind. His birthday was fast approaching and with that the so-called Renaissance. It was clear he wasn't the only one. Leah, Dunk and Sarah barely talked to each other, often disappearing to some discreet corner of the monastery to be alone with their thoughts.

As New Years Day approached, the more overcrowded the monastery became. Templars were arriving every day, some speaking in languages Zak didn't recognise or with accents unfamiliar to him. Many arrived bright-eyed, jovial and dressed to the nines, whilst others appeared unkempt, world-weary and battle scarred as if they'd just returned from conflict. Still, despite the joyful reuniting of old friends and comrades, the tension around the monastery could be cut with a knife.

More than ever, Zak felt strangers' eyes upon him, and he wasn't the only one. Dunk, Sarah, and Leah all voiced their discomfort at being what Dunk called 'monkeys in a cage', until it reached the point they rarely left the social room, except for meals and even then it was arranged for the Fraterhouse to be empty so they could eat in peace.

New Years Eve arrived and the sky was as clear as glass. A full sun illuminated the Training Yard as Zak, Leah, Sarah and Dunk gathered for Magnasword practice.

After a vigorous bout with Dunk, Zak spied two figures on the horizon heading in their direction. Pottsy led the way, followed by a much taller slender man he didn't recognise wearing a long ceremonial robe, his hood high to offset the icy wind that billowed in from the ocean.

As he approached, the stranger pulled down his hood to reveal long grey hair tied back in a ponytail and a thin but neatly trimmed goatee beard. His blue eyes were set beneath caterpillar eyebrows, but, other than his enormous height, the most striking thing was a deep scar that cleaved his left cheek from eye to chin. Ordinarily, this one detail would have been an unnerving sight, but the man's smile radiated such warmth it only added character to his face.

'Good morning, everyone,' Pottsy said. 'You have a visitor.'

Dunk studied the tall stranger. 'Is it Gandalf?'

Sarah looked shocked. 'Don't be rude, Dunk!'

'Only having a joke,' Dunk said. 'You don't mind, do you, Mister?'

'Not at all,' the tall man said in a deep, silky voice. 'And Gandalf is certainly better than *Dumbelbore* which I get repeatedly at Perigorn Castle. The truth is I'm not remotely exciting enough to be a literary figure and I'm certainly not magical. I am, however, William Brockenhurst.'

Zak recognised the name. 'You're the Templar Grandmaster.'

'I am, indeed. And you must be Zak Fisher?'

'Yeah.'

'John Kurnan thinks very highly of you.' One by one, Brockenhurst's gaze met the others. 'You must be Andrew Duncan, Leah Emerson and Sarah Miller. It's a great honour to finally meet you all.'

'So you've come to see us grow wings?' Leah said.

'Like everyone else, I have no idea what'll happen over the next few hours, Leah,' Brockenhurst said. 'According to the archives previous Watchers have received a range of powers. No wings as far as I'm aware but we really don't know. What I do know is that history will be made at Avernon tonight.'

Dunk didn't look so sure. 'I'm sorry but I don't reckon this whole rebirth thing is gonna happen. I hope we'll still get birthday presents, though.'

Brockenhurst smiled. Of course you shall, Andrew. It wouldn't be a birthday without presents. Anyway, I just wanted to meet you all and to let you know that I'm your humble servant if ever you should need me.'

'Thank you, Mister Brockenhurst,' Sarah said.

Brockenhurst looked at Pottsy. 'Ichabod, it's rather

chilly on my old bones so shall we get back to the warmth? I have a small matter to discuss with you over a bottle of oak-aged port and a roaring fire.'

'What a super idea,' Pottsy replied.

Brockenhurst turned back to the group. 'Now as you are aware there's something of a party tonight, so I must warn you I'm wearing my Cornish kilt which means my knees shall be making a rare public appearance. And if you consider my face frightening wait until you see them – they'd scare the scales off a Scorpoid.' With a chuckle, he turned about and he and Pottsy set off back to the monastery.

Zak and Dunk watched them leave.

'That is one massive fella,' Dunk said. 'What do you reckon six feet seven?'

'At least,' Zak replied.

'And who do you reckon gave him that scar?'

'No idea,' Zak replied. 'But if it was a demon I bet they're not around to brag about it…'

*

As morning became afternoon, the four of them became ever more pensive, barely saying a word to one another. And Zak knew the others felt the same as him: the Renaissance was bad enough, the last thing they wanted was a party with them as the centre of attention.

It was a night Zak wasn't looking forward to at all. Still, he knew he had no choice and, at eight, left his room to meet the others in the dormitory entrance. Not one of them smiled, laughed or even chatted as they walked over to the Chapter House, the wind whistling in their ears.

As they entered the hall they could see it was already heaving with Templars, sitting at tables buckling under the weight of large jugs of wine and ale. On the south wall was a long table laden with food in what resembled a medieval banquet.

'Reckon we'll get any of that beer?' Dunk said.

'Can't see it, somehow,' Zak replied.

Zak stared over at the top table. William Brockenhurst was in deep conversation with Mister and Mrs Gudrak, and beside them were Pottsy and six other Templars he'd never seen before, four men and two women.

As they found an empty table, Pottsy leapt from his chair and raced over.

'The guests of honour have arrived,' Pottsy said.

'Is any of that booze for us, Pottsy?' Dunk asked, a glint in his eye.

'A vast range of soft drinks is available for you, Mister Duncan.'

'As mixers?'

'I'm not sure you should even know what that term means,' Pottsy replied. 'But not one of you will be having alcohol until you are an appropriate age. Although we are a clandestine organisation, we still try to obey the laws of the land when we can.'

'Spoil sport,' Dunk muttered.

''If it's any consolation, Mabel has outdone herself with the food. The fare on offer tonight is simply spectacular. There are even some excellent Hellian dishes Mister Gudrak has prepared for us – he's quite the chef, I'll have you know. Furthermore, the entertainment doesn't stop with the food. I've arranged for some prize bingo, followed by a disco later on and, should you be interested, I've brought my Karaoke machine should any of you wish to perform a number.'

'Karaoke?' Dunk laughed.

'Yes,' Pottsy replied. 'I adore Karaoke. If I do say so myself I could've been quite the frustrated rock star.'

'You are so weird, Pottsy,' Dunk said.

'I do hope so,' Pottsy grinned. 'Anyway, have a think about a song. Maybe you could do one as a four piece? I know, two girls, two boys - what about an Abba number?'

The suggestion was followed by silence.

'Ah, well,' Pottsy said, disappointed at the lack of enthusiasm. 'Have a think about it.' As he walked back to the head table, he could be heard singing 'The Winner Takes it All' in a tuneless voice.

'That guy's ace,' Dunk said to Zak. 'He's as batty as a box of bits but you can't help but love him.'

It was then Zak felt eyes upon him. He looked to an adjacent table and saw Sid and Irene staring at him. Sid wore a look of that seemed to mix pride with deep concern. Irene's face, on the other hand, revealed merely worry, her eyes coloured with extra make up as though she'd recently been crying but was at pains to conceal the fact.

As he reached his seat, Pottsy turned to the hall, extended his arms and waited for a hush to cloak the room.

'Good evening, everyone,' Pottsy said. 'And may I welcome you all. For once I won't be bore you a second longer than is necessary. Instead, I'll be yielding the floor to someone considerably more stimulating than I... ladies and gentlemen, I give you our Grandmaster, William Brockenhurst.'

Applause echoed through the room.

William Brockenhurst got to his feet. He surveyed

the many smiling faces. 'Friends, comrades, brothers and sisters in arms - welcome to you all. I'm aware it's the first time some of you have returned to earth for many years and it does me good to see so many of you safe and well. Unlike our good friend, Ichabod, however, I don't enjoy public speaking so I'll get straight to the point. We are gathered here tonight because of these four remarkable young people.'

He looked at Zak and the others.

'Tonight, within the confines of these hallowed halls, a legendary happening shall occur: The Renaissance of the Watchers, an event this earth has not seen for a thousand years. Yes, we've all read the Chronicles of Hywel of Monmouth, we've all studied the transcripts of André de Champagne in the archives at La Rochelle, and I'm sure many of us have talked in whispers about this night since we were children. Indeed, as children I'm sure many of us fantasised it was *we* who were the Watchers… I know I did. Still, I think as adults we can all appreciate how different the truth is from those childhood fantasies, and how frightening this must be for Zak Fisher, Sarah Miller, Leah Emerson and Andrew Duncan.'

The room fell silent.

'Now as Templars we've seen and experienced much, from the battle of Banidor to the uprising at Brenkyk; defending the Fort at Akron, to the Gripper Onslaught at the Wexliath Pass. We have witnessed conflicts most men and women, even those in the non-Templar Armed Forces, couldn't imagine. Yet for all the amazing things we've seen no one alive has ever witnessed the miracle that will happen here tonight. The hand of God will truly touch these four young people, they shall experience something celestial, something divine. And with those powers they shall battle evil for the defence and liberation of not one but two worlds… and for that we thank them. So with that in mind I ask you to stand, raise your glasses and toast the Watchers: *Shadow Passes, Light Remains… Transit Umbra, Lux Permanent.'*

Every Templar in the room rose from his or her chair, glass in hand, and repeated Brockenhurst's words.

'*Shadow Passes, Light Remains… Transit umbra, lux permanent.'*

As the Templars sat down, Zak scanned the room; he saw Sid, Irene, Mister and Mrs Gudrak, Big Al, Kelly, Pottsy, Mabel and many other faces he'd begun to know well, faces that belonged to people he cared about deeply.

And although he had no idea what would happen over the next few hours, he knew he'd cope with it. His friends, his family, his extended family surrounded him, and that was all he needed to overcome all that would follow.

Whatever that was.

- Chapter 26 -
The Renaissance of the Watchers

All told, the New Years Eve party was a somewhat muted affair. Although everyone tried to maintain a playful atmosphere, a solemnity hung over the night like a heavy fog, seemingly stopping anyone having a particularly good time. Even Pottsy's karaoke turn went down like a lead balloon leaving him in a rather huffy mood for the rest of the night.

Zak knew it was all because of the Renaissance. No one said it directly, of course, but the constant stream of sympathetic looks he and the others received left him in no doubt everyone was concerned as to what would happen at the stroke of midnight.

In the end, Zak was relieved when William Brockenhurst approached them and suggested that they go to bed.

It was 11.30pm when they entered their dorm and went to their rooms, saying nothing to one another. It had been decided their mentors would stand guard outside their room as they slept, and with Kurnan absent it was Sid who volunteered for the job.

As Zak entered his room, he turned to Sid, who followed him inside. 'Sid, I really don't need you to guard me overnight.'

Sid picked up the desk chair. 'Well, I am, son,' he replied. 'And I ain't having no arguments about it.'

'Seriously,' Zak replied. 'We're in a fortress, surrounded by battle hardened Templar Knights... do you really think I'm in any danger?'

'I know where we are,' Sid replied. 'But I won't sleep anyway, no matter where I am. I might as well be with you, just in case.' He walked back into the corridor and placed the chair to the right of Zak's bedroom door. Then he sat, withdrew his Magnasword and rested it on his lap.

'Then goodnight, Sid.'

'Goodnight, lad. You know where I am if you need me.'

Zak closed the door. As he threw on his shorts, shirt, and climbed into bed he felt a knot well in the pit of his stomach. He glimpsed the clock: *11.58am.* Just two minutes until his fifteenth birthday... *and the Renaissance.*

In that moment he considered how most other kids would feel just before their birthday, the excitement of getting another year older, another day closer to being able to drive, to leaving school, but not him.

A clang from a distant clock coloured the night, striking the midnight hour. The world would be celebrating a New Year, and the promise of a new future.

The chimes continued. He lay there, waiting.

Waiting.

He was fifteen now. A new day had begun, but there was no sign of pain, no indication anything was any different, and certainly no rebirth.

There was no Renaissance.

He felt part relieved, part thankful. It was all a lot of fuss over nothing.

And then, just as the clock's final strike pealed... it happened.

Pain.

Astonishing pain.

Days later, he still wouldn't be able to identify whereabouts on his body the pain struck first - was it in his head? His hands? His skin?

He couldn't say.

But come it did.

And it was pain unlike anything he had ever felt.

His bones felt like they were being stretched every which way, snapped in two, healed momentarily, and then snapped again. Every nerve in his body screamed as though a pin pierced his flesh time and time again. His skin felt like it was stretched to the point of tearing.

And there was no respite.

The pain kept coming, in waves, reaching every part of his body. And in the rare moments it abated, he could hear distant screams. Was it Dunk? Sarah? Lea? All three? He couldn't tell.

Sometimes, in the blurred vacuum between consciousness and unconsciousness he could make out the image of Sid standing over him, in tears, often praying, trying vainly to comfort him.

But Sid couldn't help.

No one could.

And then, at some point in the dead of night - he had no idea when - everything went black.

As black as space itself.

*

Zak woke with a start. How long he'd been asleep was anyone's guess. The pain was a distant memory now. He glanced at his clock: **8.00am.** He looked over and saw a sleeping Sid at his bedside, snoring lightly.

The moment Zak sat up, however, Sid's eyes shot open.

'Zak?' Sid said croakily. 'You're awake.'

Zak nodded.

Sid scooped up Zak's hand. 'Oh, my boy... my wonderful boy. Yeh've done it. It's all over now. How d'you feel? Are y'alright?'

Zak considered the question, giving himself enough time to respond honestly. 'Good,' he said eventually. 'I feel good.'

But, in reality, *'good'* didn't do it justice.

'Actually, I feel great,' Zak added. 'Really great.'

And he did. A sense of power filled him, one unlike he'd ever felt before - a raw, physical power, affecting, enhancing, improving every one of his senses. He couldn't explain it. He couldn't put it into words.

But he felt different.

'Thank God,' Sid replied. 'I'll be frank - there were times I thought you were a goner.'

'How long did it last?'

'Two... three hours, maybe longer... and then you slept.'

Zak shifted himself onto his elbows. 'And the others... are they okay?'

'I haven't heard owt to the contrary.'

'So I didn't get wings then?'

'Shame that, eh?' Sid chuckled. 'Anyway, Happy New Year to you and a Happy Birthday.'

'Cheers. And a Happy New Year to you.'

'Your birthday presents are all in the Chapter House. You can open them later. For now, can I get you anything?'

'Some water, please.'

Sid approached the sink, picked up a glass and filled it, before returning to Zak's side.

'Thanks,' Zak said. He took the glass. Barely applying any pressure, it shattered in his hand. Water drenched him.

'That's all right, son, I've got it.' Sid began to pick up fragments of glass. 'Accidents happen.'

Zak was still stunned. 'How could it have broken?'

'I guess you're stronger than before. Yer gonna 'ave to get used ter that.'

Zak nodded. 'I guess.'

'Here.' Sid passed over the towel.

As Zak reached out to take it he caught sight of the palm of his right hand. In its centre was a circular symbol that had never been there before. Taken aback, he said, 'Look at that, Sid. How weird is that?' He held up his hand and showed Sid.

Sid's face creased with astonishment. His lips trembled slightly, as he spoke. 'It's not entirely unexpected, son, is it?'

Zak looked perplexed. 'You expected me to wake up with a circle in the middle of my hand?'

'Not your hand, necessarily,' Sid replied, 'but somewhere.'

'And why would you expect a circle to appear on my body?'

'Coz it ain't simply a circle, is it?' Sid replied.

Zak stared at the mark again. 'Then what is it?'

'Yer a bright kid... surely you can guess?'

Zak really had no idea. 'No.'

Sid flashed him the warmest of smiles. 'It's a halo, son.'

.

- Chapter 27 -
Guppingham's Legacy.

Sid's expression changed as if suddenly remembering something important. He pulled out his phone and looked at it. 'We've gotta go.'

'Go where?'

'Brockenhurst's asked to see you the moment you woke up. I've had a text message to say the other three are already there.'

'Why?' Zak asked. 'What's going on?'

'Don't know,' Sid replied. 'I just know the big guy asked for you to meet him first thing. So let's make moves.'

Zak leapt out of bed and threw on some clothes. More than anything he wanted to check Dunk, Leah and Sarah were okay.

A few minutes later, they were walking at a brisk pace across a courtyard and up the north facing cloister. Templar Knights were everywhere, leaving in droves; many headed toward the underground car park, leaving Avernon for who knew where.

Sid and Zak passed a small oratory obscured by ivy and entered a stone building with a convex roof of black slate. They walked down a passageway to a heavy oak door, which Sid pushed with both hands.

As the door swung open, Zak saw a familiar figure smiling back at him.

Sarah was sitting on a leather couch, Leah and Dunk beside her, opposite a table buckling under the weight of bacon sandwiches, pastries and two jugs of apple juice.

His concerns for their welfare vanished. *They looked healthier than ever.*

Sitting behind a large desk, William Brockenhurst flashed Zak a warm smile. 'And a happy birthday to you, Zak.'

'Thanks.' Zak looked over at Dunk, Sarah and Leah. 'How are you all?'

'We're fine,' Sarah said. 'We all feel really good.'

'Better than good,' Dunk said. 'Bloody ace.' He raised his right hand, showing the circular mark in his palm. 'Have you got one of these?'

Zak raised his hand to show his.

'Somethin' else we've got in common then,' Dunk replied. 'Have you tried out your new powers yet?'

'What powers?' Zak asked.

'You'll see,' Dunk replied. 'They're awesome. I reckon we're officially superheroes. I jumped on the dorm roof as easily as jumping on a park bench. And we're stronger than before. Not Hulk strong, but definitely up there with Captain America, I'd say.'

Zak remembered the shattered glass.

'No wings though,' Dunk continued. 'And it turns out Leah's well miffed she didn't get any.'

'I decided it would be pretty cool to fly,' Leah said.

'It was agony though, wasn't it?' Dunk said.

'I've never felt anything like it before,' Zak said.

'It was like being on fire,' Leah said, 'for hours.'

'But it's all over now,' Brockenhurst said. 'And these additional powers make you less vulnerable than before, but, and this is very important, never forget you are not invincible, you are not immortal – far from it.' His eyes locked on Dunk, his next words clearly aimed at him. 'So don't do anything that might endanger yourselves in any way, shape or form.'

Dunk returned a mischievous grin. 'And here was me gonna jump out of a plane without a parachute to see if I'd survive.'

Leah's face ignited. 'Try it. I'd happily push you if you chickened out at the last second.'

Dunk stuck his tongue out at her.

'No one is jumping out of any planes, and no one is pushing anyone else out of them either,' Brockenhurst replied. 'But I am being serious now, please don't do anything silly. You're all too valuable to lose in a stupid accident.'

'You don't have to be worry 'bout me, boss man,' Dunk said.

'Ah, but I do worry, Andrew,' Brockenhurst said. 'I worry about all of you. That is the very least I can do. You are *all* miracles.'

'They are indeed,' Sid said. 'Now I reckon it's time I said my cheerios. I'm sure you've got private business with this lot, William, so I'll get back to Irene. You can guarantee she won't have slept a wink last night.'

'You do that, Sid,' Brockenhurst replied. 'And a Happy New Year to you both.'

'Happy New Year to you all,' Sid said, before leaving the room.

As the door closed, Brockenhurst surveyed the group. 'Anyway, I suppose I should explain why I've summoned you to what can only be described as a secret meeting. In fact, only twenty people in history know what I'm about to do, and all of them have long since passed away.'

Zak's eyebrows arched. *Only twenty people in history.*

Brockenhurst reached into the desk drawer and pulled a package into the light. Swaddled in a raggedy brown cloth, a crimson red wax stamp secured the material into place.

'What's that?' Dunk asked.

Brockenhurst's reply surprised them all. 'I have no idea,' he said. 'But what you're looking at is one of the most intriguing artefacts in history.'

'Why?' Sarah asked.

'Whatever object is inside this cloth was placed there over seven hundred years ago and has not seen the light of day since. Pottsy has told me you're aware of Sir Robin Guppingham?'

'He was the Grandmaster that built Avernon,' Sarah said. 'He was believed to be the last one to be in possession of the Seal of Solomon.'

Dunk's eyes enlarged. 'Is that it? Is that the Seal?'

Brockenhurst shook his head. 'I don't think so.'

'How do you know?' Leah asked.

'Because Sir Robin said it wasn't when he passed it to his Grandmaster successor, Sir Robert Shawbury.'

'Then maybe it's a marker that tells us where the Seal is?' Dunk said.

'It may well be,' Brockenhurst said. 'It may be a map that leads you directly to it. The fact is I don't know.' He held up the package. 'What I do know is that it's been passed down from Grandmaster to Grandmaster under the strictest assurances that its existence would never be revealed to anyone… not even other Templars. And that's precisely what's happened. There's not a single Templar Knight alive that knows this handover is taking place.'

'Whoa,' Dunk said.

'*Whoa* indeed, Andrew, ' Brockenhurst replied.

'So why are you showing it us?' Zak asked.

'Because it's yours. Guppingham gave instructions for it to be given to the Angels the day after the Renaissance.'

'Why?' Dunk asked.

'I have no idea.'

'Come on, Wilbo, you must've been tempted to take a peek?' Dunk said.

'No,' Brockenhurst replied. 'And my name is William if you don't mind.'

There was just enough threat in Brockenhurst's voice to wipe the grin from Dunk's face.

Sarah leaned forward. 'So what would've happened if a Grandmaster died suddenly and didn't leave it to his successor?'

'We leave detailed instructions in our wills as to what should happen to it,' Brockenhurst said. 'But thankfully that's not happened.'

'Then open it,' Dunk said eagerly. 'Let's have a gander.'

Brockenhurst's long fingers trembled as they found the wax stamp. He hesitated. 'I can't begin to tell you how momentous this small act is,' he said in a quiet voice. 'For seven hundred years, through countless conflicts and interplanetary skirmishes, this one object has been in the possession of the Grandmasters, sealed, and unopened.'

He took a last lingering look at the package before snapping open the wax. He unwrapped the top layer, exposing a second layer of cloth beneath. He pulled away the second layer and a small metal box was revealed.

The box radiated an eerie glow as though it had been polished that very day.

Brockenhurst exhaled and set the box on the table so everyone could see. Slowly, he pushed open its lid.

Everyone leaned in to peer inside. Straightaway, five expectant faces creased with disappointment.

'It's empty,' Dunk said.

But then Zak looked more closely at the box's base. Etched faintly into the panelling was what looked like text and a small symbol:

Liʒtne thou myn iʒen and Y schal biholde the merueils of thi lawe

On this stoon Y schal bilde my chirche

'What language is that?' Leah asked.

'Middle English, I believe,' Brockenhurst said.

'What does it mean?' Leah asked.

'I don't know,' Brockenhurst replied. 'Ancient languages were never my forte.'

'Let's worry about the words later,' Dunk said. And he picked up the box and started examining it closely. 'There's probably a secret compartment.'

'Perhaps there is,' Brockenhurst said. 'But what I do

know is I've seen all I need to see. My job is done. Find out what the words mean. Find the secret compartment if there is one. Whatever you do with the box is completely up to you. However, Guppingham did say it should be passed to the Archangel for safe-keeping.'

'The Archangel?' Sarah said.

'Yes,' Brockenhurst replied. 'On the three occasions the Renaissance has occurred one Angel has always been chosen the Archangel – the Angel leader. I suggest it's time you elected one of you for that role.'

'We don't have a leader,' Zak said. 'We don't need a leader.'

'Perhaps not,' Brockenhurst said. 'However, there will be occasions in the coming weeks, months and years where you may need one person to make decisions that cannot be voted on by the collective. In my experience it's impossible to fight a war without a leadership structure in place. And I've had more experience of war than I care to mention.'

'But we're not at war,' Leah said. 'I mean, I know the Templars are but – '

'- War is coming to Earth,' Brockenhurst replied. 'Make no mistake about that. And it is a war that could affect every man, woman and child on this planet. I wish that wasn't the case but it just is.'

No one said a word.

'So how do we decide on which of one of us is the leader?' Leah asked.

'That's up to the four of you,' Brockenhurst said.

'Then we should vote on it,' Sarah said.

'It's okay,' Dunk said. 'I'll do it. I don't mind.'

'No you won't,' Leah replied quickly.

'Why?' Dunk replied. 'I'm the best man for the job.'

'Who says it should be a man you sexist pig?' Leah said. 'Maybe I'm the best leader... maybe Sarah is?'

'Okay,' Dunk replied. 'Well let's vote on it.'

'It is the fairest way,' Brockenhurst offered. 'But remember whoever takes on the mantle is accepting the most difficult of roles. Decisions made by that person could affect the life and more notably the death of others. Such is the nature of wartime leadership.'

'That's why it should be me,' Dunk said.

'Perhaps it should, Andrew,' Brockenhurst replied. 'However, the fact you think it should be you is perhaps why it should not. Often in life those with the loudest voices become leaders but rarely make the best ones. After all, mere volume alone cannot improve a poor command.'

Dunk was unsure whether he'd been insulted or not.

'Anyway, you should go away and think about it,' Brockenhurst continued. 'There's no immediate rush. I suggest you return to your social room and relax or go and open your birthday presents in the Chapter House. Perhaps, Zak, I could entrust this to your care for now?'

He passed Zak the box.

'And please,' Brockenhurst said. 'Don't let anyone see it. It seems obvious its secrets have yet to be revealed.'

Zak held the box in his hands. Then one by one he, Dunk, Sarah and Leah left the room.

- Chapter 28 -
Follow The Leader

Zak led the way out of the corridor and into daylight. All the while, he couldn't take off his eyes off the box. It was such a small, unremarkable object yet its significance could not be understated. It had meant so much to the highest ranked Templars for over seven hundred years.

Firstly, they decided to go to the Chapter House to open their presents, which they took back to their dorm rooms, before meeting up in the social room, where Zak placed the box on the table in the centre of the room. Although he, Sarah and Leah were keen to discuss it, Dunk had something else on his mind entirely.

'Shall we do this vote then?' Dunk said.

'What's the rush?' Zak replied.

'There's no rush,' Dunk said. 'But we might as well get it out of the way.'

Leah frowned. 'Because you think it should be you and you want to start bossing us around.'

'No,' Dunk replied. 'But maybe the old Wilbo has a point. We've all learnt military strategy as one of the barmy things our barmy foster families taught us, and we all know a military outfit needs a leader. And yes, whether we like to think of it or not, that's what we are - *a military outfit.*'

No one said a word.

'Okay,' Leah said to Dunk. 'Then let's do a vote. At least that way it might shut you up.'

'But whoever is chosen – well, that's it,' Sarah said firmly, folding her arms and staring at Dunk. 'There can be no recount. We all agree to abide by that decision… no sulking or little strops if it doesn't go your way.'

'She's talking about you,' Leah said to Dunk. 'In case you didn't get that.'

'I don't sulk,' Dunk replied.

'You're like a bratty toddler most of the time,' Leah said.

'Rubbish,' Dunk replied. Anyway, let's do it. Let's see who the winner is.'

'It's not a game show, Dunk,' Sarah snapped. 'There's no winner. Whoever gets picked has a huge responsibility. It's not something any of us should agree to do lightly.'

'Then you can turn it down if you're picked,' Dunk said. 'Ok. I'll start. I'd like to vote for myself.'

'Shocker!' Leah said.

'I genuinely think I'm best suited to the job.'

'Why do you think that?' Sarah asked.

'Dunno. I just do. Now, go on Zak. Who do you think?'

Zak thought for a moment before his mouth formed a name. 'Sarah.'

Dunk looked like he'd swallowed a wasp. 'Are you kidding?'

'Not at all. Sarah should be leader,' Zak said. 'She's

the best person for the job.'

'Me?' Sarah said, surprised. She scowled at Dunk. 'Oh, and no offense taken.'

'Yeah, definitely,' Zak replied. 'You're kind, decent, caring and the smartest of all of us. You always make sound, considered decisions, and you think of others before yourself... that's what the best leaders do. So yeah, I think you'd make a great leader.'

Sarah blushed. 'Thanks, Zak.'

'I'm all of those things,' Dunk said.

'Yeah, right,' Zak said dismissively.

Dunk turned to Leah. 'And what about you? I guess you'll vote for yourself.'

'No,' Leah replied, looking at Sarah. 'Zak's right. You are all those things, Sar. But I still think Zak should be the leader. So my vote's for him.'

Dunk's infuriated expression suggested it was over. He knew he'd lost. 'And Sarah?'

Sarah didn't hesitate. 'Zak.'

The instant his name hung on the air, Zak knew he'd been chosen. Still, he didn't feel any sense of celebration. He wasn't even sure he wanted the job.

'So well done, Zak,' Sarah said. 'I guess it's you.'

'Good choice,' Leah said. 'Are you okay with that, Zak?'

'I guess,' Zak replied. 'I mean... if that's what you all want.'

'Not really,' Dunk muttered sourly.

'Well, he's the leader,' Sarah said. 'So that's that.'

'He was my second choice, anyway,' Dunk said. 'So what's your first command then, boss?'

'I'm not about to give any commands,' Zak replied. 'And don't call me *boss*.' He nodded at the box. 'But I do think we need to concentrate on this. First step is to figure out what the words and the symbol mean. Thoughts, anyone?'

He opened the box to reveal the message inside.

Liȝtne thou myn iȝen and Y schal biholde the merueils of thi lawe

On this stoon Y schal bilde my chirche

'Well surely the symbol is supposed to represent the Seal of Solomon?' Leah said. 'It looks like a ring that's radiating some kind of power.'

'Yeah. I thought that,' Dunk said.

'As for the text,' Sarah said, studying the words. 'Well, the library has to be our first stop. I'm sure many of the manuscripts in there are written in Middle English so there's bound to be plenty of translation books. Plus it's not so different from modern English. You can already see some words are recognisable, like 'thou', 'and', 'the' 'of'. 'Lawe' probably means 'Law'. I think it'll be pretty easy to translate once we get started.' She looked at the others. To her annoyance she saw Dunk wasn't listening. Instead, he was typing something onto his phone.

'For heaven's sake, Dunk,' Sarah said. 'Are you really on your phone at a time like this?'

Dunk looked up, surprised to hear his name voiced in such an angry tone. 'What?'

Sarah glared at him. 'Seriously, we're trying to

determine why we've been left a seven hundred year old box and you're more interested in checking your Snapchat?'

Dunk looked hurt. 'I wasn't on Snapchat. I was on Google and I've solved it.'

'Solved what?' Sarah said.

'I know what the words mean... I found a great Middle English to Modern English translator... only took me a few seconds to crack it.'

The excitement left Sarah's face. She'd clearly been excited by the prospect of library research. 'Go on then,' she huffed. 'What does it say?

'Both sentences are from the Bible,' Dunk said. 'The first one is Psalm 119:18. It says, *"Open my eyes that I may see wonderful things in your law."'*

'Oh, right,' Sarah mumbled.

'And the other sentence is Matthew 16: 18,' Dunk said, 'and means *"on this rock I shall build my church."'*

Zak looked taken back. 'Well done, mate. Fantastic.'

'See... I'm not just a pretty face,' Dunk grinned.

'Not even,' Leah said.

'So how does it help us?' Dunk said. 'It's not exactly *X Marks the Spot.'*

'Well, Avernon has a church in it,' Leah said, 'and it's built on a massive rock so it might mean the Seal is here after all.'

'So what about the first quote?' Dunk said.

'Maybe we need to "Open *his* eyes" to find the Seal. Guppingham's eyes, I mean.'

Dunk looked confused. 'You're saying we need to find his eyes?'

'Not literally,' Zak said.

'Good,' Dunk replied. ''Cause they'll have long since

been worm food.'

'But maybe the ring's been buried *with* his eyes,' Zak said, 'as in we need to find his coffin.'

'Then let's find out where he's buried,' Dunk said.

Sarah didn't look convinced. 'Don't you think that's a bit obvious?'

'Why do you say that?' Zak asked.

'If the Seal of Solomon is such a powerful artefact, one that can determine the fate of mankind, surely he's not going to hide it somewhere as obvious as that. It's the first place anyone would look.'

'Maybe it *is* obvious,' Dunk said. 'But we're stuck for any other ideas, so I say we find the dead guy.'

'Then let's track down Pottsy?' Zak said. 'If anyone knows where Guppingham is buried it'll be him.'

At that moment, a sharp breeze caused the fire to flicker. The door opened and Big Al's massive frame entered.

'Happy birthday, kiddies!' Big Al said, his gruff voice warm and welcoming.

Dunk looked surprised to see his mentor. 'I thought you were going to Perigorn Castle after you left me this morning?'

'I'm just leavin',' Big Al replied. 'I just wanted to check on the rest o' ya before I went. Is that all right with you, boss?'

'I guess,' Dunk replied. His eyes were suddenly drawn to the ivory handled Magnasword that hung from Big Al's side. 'What's happened to your usual Magnasword?'

'Ain't you the nosey parker?' Big Al replied. 'I broke the grip on mine, so I'm using this old one while it's gettin' fixed. So... how are y'all?'

'We're good, thanks,' Sarah said.

'Anyone get wings?' Big Al asked.

'Not exactly,' Dunk replied. 'But we've all got superhuman powers now, so don't mess with us?'

'Superhuman powers or not, I'll go toe to toe with you anytime if ya want.'

Dunk took in Big Al's colossal size and thought better of it. 'I wouldn't wanna hurt you.'

'Don't do me no favours,' Big Al said with a grin. He approached the fire and spread out his plate-sized hands, embracing the warmth. 'So what kind o' powers did you all get?'

'Well... we're stronger and faster than before,' Leah said. 'We're not sure about anything else yet.'

'But we do think we're closer to finding the Seal of Solomon,' Dunk said.

Big Al's jaw fell open. 'Wha' d'ya mean?'

'Brockenhurst gave us something only Grandmasters have known about for seven hundred years, something we think is to do with the Seal.'

'What kind of somethin'?'

Dunk picked up the box and held it up. 'This.'

Big Al's eyes widened. 'And was the Seal of Solomon in it?'

'Well, no,' Dunk replied. 'It's empty.'

'What good is an empty box?'

'We're not sure yet,' Dunk said, 'but there are a couple of phrases carved inside in Middle English. They might be markers.'

'What did the words say?' Big Al asked.

'*Open my eyes that I may see wonderful things in your law*,' Dunk said. 'And *on this rock I shall build my church*.'

Big Al looked none the wiser. 'And what do they

mean?'

'We don't know,' Zak said.

'But we think the Seal might be here at Avernon with Guppingham,' Dunk said. 'Maybe in his coffin? You wouldn't know where he was buried would you?'

'No,' Big Al replied. 'But Pottsy should know.'

'Yeah. We're off to find him now,' Dunk said.

A curious glint flickered in Big Al's eyes. 'Then I hope ya do find it,' he said. He hesitated for a moment. 'And *soon*.'

Zak noticed the change of tone. "Why soon?"

Big Al hesitated as though he wasn't sure whether he should continue. 'Coz somethin's happening out there,' he said, gesturing toward the window as if spying something beyond the glass. 'I don't know wha', but many of the Templars are worried. Don't tell anyone I told ya this, especially not Pottsy or Brockenhurst, but I've heard the Hellfire Club are organising a big attack somewhere in Britain.'

'An attack... where in Britain?' Sarah asked.

'Nobody knows,' Big Al said. 'I shouldn't even be telling ya... and maybe it's just a rumour...' Firelight gleamed in his eyes, turning them blood red. 'But word on the street is there could be hundreds o' Hellians flooding into the country as we speak. Findin' the Seal of Solomon might give us the edge we need if it is true. Oh, and there's summat else.'

'What?' Dunk asked.

Big Al paused before he spoke. 'Be careful who you tell about any of this.'

'Why?' Zak said.

'I ain't sure who can be trusted anymore.'

'Why d'you say that?'

'Because things are gettin' messed up out there. Some Templars may not be what they seem. There's mutterings some might've been –' He hesitated, ' - *turned* by the Hellfire Club.'

'You mean working for the baddies?' Dunk said.

'Surely not?' Leah said.

Big Al sighed heavily. 'A lot o' 'em have families. All it takes is a family member gettin' kidnapped and a person will do just 'bout anythin' to keep 'em alive. But it might be bunkum. These are dark times and all kinds o' stuff is bein' said by all kinds o' people, most of which is probably a crock o' crud.'

'Who do you trust?' Dunk asked.

'Not as many as yeh'd think. John Kurnan, Kelly Barnes, maybe a couple more, but that's about it.'

'But Kurnan isn't here,' Zak said.

'And why Kelly?' Sarah asked.

'The kid's got no family,' Big Al replied. 'Reptilaks murdered her parents when she were a nipper, so she got a big damn grudge. Plus, she helped ya with the Gripper attack. If she were on the other side she wouldn't have done that. Still, if you do track down the Seal maybe you should keep it to yourself.'

Zak didn't really know what to say to that. Since arriving at Avernon he'd never questioned the integrity of anyone, and the idea a Templar could be in league with Hellians was unthinkable. But Big Al had made a good point. Other than Sid and Irene, who else could he really trust?

Furthermore, he was responsible for the group now and all decisions related to their welfare were down to him.

In that moment, being Archangel felt the loneliest

job in the world.

- Chapter 29 -
A Memory Stirs

'You want to know where Sir Robin Guppingham is buried?' Pottsy said, looking up with surprise from his office desk. Realisation spread across his face. 'You're looking for the Seal of Solomon, aren't you?'

'Nah. We just want to see the bones of an old dead bloke and he seems as good as any,' Dunk replied. 'So is he at Avernon?'

'You should be resting after last night, not searching for a mythical talisman.'

'Please,' Zak said. 'We just need an honest answer to a simple question.'

'Then no,' Pottsy replied. 'He's not here. Guppingham's body is not even on this planet. He was killed in the Terranid War on the Hellian Island of Perlina. The Chronicles state he was buried where he fell.'

Zak felt deflated. 'Oh.'

'So you can call off your search now and concentrate on something more constructive. I've got some plants that need potting if you're stuck for something to do?'

'We're not that bored,' Dunk replied. He turned to Zak. 'Anyway, mate, we knew it was a long shot.' His eyes twinkled. 'So why don't we go to the Training Yard and check out our new superhuman powers?'

Zak smiled. 'Sounds good to me.'

*

Putting the Seal to the back of his mind, Zak and the others walked to the Training Yard. Snow fell from a misty sky, painting the landscape a shimmering white.

Zak barely noticed any of it. He was filled with nervous anticipation. What was his body capable of doing?

He couldn't wait to find out.

*

The next two hours passed in a feverish blur.

His body had never been capable of such amazing things. He ran and jumped and vaulted around the yard with a newfound zest. He heaved boulders into the air, far beyond the usual capacity for someone his age and size; he pitched rocks into the ocean at such distances they vanished on the horizon before hitting the water. His speed, dexterity, agility had improved beyond belief. He felt liberated, unshackled from the limits of his former self.

He accomplished feats no human had ever done. But then, in a sobering moment, something struck him, something he'd never considered before.

He wasn't really human at all.

*

After lunch, Zak and the others retired to their rooms, each of them tired after three solid hours of the most punishing exercise.

Lying on his bed, Zak listened to the wind pummel his window and his mind drifted to the mysterious box. Why had Guppingham left it for them? Was it a marker to the Seal of Solomon? If so, how would it help them find it?

He reached over and picked it up. Turning it in his fingers, he studied its contours. Opening the lid, his eyes scanned the words again, their translation filling his mind.

Open my eyes that I may see wonderful things in your law.

On this rock I shall build my church.

Again and again, he contemplated every word, every syllable. What did it all mean? Then his gaze found the symbol.

And as he studied it, something stirred within him.

He felt sure he'd seen it before. It seemed familiar as if once observed in a long forgotten dream.

Slowly, a memory formed. His heart thumped in his chest.

Furthermore, the symbol and the words fused as one to form a distinct image, one he hadn't considered since first arriving at Avernon.

An image that left him convinced as to the whereabouts of The Seal of Solomon.

*

Zak leapt off his bed. Within seconds, he was banging on Dunk's door so hard it almost shattered its hinges.

Dunk opened the door. He yawned as if woken from a long nap. 'What's with the racket?'

'I know where the Seal is.'

Dunk's yawn morphed into a gasp. 'W-what?

Where?'

'Let's get the girls,' Zak replied. 'We'll discuss this as a group.'

Within minutes they had rounded up Leah and Sarah and were back in the social room.

'Go on then,' Dunk said impatiently. 'Why d'you think you know where the Seal is?'

Zak raised the box high. 'It's the symbol,' he said. 'I've seen it before.'

'Where?' Sarah asked.

'After Kurnan took me from Addlebury we went to a safe house in Wales. When I say house, it was actually an old church in the middle of nowhere. Anyway, I met this oddball priest called Father Edward and he showed me around the chapel, which was jam-packed with these crazy symbols. Father Edward said the place was built about seven hundred years ago. Anyway, I saw this statue of a Templar Knight.' He opened the box and pointed at the symbol to stress his next point. 'This symbol was carved on the Knight's shield. Now the statue's face was angled down, toward the ground as if in prayer. If its eyes were *open* he'd be looking directly beneath him. Also, there was a plaque at the bottom of it with a quote by Virgil, the Roman Poet.'

'What did the quote say?' Sarah asked eagerly.

'I don't remember the Latin, but the translation was *'The descent to Hell is easy.'*

'And the Seal is supposedly a doorway to Hell,' Sarah said. 'So Hell would be easy to get to if you used it.'

Zak nodded. 'And remember when Pottsy first told us about Guppingham... he said he was an architect. So it ties in with the words *'On this rock I shall build my church.*' Saint Catherine's Chapel was literally the church he built.'

Dunk clapped his hands. 'There you go. That's me convinced.'

'You think the Seal is underneath the statue?' Sarah said.

'I do,' Zak replied. 'And it does make sense Guppingham hid it there. Let's face it, the only way the church and statue become significant is if you've seen this box, and as the Grandmasters kept it to themselves then no one else has... *until us.*'

'Looks like we're off to Wales,' Dunk said.

'I reckon so,' Zak said.

'Then how are we going to get there?' Leah asked.

'We'll take an Aquacar,' Dunk said.

'By *take* you mean *steal*?' Sarah said.

'Err, okay. If you insist,' Dunk replied sarcastically.

'Do you know the amount of security they have here?' Leah asked.

'And besides... who's gonna drive it?' Sarah added.

'Me,' Dunk replied. 'I can drive anything. No sweat.'

'And what if we're stopped by the police?' Sarah said. 'You're fifteen with no licence.'

'The way I drive the police would never keep up.'

'You're not driving there, Dunk,' Zak said. 'There must be another way.'

'We could ask Big Al to take us,' Sarah suggested.

'He's gone to Perigorn Castle,' Dunk replied.

'Kelly then,' Leah said. 'Big Al trusts her. And I do, too. She helped us out with those Grippers remember.'

'Yeah, she really saved our bacon there,' Dunk said, looking at Zak. 'I'm sure Kelly would do it.'

'Maybe,' Zak said. 'And I do trust her but I'm not

sure we should get her involved. She could get in serious trouble if we're wrong.'

'Do you really think we're wrong?' Sarah asked.

'No,' Zak replied. 'I know it's there.'

Sarah looked hesitant as she spoke her next words. 'Let's just say you are right and the Seal of Solomon is at Saint Catherine's... then maybe - just maybe - we should leave it where it is.'

Dunk looked at her as though she'd lost her mind. 'Why the hell would we do that?'

'Because maybe we're opening up a can of worms if we do get it,' Sarah said. 'Maybe one that shouldn't be opened. The way I see it -'

'- Don't be bloody daft,' Dunk cut in.

'Be quiet, Dunk!' Zak said firmly. 'Let her speak.'

Sarah's eyes met Zak's. 'As you said we're the only ones that know it's there. Lord Ballivan wouldn't have a clue because he hasn't seen the box. He couldn't understand the significance of the words and the symbol even if he knew about the statue at Saint Catherine's.' She took a deep breath. 'So maybe it's best we leave the Seal where it is. Let's face it, once the Seal's out in the open, who knows what the repercussions will be?'

Zak pondered this for a moment. 'That's a fair point,' he said. 'But it's not as simple as that. Yeah, we don't know what the repercussions will be, but we do know the Seal may be powerful enough to help win the war. That's why Lord Ballivan is searching for it. With that in mind, surely we have a duty to get it?'

'Agreed,' Dunk said without hesitation. 'Then that's settled... let's ask Kelly to take us to Wales and get the Seal.'

All eyes fell on Zak as his mouth formed a response.

'Okay. Let's ask her.'

*

Her fingers typing at the speed of light, Leah sent a text to Kelly, and five minutes later she entered the room to be confronted by four nervous faces.

'We need to talk to you,' Zak said. 'It's important.'

'I assumed it would be,' Kelly said. 'I've never been summoned by the Angels before.'

'We know where the Seal of Solomon is,' Zak said bluntly, 'and we need you to help us get it.'

Kelly appeared on the verge of fainting. 'You know where it is?'

'Yes.'

'Where?'

'Saint Catherine's Chapel... South Wales. It's about four hours away.'

'How do you know it's there?'

'That's a long story and we'll tell you on the way,' Zak replied. 'Can you get an Aquacar and take us?'

'When?'

'Now,' Dunk said. 'This second.'

'And no one else can know about it,' Leah said.

Kelly thought for a second. 'I have to tell Pottsy.'

'Big Al suggested we keep it to ourselves,' Dunk said. 'And I trust Big Al.'

'But I'd get in so much trouble,' Kelly said. 'Pottsy would kill me.'

Dunk waved his hands dismissively. 'Any trouble you'd be in would soon be forgotten when they know you helped get the Seal of Solomon. You'll be a hero.'

'I'm not a hero,' Kelly said firmly.

'Fair enough. But will you take us?' Leah asked.

Exhaling heavily, Kelly paced the room, an internal

battle clearly raging inside her. Eventually, she stopped in her tracks, and said, 'Okay... I'm in.'

'And you're okay with Pottsy killing you?' Dunk grinned.

Kelly smiled back at him. 'He can try, but I am tougher than I look.'

'Then let's get going,' Dunk said.

'Not now,' Kelly replied. 'It'll have to be tonight, when it's dark. Plus, I need hours to prepare. How does ten sound?'

'Good to me,' Dunk said.

'What is there to prepare?' Zak asked.

'I've got to try and give us a twenty minute window to get out of Avernon without anyone noticing. To do that I'll need to adjust the security settings on the perimeter codes, the motion and proximity sensors, the moni-cams, and the pulse radar.'

'And you can do all that?' Sarah asked.

'I've been well trained.' Kelly nodded. 'Of course, that's not going to stop the Aquabay Night Guard raising the alarm if they see us nicking a car.'

'There's a Night Guard?' Zak asked.

'There are always two Templars day and night guarding the Aquabay,' Kelly replied. 'But you let me worry about them.'

'Thanks, Kelly,' Leah said.

Stone-faced, Kelly scanned the group. 'You meet me at the main Aquabay security door at bang on ten. I'll do the rest.' Her voice adopted a low, reverential tone. 'I promise. If it's there... we'll get the Seal of Solomon tonight!'

*

For the rest of the day, Zak couldn't decide if he was

anxious, nervous, excited or a combination of the three. Despite this, he felt certain they were making the right decision. He would have preferred to tell Pottsy or Brockenhurst but something in Big Al's voice returned to him repeatedly, something that genuinely concerned him.

"I ain't sure who can be trusted anymore."

The hardest thing for Zak to deal with, however, was the fact he couldn't tell Sid or Irene. Although he had a sneaking suspicion Sid would support their plans, he had no doubt Irene would bind him to his bed with barbed wire if it prevented him making the trip.

Indeed, the Renaissance had made Irene even more protective of him than usual. After lunch, she spent the afternoon clucking and fussing over him and not letting him out of her sight, even insisting he join her and Sid for dinner. In the end, he felt suffocated and left his food without finishing, claiming he needed an early night after the previous night's events.

Leaving the Fraterhouse, Zak felt specks of rain drum his face. By the time he returned to his room, the rain pounded the ground and an unforgiving wind shook the dormitory.

He showered and dressed in a sweater, jeans and trainers. As he got ready, his eyes returned to the clock again and again; each second passed more slowly than the last. At nine forty five, he filled a water bottle and tossed two chocolate bars in his backpack. With the rain still hammering the roof, he pulled the waterproof poncho from his wardrobe and threw it on.

As he slipped his phone in his pocket, a knock shook the door. He opened it to see Dunk, Leah and Sarah, each wearing their rain ponchos, too.

'Hey, it's official,' Dunk said. 'We must be superheroes - we've even got a uniform. From now on we're *The Poncho Posse.*'

Zak forced a chuckle, although he was too nervous to offer anything that resembled a genuine laugh. He threw his backpack over his shoulder and moved toward the door.

'Have you got your Magnasword?' Dunk asked.

'No,' Zak replied. 'Why would I need it?'

'Get it,' Dunk said. 'You know what happened the last time we all left Avernon together.'

Zak collected his Magnasword holster and fastened it to his waist. Then he slid his Magnasword into it. As he left the room, all that filled his mind was how he hoped beyond hope he wouldn't need it.

- Chapter 30 -
Road Trip

The rainfall didn't let up as the group entered the central cloister. There wasn't a soul around and the perimeter walls, usually manned by Templars, were deserted.

Zak glanced at his watch as they approached the door that led below to the Aquacar bay. It was exactly ten.

Dunk reached the door first and pushed it open. A familiar face greeted them. Kelly wore a wide smile, her features illuminated by a single light bulb above.

'Quick, come on in before anyone sees,' Kelly said, ushering them out of the rain.

'Did you get everything done?' Dunk asked, pulling the soaking rain hood off his head.

'And more,' Kelly replied. 'The cameras are all on a nano-loop and the pulse radar is down. We definitely have the twenty minute window we need.' She grinned. 'I know it's wrong, and I'll probably get in heaps of trouble, but I am so buzzing about all of this.'

'What about the Night Guards?' Sarah asked,

concerned.

But Kelly didn't hear the question. She was already hurrying down the narrow steps, two at a time. Everyone followed. The sound of the ocean grew louder as the rainfall above became more distant.

Zak's pulse raced as he trailed Kelly down the hundreds of steps. As he emerged into the Aquacar bay, he scanned the area and saw at least twenty identical Aquacars parked there – all black Bentleys.

Ahead, he watched Kelly turn and walk purposefully to her left. Then, from a far room in the corner, two Templars emerged - one male, one female - and approached her.

The female Templar looked at Kelly, before noticing Zak and the others at her rear. Confused, she said, 'Kelly... what going on?'

'Hi, Carol,' Kelly replied brightly. She gestured to the group behind. 'I'm taking this lot on a road trip.'

Disbelief crossed the Templar's face as she glanced at her male counterpart. 'You're doing what?'

'We're off on a jolly to Wales,' Kelly replied.

'We haven't been informed of - '

The Templar didn't finish her sentence when Kelly raised a pistol from beneath her poncho. Like lightning, she took aim and pulled the trigger.

PHIKK!

A dart skimmed the air, piercing the female Templar's neck. Immediately, she collapsed to the floor. The male Templar pulled free a dart gun, but Kelly was too quick. She adjusted her aim and fired again.

PHIKK!

The dart spat out of the pistol's muzzle, impaling itself in the man's neck. He crumpled to the ground.

Zak could not believe his eyes.

Kelly returned her gun to a holster beneath her poncho and smiled at the others. 'Now I really am going to be in serious trouble. They'll probably send me to the *Fort* for this.'

Leah struggled to breathe. 'W-what have you done?'

'Oh, they'll be okay,' Kelly replied. 'I used stun darts, soaked in Sodium Mentantathol.' She said this so matter-of-factly it was hard to believe she was standing over two lifeless bodies. 'Well, Carol and Danny weren't going to let us out of here so what else could I do? But don't worry about it. They'll be right as rain when they come round tomorrow morning, by which point I'm hoping we'll be back.'

'Err, okay,' Dunk said, uncertainly.

'Help me move them, Dunk.'

Kelly sprinted over to the female Templar and seized her shoulders, pulling her toward a door in the wall. Dunk grasped the male Templar and followed suit.

Kelly opened the door to reveal a storeroom. She dragged the Templar inside, sitting her up against the wall. Dunk did the same. Then they returned to the group.

'Now which car do you want?' Kelly said.

'Can I drive?' Dunk asked.

'No, but for that you can sit in the back.' Kelly looked at the nearest car to them. 'This one will do.'

Removing a small device from her pocket, Kelly pressed a button and the car burst into life. She opened the driver's door. 'Get in the front, Zak. You've been there before.'

'I don't know the way though,' Zak replied, climbing onto the passenger seat.

'Don't worry,' Kelly replied. 'These babies drive themselves. I could just type in Saint Catherine's Chapel and it would take us there itself. We could all have a nice kip and wake up in Wales.'

'Really?' Zak said, amazed.

'Yeah. They've got a self-steering function that's controlled by an AG-satellite – it's real state of the art stuff. It certainly beats your average sat-nav.'

Kelly flicked another button on her remote and the engine turned over. Taking the wheel, she pressed her foot on the accelerator.

The Bentley drove off, turning onto a ramp that descended into blackness. A second later, there was a burst of white light and they were powering along a long tunnel that extended into the distance, its panelled walls lit by a sequence of strip lights.

'I can't believe we're doing this?' Dunk said. 'This is so cool.'

'I just hope we're doing the right thing,' Sarah replied.

'I think you are,' Kelly said.

The Bentley hurtled along faster than a train. The tunnel went on for miles, as straight as an arrow.

As the tunnel appeared to be coming to an end, Kelly hit a button on the dashboard and a wide doorway opened up ahead. Seconds later, they rocketed through it into the open air. Rain pelted the windscreen and a stiff wind rocked the car.

Zak glanced in the rear-view mirror to see they had emerged atop a rocky outcrop on the cliff. The doorway closed automatically, until once more it was camouflaged seamlessly with the existing rock.

A few moments later, the Bentley approached the

gates and high electrified fences that marked the Templar-owned land.

Kelly hit a purple button on the dashboard and the gates ahead opened. The Bentley sped through them and onto a dark, winding road.

The further they drove from Avernon, the more Zak found himself glued to his phone. He knew the second their disappearance was uncovered Sid and Irene would phone him.

But he hadn't had a single message.

With each passing mile, the conversation in the car dwindled to the odd remark, before culminating in complete silence; each of them seemingly lost in their own thoughts, contemplating what, if anything, they would find at the end of their journey.

*

It was two in the morning when Saint Catherine's Chapel appeared on the horizon. The rain stopped and a brilliant moon brightened the landscape, making it gleam like glass from the recent rainfall.

'So that's it?' Dunk said.

'Yeah,' Zak replied.

'This is really happening,' Kelly said excitedly.

'Should we wake Father Edward and explain what we're doing?' Sarah asked.

'No, Zak replied. 'He was emotional enough when he met just me. He'd have a cardiac arrest if he met you lot. No, I say we just get in there, get the Seal, and get out.'

'We're still sure this is the right thing to do, aren't we?' Sarah asked.

Surprisingly, it was Kelly that answered. 'No question about it. This is a momentous night. Make no mistake about it, getting the Seal will you change the course of the war for the better.'

'And it's all thanks to you for bringing us,' Dunk said to Kelly.

'Don't be mad,' Kelly replied. 'The honour is mine. In some ways I think my whole life has been building up to this point.'

Kelly stopped the Bentley at the entrance to the chapel. As she removed her hands from the wheel, Zak could see she was trembling.

'Right, kids, go and do your thing,' Kelly said in an unsteady voice. 'I really hope we haven't come all this way for nothing.'

'We haven't,' Leah said. 'I'm sure of it.'

'You've gotta come in, Kelly,' Dunk said. 'You've gotta be there when we find the Seal.'

'No,' Kelly said. 'I'll wait here. It's your moment. This is all about you.'

'It's about you too now, Kelly,' Zak said. 'Come with us.'

Kelly shook her head. 'No. I'm honoured enough just to be a part of it. Now go and get that ring.'

'We won't be long,' Dunk said.

The group left the car.

Zak approached the chapel's entrance and turned the iron ring handle. The door opened with a soft creak. They entered to find the room cloaked in darkness. Zak saw a light switch on his right and flicked it on.

A muted orange light painted the chapel, casting long shadows over the columns and pillars, which were covered top to bottom in ancient symbols.

'Wow,' Dunk gushed. 'You weren't wrong about the symbols, Zak. They're everywhere. It's mad!'

'Even Avernon isn't as weird as here,' Leah said.

'It's amazing,' Sarah said, awestruck.

'It is,' Zak replied. 'But we're not here to sight see. Follow me.' Approaching the statue of the Templar Knight, he thought it more imposing than he remembered.

'It's massive,' Leah said.

Zak dropped to his knees and studied the statue's base. 'There's no sign of a door or an opening.'

'Then we'll have to move it,' Dunk said.

'And how will we do that exactly?' Sarah asked, doubtfully.

'Like this,' Dunk said. Without hesitation, he gripped the statue around its middle, bent his knees and took the strain. Teeth gritted, he pushed upward. COMMEEE ONNNN!' he shouted.

The statue barely moved an inch. Dunk tried again, yelling louder this time, but it didn't make much of a difference. In the end he gave up, panting wildly. 'Yeah, I think it's safe to say it'll take a team effort.'

Together, they surrounded the statue. One by one they clasped a part of it. Glancing at each other, they each nodded silently to show they were ready.

'Okay,' Zak said. '3 – 2 – 1… GO!'

With a loud collective grunt, they lifted. The statue rose off the floor. They each took a small step, then another. It was the heaviest thing any of them had ever lifted, but it was moving slowly, steadily, edging away from its original position.

Zak's shoulders and arms seared with pain. Twenty seconds later, he yelled, 'That's enough… drop it.'

They released the statue. With a thunderous *whump*, it met the floor in a thick puff of dust.

Zak took a step back, his every fibre thankful for shedding the weight. His gaze found the patch where the statue had been. A stone hatch three feet square with a small brass handle had been uncovered. His eyes widened further. Painted onto the stone, as clear and vivid as if it been applied that day, was an intricately designed pictogram.

'I've seen that symbol before,' Sarah said.

'You have?' Zak asked. 'Where?'

'The moment Pottsy mentioned the Seal I began to research it myself,' Sarah said. 'I saw this symbol in a manuscript in Avernon library. Apparently, it was designed by King David, and his son, Solomon, had it replicated in gold on the ceiling of the First Temple in Jerusalem.' Her eyes found Zak's. 'It's the symbol for the Seal of Solomon. You were right. It's here.'

Excitement flashed in Dunk's eyes. 'Then what're we waiting for? Let's go and get it.'

Zak exhaled nervously, before dropping to his knees. His fingers curled round the handle and he pulled it. The door was heavy – very heavy – but it opened slowly, revealing a cavernous hole below. He stared down and in the gloom saw a series of steps that led deep underground. Pulling out his phone, he hit the torch key. Suddenly, light was everywhere. He looked up at the others. 'I guess this is it then?'

'After you,' Leah said, smiling.

His heart pounding, Zak descended.

- Chapter 31 -
The Wolf in Sheep's Clothing

Stepping off the bottom rung, Zak found himself in a passageway, barely a metre wide, its low ceiling reinforced by thick wooden beams. He doubled over to avoid banging his head. Raising his torch before him, he saw the shaft extended about fifty feet to an antechamber. Strangely, a soft blue light emanated from an unseen source within.

His trainers crunching on dirt and grit, Zak led the others down the passageway. It was cramped, awkward and the air was stale and as thick as smoke.

'Tell us what's up there, Zak,' Dunk said. 'We can't see a thing.'

'There's a room with a weird blue light coming from it,' Zak said.

In no time at all, he reached the passage's end and turned off his torch. He entered the antechamber.

To his surprise, it was much bigger in height and width than the tunnel and he straightened himself to his full height. As he scanned the room's interior, he saw a stone altar set against the north wall, adorned with three silver candlesticks and a golden plate, in the centre of which was the source of the blue light: *a small ring.*

The breath caught in his throat.

They had found the Seal of Solomon.

Zak sensed the others beside him. No one moved a muscle as they stood there in silence, each mesmerised by the artefact before them.

'It's here,' Leah breathed.

'It really is,' Sarah added.

'Go on then, Zak,' Dunk said. 'You found it, you get it.'

'Hang on,' Sarah said. 'Should he even touch it?'

'Yeah, we haven't a clue how it works,' Leah said.

'If he touches it and it teleports him to another planet,' Dunk said, 'he'll know better than to do that again.' He chuckled.

Zak didn't find it vaguely funny, but he knew he had no choice. Approaching the altar, he picked up the ring. Entranced, he studied it closely, his face coloured a shimmering blue. It was so exquisite, divine, unlike anything he'd ever seen before.

'Right, we've done it,' Sarah said. 'Now let's get back to Avernon.'

'Agreed,' Zak replied. He slipped the ring in his pocket.

Immediately, the room fell into darkness.

Zak flicked on his phone again and illuminated the tunnel. Bending over, he advanced back up the passageway. He scaled the steps, the air becoming cleaner with each stride. The moment he emerged into the chapel, however, something happened that froze his spine.

He heard a voice he didn't recognise - a chilling female

voice.

'So, Zak Fisher, you did it.'

'Who's there?' Zak replied, glancing left and right.

As Dunk, Leah and Sarah joined him, a willowy figure sloped out of the shadows about twenty feet away. As it stepped into the half-light, Zak's eyes nearly popped from his head.

Standing upright on two powerful legs, the creature had black, fibrous skin and a long, whip-like tail that coiled the air languidly. Feminine curves added elegance to her muscular physique, and there was something almost human about her face, with pronounced cheekbones, gleaming white teeth, and magnetic, dark blue eyes.

He didn't recognise the species from any of his Demon-lore classes or the textbook, *'Demons and Demonilla.'*

There was movement behind the creature's shoulder. Beasts were crawling out of the gloom, scaling the walls and scuttling across the ceiling like giant insects. He recognised these immediately: *Arachnoids.*

To make matters worse, more creatures joined them - a second species. Walking on two legs, they were tall, powerfully built with green skin, yellow eyes with vertical slits for pupils and long tails. Elongated jaws dominated their angular faces and blood-red forked tongues flicked in and out of their thin lips. Each wielded a curved sword.

Zak knew them, too: *Reptilaks.* He did a mental count. They were outnumbered at least five to one.

Zak, Sarah, Dunk and Leah watched silently as the opposing force surrounded them, filling the chapel. As one, they pulled free their Magnaswords and extended them, their blades gleaming like lasers.

'Now you've already lost,' the creature said. 'So lower your weapons and let me introduce myself: I am Dreanda.'

'I couldn't give a toss who you are,' Dunk said. 'And if you think we've lost already you don't know us very well.'

'Ah, but I do know you. I know you all very well,' Dreanda sneered. 'I've had your bedrooms and your social room *bugged* for quite some time now.'

'What are you talkin' about?' Dunk asked.

Dreanda opened her mouth to speak, but instead of her normal voice they heard one they'd heard a thousand times before.

'Hi, kids.'

Zak was stunned. *Dreanda was speaking in Kelly Barnes' voice.*

Dunk looked confused. 'I don't get it.'

An ugly smile curled on Dreanda's mouth. 'Then do you get this?' With that, her face began to change. Her bones undulated beneath her dark skin that rapidly lightened in colour, her blue eyes became brown, and hair sprouted from her scalp, thick and golden, stopping when it grazed her shoulders.

Leah gasped in horror.

Kelly Barnes was staring back at them.

'Now do you understand?' Dreanda said.

'You're a Morphean?' Sarah said. 'A shapeshifter.'

Promptly, Zak recalled John Kurnan telling him all about Morpheans.

'I think that's obvious, don't you?' Dreanda purred, transforming back to her natural form. 'And isn't it handy the Templars believe my kind to be extinct. The fact is, I was born and raised on earth, and have trained my whole life for this very night.'

'W-where's the real Kelly?' Leah stammered.

'You've never actually met her, 'Dreanda replied. 'She was murdered in London so I could take her place. I've been Kelly Barnes ever since I turned up, beaten and bruised, at Avernon in November.'

'But Doctor Pudgbury gave you a full check up,' Sarah said. 'Or was he in on it?'

'Obviously, he discovered I was a Morphean, but when I told him we'd kidnapped his grandson and daughter he wasn't about to divulge my little secret.'

'And did you kill him?' Zak asked.

'I had no choice,' Dreanda said. 'I just couldn't trust him to stay silent any longer. Now let's get to business, shall we? Put your Magnaswords down and pass me the Seal of Solomon.'

'That's not gonna happen,' Dunk said.

'I suggest you do,' Dreanda said. 'You see, the Templars have already lost. Even as we speak Avernon is overrun with my kind. Lord Ballivan took Avernon a few hours ago.'

Zak's heart sank.

'That's impossible,' Leah said. 'That place is a fortress.'

'Ordinarily yes,' Dreanda replied, 'but you gave me plenty of time to weaken their defences, didn't you? So this whole thing is really your fault. Any blood shed tonight is on you.'

Fear swept through Zak. *Sid and Irene were at Avernon.*

'Can we get to the fighting bit now?' Dunk said.

'There'll no fighting here,' Dreanda said. 'But I will

be taking you back to Avernon for Lord Ballivan to pass judgement on you.'

Simultaneously, Zak, Leah, Dunk and Sarah's phones buzzed. They looked at each other, confused.

'Perhaps you should take a long hard look at your phones before making your next move,' Dreanda said coldly.

Speechless, they all raised their phones and opened the message.

As an image formed before him, Zak felt sick to his core.

A young girl was kneeling on the lawn at Avernon, her hands tied behind her back.

Terrified, Anne Dixon stared directly into the camera lens, her clothes torn, her mouth bleeding, her eyes raw from tears.

- Chapter 32 -
The Battle of Saint Catherine's

Zak's insides boiled. He knew everyone was looking at him, waiting for him to react. Coolly his gaze found Dreanda's, and he said in a low menacing voice, 'If you hurt her you'll be sorry.'

Dreanda smirked. 'No one wants to hurt her. She's nothing. Her life is meaningless to us… but it isn't to you. Whether she lives or dies is now in your hands. Now pass over the Seal!'

A million scenarios flitted through Zak's mind.

How should he play this? It seemed to him that even if he followed Dreanda's instructions to the letter, he could only envisage one outcome. 'It doesn't matter what we do…' His voice was emotionless. 'You'll kill Anne, you'll kill Sid, Irene, everyone at Avernon, as you've done with Kelly and Doctor Pudgbury…'

Dreanda's tail whipped the air angrily and she screamed, 'GIVE ME THE SEAL!'

Zak's face remained impassive. He stood there,

stock-still, like a statue.

The seconds passed.

Dreanda regained her composure. 'As you're not in any rush to comply, perhaps I should employ another tack.' She nodded at an Arachnoid to her left.

The Arachnoid extended its front limbs and lifted a large mass that was cloaked in shadow. He hurled it at Dreanda's feet.

Father Edward landed heavily with a muffled grunt. His hands and mouth were bound with tape; his forehead bled profusely from a gaping wound.

Dreanda ripped the gag from Father Edward's mouth. 'Priest… tell them to do as I ask and I may spare your life!'

Father Edward trembled with fear. As he processed these words, however, his terror morphed into resolve.

'ZAK… NO!' Father Edward shouted over. 'Don't do as *it* says.' He looked up at Dreanda, whose eyes were wild and dangerous. 'Do what you will with me, *monster*!'

'Then it is my will I have your head,' Dreanda said to Father Edward.

'NO!' Zak yelled.

Dreanda nodded at a Reptilak, who raised his curved sword high. 'It seems, Zak Fisher, you have a simple decision to make: pass me the Seal and the good priest will live.'

'Father Edward isn't dying today,' Zak replied. 'But I shall give you something… the opportunity to surrender.'

'Surrender?'

'Yes.'

'Do you really think you can defeat us? Don't forget

I've seen you train. I know your strengths and weaknesses.'

'Things have changed a bit lately,' Zak replied. 'I thought you'd heard.'

'Your arrogance overwhelms me.'

'It's not arrogance.'

'What is it then?'

'Confidence,' Zak said. 'Now will you surrender?'

'I think not, but I'll give you one last chance. The Seal or the Priest?'

As Zak appeared to mull this over, he glanced at the throwing knife concealed in Leah's left palm. 'Have you got a shot, Leah?' he said under his breath.

Leah gave an almost imperceptible nod.

'Take it,' Zak said to Leah.

In a flash, Leah pitched the knife at the Reptilak standing over Father Edward. It cut the air, plunging into the Reptilak's forehead. The creature crumbled to dust.

Zak turned toward the closest Reptilak and threw his Magnasword, piercing the creature's breastbone. As the Reptilak disintegrated, he raced over and caught the sword before it landed. Another Reptilak charged at him. With a swipe of his Magnasword, the threat had gone.

At the same time, Leah, Dunk and Sarah burst into action.

Dreanda stared furiously at the battle. Eyes wild, she glared at Father Edward. 'So be it. You will perish, priest.' She drew her Magnasword and raised it high.

Zak saw this. With the briefest run-up, he bounded through the air, his newfound strength carrying him a astonishing distance. He landed deftly, his sword extended, stopping Dreanda's blade before making contact with Father Edward's neck.

'I told you he's not dying today,' Zak said, forcing Dreanda's sword away from Father Edward.

Dreanda swiped at Zak's head, but he ducked, the blade missing him by a whisker. Gripping his Magnasword with two hands, he thrust it at Dreanda's chest.

She parried the attack, whirling round and attacking again.

Again, Zak dodged the strike, counter-attacking with a jab, but his shot was blocked.

In a blur, the two of them fought relentlessly, at speeds the eye could barely follow. Neither gave way to the other, neither yielded for a second.

As the fight thundered on, however, Zak could sense Dreanda was tiring. 'Stop this,' he said. 'You won't beat me. And I don't want to kill you.'

Panting loudly, Dreanda growled, 'But I *want* to kill you.' She swung at his neck, but Zak predicted the move.

Zak swung again, but Dreanda blocked the shot. She was panting harder now, her strength fading fast.

In that moment, Zak knew he could finish the fight if he wanted. 'This is over,' he said. 'You know that.'

'Nothing's over,' Dreanda fired back. And then the strangest thing happened. Her face transformed into a human one. Suddenly lined with age, her skin turned a shade of pink, as hair grew from her scalp, styled and stylish.

In that instant, Zak's strength deserted him.

He was staring at Irene Shufflebottom.

'Now stop this right now, Zak, my dear,' Dreanda said, imitating Irene's voice perfectly.

Zak head spun. He knew it was Dreanda, but the face, the voice was entirely that of Irene's. He let his guard down.

Dreanda noticed. She attacked with a ferocious strike to his neck.

Zak collected himself just in time to sidestep left and swiftly brought up his blade, targeting Dreanda's chest.

This time Dreanda didn't see it coming. As the Magnasword struck, Irene's face vanished, replaced by Dreanda's, which displayed merely shock as it froze in a death mask.

Her body dissolved to powder.

Barely taking time to catch his breath, Zak waited for another assault from a different foe but it didn't happen. Scanning the scene, he saw the church was thick with dust. There was no movement anywhere.

The battle was over.

In that instant, Zak felt a rush of panic. Had Dunk, Leah or Sarah been injured or worse? As the fog settled, however, he saw all three standing there, panting and weary, but unharmed. Feeling relieved, he turned to Father Edward and ripped off the priest's bonds.

'T-thank you, Z-Zak,' Father Edward stuttered.

'That's okay. How badly are you hurt?'

As the words lingered, Father Edward's eyelids twitched and he lost consciousness.

For a moment, Zak felt helpless. However, a moment later, Sarah sprinted over and dropped to her knees. She leaned over Father Edward's body and extended her fingers an inch or so above his head.

Zak watched, enthralled, as Sarah's open palm traversed his forehead slowly, before massaging his temples in small, concentric circles. Her breathing became shallow, her eyes closed in deep concentration. Tiny flecks of electrical charge emanated from her fingers, feeding into the Father Edward's skull, healing the open wound before their very eyes.

Zak glanced at Dunk and Leah, who wore shocked expressions as if they too had never seen anything like it before.

'Whoa!' Dunk gasped.

Almost immediately, Father Edward's eyes snapped open. He stared at Sarah, his eyes misting over as if knowing instantly he had been involved in something extraordinary.

'Hello, Father Edward,' Sarah said softly. 'I'm Sarah.'

'Hello, my child,' Father Edward replied.

'Do you feel okay now?' Sarah asked.

Father Edward took a moment before offering a response. 'Never better,' he replied sincerely.

Sarah smiled with satisfaction.

'Wow, Sar. You really do have healing hands,' Leah said.

'Can we all do that?' Dunk said.

'I don't know,' Sarah replied. 'I've been able to do it since I was a child.'

'And can you cure anything?' Leah asked.

'No,' Sarah said. 'Just minor stuff. But I'm great at getting rid of headaches.'

'That would be useful if any of us ever had them,' Dunk said.

Father Edward's gaze scanned the empty church. 'Did - did we win?'

'Sure did,' Dunk said.

'Praise the Lord,' Father Edward said.

'Just praise me if you want, Father,' Dunk said.

'Yeah, Dunk the Destroyer did it all,' Leah said sarcastically. 'The rest of us just watched.'

At that moment, Zak remembered all that was happening at Avernon. 'Father Edward, we have to go now - Avernon's under attack.'

'Then of course,' Father Edward replied. 'But before you do can I just ask one thing - did you really find the Seal of Solomon here?'

Zak searched his pocket and withdrew the ring, which emitted a soft blue glow that illuminated all of them.

Father Edward gasped. 'Will the wonders of this night ever end?'

'Let's go,' Zak said to the others. 'You take care now, Father Edward.'

'And you, Zak. I shall pray for Avernon and I shall pray for all of you. You truly are divine, you are at one with God.'

Zak nodded over at church - the pews, the altar, the pulpit were all coated in the residue of all the Hellians. 'Sorry about the mess.'

'No matter. I have an excellent Dyson Cyclone V10 vacuum cleaner which will sort this place out. It's nearly as much a miracle as the four of you.'

Zak smiled. Then he noticed Dreanda's bone-handled Magnasword on the floor. It occurred to him it had almost certainly belonged to Kelly Barnes.

Exhaling heavily, he picked it up, and turned to the others. 'Dunk... looks like you get your chance to drive after all.'

'Wicked.' Dunk grinned. 'Now you're gonna see something really special...'

- Chapter 33 -
Return to Avernon

Zak agreed that for once Dunk wasn't exaggerating.

After hot-wiring the car with worrying ease, Dunk took his place behind the wheel as if born there.

The Bentley sped off in a billowing cloud of fumes and soon powered over the landscape at speeds the car hadn't seen before.

As the Bentley cut the night, Zak stared at Kelly Barnes' Magnasword. Sadness welled within him. He had never met Kelly, never known her true personality, and he never would. Her corpse lay on the bed of the Thames and would never be found. The Magnasword was all that remained of her, a testament to a courageous life prematurely ended by a malevolent foe.

'Dreanda really played us, didn't she?' Leah spat out.

'She played everyone,' Zak replied. 'We should've picked up on it.'

'It's not our fault,' Sarah said. 'She was a Morphean; even the Templars thought they were extinct. No one was prepared for it.'

Zak contemplated this for a second. 'What amazes me is the amount of training she must've had to infiltrate the Templars so easily. She must've been trained in all their procedures, their rules, their systems, their weapons, not to mention the names of the Templars at Avernon.'

'She said she'd been training her whole life for it,' Sarah said.

'And she really must have,' Zak replied.

'Plus, she must know scumbags inside the Templar organisation,' Dunk said. 'It's the only way to get that kinda information.'

'I agree,' Zak replied. 'Kurnan once told me the Hellfire Club were everywhere. He wasn't wrong.'

'I still don't get is why she turned up to help us with the Gripper attack?' Leah said. 'There's no way we could've beaten them without her help.'

'Maybe she did it to back up her cover?' Zak said. 'Maybe someone in the Templars suspected she wasn't all she seemed? Let's face it, after helping us no one would ever question her loyalty to the Templars or us again - all it took was to sacrifice a few Grippers and her allegiance to the cause can't be questioned.'

'Maybe you're right,' Leah said. 'What I do know is that it'll be hard to trust anyone from now on.'

'Big Al warned us about trusting people,' Dunk said. 'He was bang on right.'

As Zak's fingers traced the contours of Kelly's Magnasword, something occurred to him, something that chilled his bones.

'Big Al didn't say that.'

'What are you talkin' about?' Dunk asked, perplexed. 'We were all in the social room when he did.'

'That was Kelly,' Zak replied. 'She must have transformed into him to find out everything about the

Renaissance, about our new powers. If you remember rightly she was asking all about that kind of stuff. Maybe she was asking to let Lord Ballivan know what he was up against.'

Dunk looked stunned. 'How d'you know it was her?'

'Because of this,' Zak replied, holding up the sword. 'Do you remember you asked why Big Al didn't have his usual Magnasword and he said he was getting the handle fixed. It was this Magnasword he was holding: Kelly's Magnasword. Dreanda was Big Al. There's no doubt about it in my mind.'

Dunk glanced at the sword. A sharp nod suggested he knew Zak was right. 'What a bloody devious cow.'

'And come to think of it,' Zak said. 'It was Big Al that persuaded us to go to Saint Catherine's Chapel alone, and not tell anyone about anything... to not trust Pottsy or Brockenhurst. In fact, he said only to trust Kelly.' He chuckled sourly. 'Dreanda played us good and proper...'

Fortunately, the roads were deserted. There was no sign of the police anywhere. As they passed the county boundary and entered Cornwall, the conversation dwindled to the odd comment and a sombre mood filled the car.

It was clear they each had only one thought on their mind: *Lord Ballivan's conquest of Avernon.*

'So what's the plan when we get there?' Leah asked.

'We give every single Hellian a damn good kickin',' Dunk said. 'We send them to Hell, and not their Hell either, we send them to our old school, fire and brimstone, Satan's pitchfork up the bum, Hell.'

'I'm not sure it's that simple,' Zak replied.

'Why not?'

'We beat twenty or so of them at Saint Catherine's,' Zak said. 'But what'll we do if there are fifty of them, a hundred, two hundred?'

'We kick their asses, too,' Dunk replied.

'Do you have a plan, Zak?' Sarah said.

'Yeah, you took the top job,' Dunk said. 'Now's the time to step up to the plate. Our lives are in your hands, buddy.'

Although Dunk's words felt like a gut punch, Zak knew he was right. He had agreed to be Archangel, and it was up to him to make the best decisions for all their sakes. 'First of all,' he said, 'we need to find out exactly what we're up against, how many Hellians there are, how many Templars are still alive.'

'So how do we do that?' Leah asked.

'We need to get into Avernon unseen,' Zak said. 'We need all the information we can before we make any kind of move.'

'But how can we do that?' Leah said. 'Lord Ballivan must know by now things didn't go to plan at Saint Catherine's because Dreanda would've contacted him. So, let's face it, he'll be expecting us. And as there's only one-way in and that's through the tunnel, he'll have that guarded to the hilt. Zak, we just can't get into Avernon unnoticed.'

'You let me worry about that,' Zak said mysteriously.

*

It was nearly six when they approached the gate that marked the entrance to the Templar estate. It was also clear that Dunk had no intention of stopping at it.

Aiming the car directly at it, Dunk pushed the

Bentley to maximum speed. Then he struck it like a missile.

In an explosion of metal and plastic, the Bentley powered onto Templar land.

Dunk whooped. 'THAT WAS AWESOME!'

Zak grinned. 'Now don't slow down.'

'Zak, we can't use the tunnel!' Leah said urgently.

'We're not,' Zak replied.

'Tell me we're not swimming there,' Dunk said.

'Nope.'

'Then what are we doing?' Leah asked.

'You'll see,' Zak replied.

The Bentley zoomed down the road at over two hundred miles per hour.

'What are you doing, Zak?' Sarah said, concerned.

'The one thing that might give us that element of surprise.'

For the first time there was anxiousness in Dunk's voice. 'You do know we're gonna run out of road soon, don't you?'

Zak shrugged. 'You wanted to see if you'd survive jumping from a plane? This is as close as you're going to get.'

'What're you talkin' about?' Dunk asked.

The cliff edge was fast approaching.

'SERIOUSLY, ZAK!' Leah yelled. 'WHAT ARE YOU DOING?'

Zak didn't reply.

They were twenty feet from the cliff edge now.

Leaving it to the last second, Dunk spun the wheel right, steering them from danger, but Zak anticipated the move. Leaning over, he forced the wheel front.

Facing an oil-black sky, the Bentley powered off the

cliff.

Leah's scream slashed the air. As the car plunged toward the water, Dunk's scream fused with hers.

Remaining calm, Zak pressed the same green button he'd seen Kurnan push months ago. Immediately, the undercarriage grumbled and groaned, tilting them upward, maintaining a horizontal position.

Just then, seconds from impact, a power surge propelled them forward. Suddenly, they were skimming along the ocean like a pebble. The car headlights illuminated the choppy water ahead.

Dunk's howl of terror became one of exhilaration. 'WHOAAAAA!'

Zak laughed.

'WHAT? HOW?' Leah shouted.

'This is why they're called Aquacars,' Zak said.

'You could've warned us,' Leah said.

'Where's the fun in that?' Zak replied. 'Besides, Kurnan did the same to me when I first came to Avernon. You all used the tunnel, didn't you?'

'Yes, we did,' Sarah said, still shaken. 'And I'll be using it next time, too. I don't care if it's guarded by a thousand Hellians.'

Dunk stared out at the open ocean. 'I have to say this is pretty cool. I've always wanted to drive a speed boat.'

'It is cool,' Zak replied. 'Now turn off the headlights.'

'But we won't see a thing,' Dunk replied, doing as Zak requested.

'Yeah. And no one on the island will see us...'

In darkness, the car sped along the ocean, the sound of the crashing surf masking the sound of the engine. In no time at all, Avernon appeared on the horizon, above its outline, a reddish tinge painted the sky.

'Avernon's on fire!' Leah gasped.

Zak's heart sank. 'Dunk, pull up on the beach nearest the cliff.'

Dunk steered them toward the shoreline. Entering the shallows, the water merged with soft sand. Zak pressed the button again. Instantly, a loud churning sound signalled tyres had replaced the water skis.

Driving onto the beach, Dunk cut the engine.

No one said a thing.

Zak's gaze locked on Kelly's Magnasword, but he didn't really look at it. His mind was elsewhere, consumed with dread at what they might find at Avernon. Reaching under his seat, as he had done with Kurnan, he found a dart gun. He pulled it into the open, and passed it to Sarah. 'Here,' he said. 'You're the best shot.'

Sarah took the gun, surprised. 'Err, thanks.'

Zak exited the car. Everyone followed him out and a moment later, they all stood in a circle.

'So what's the plan?' Leah asked Zak.

Stone-faced, Zak nodded at the cliff. At over three hundred feet high, its sheer face looked black, damp and imposing. 'We're climbing that.'

'What?' Leah replied, aghast.

'We need an element of surprise,' Zak said. 'That should give us it. There's no way they'll expect us to approach from there.'

'And that's because only an idiot would try,' Dunk said.

'Then I'm an idiot,' Zak replied. 'The truth is we need to get on the boundary walls without being spotted to see what's going on. There may be guards at the normal entrances so I reckon climbing them is the only way.'

'But it's been raining half the night,' Sarah said. 'It'll be like climbing an iceberg.' She shook her head. 'Seriously, Zak, it's lethal.'

Zak didn't waver. 'It's only lethal if you fall...'

- Chapter 34 -
Lord Ballivan

Inhaling a lungful of salty air, Zak stood at the cliff's base, staring upward. The roar of the sea faded in his ears as he focussed on the countless ridges and crags jutting out from the rock face.

He could do this.

He reached for a rock. The moment he did, he recalled his second foster family, the McCann's, teaching him *free climbing* in Snowdonia. Like everything else, he had taken to it like a duck to water. He gripped another rock and heaved himself up, his feet finding a ledge. Determined not to look back, he continued his ascent.

Ten feet.

Twenty feet.

Adrenaline filled him as he climbed onward.

A hundred feet.

A hundred and fifty feet.

Two hundred feet.

He could see top now, as he reached for another rock. Just then, his fingers slipped. Falling fast, he could hear Sarah scream below. Instinctively, he grasped another rock with his right hand. He held on, his muscles screaming as his body swayed like barley in the wind.

Pushing himself through the pain, he gripped another rock, his feet finding a firm toehold. Heart hammering his chest, he balanced himself, and pressed his face against the damp rock. He waited for his pulse to slow.

Then he began his ascent again. This time he was determined there would be no mistakes. Within a minute, he'd reached the summit. Pulling himself onto the dirt track that bordered the monastery wall, he lay down, panting heavily.

From the other side of the wall, he heard strange noises. Bizarre yelps, high-pitched shrieks, and countless other sounds were joined together in jubilation.

Turning on his side, he looked down to see Dunk, Leah and Sarah were nearly at the top. Reaching down, he heaved Dunk to safety.

'Jeez,' Dunk puffed. 'You and your bright ideas. And if you'd have fallen another few feet you'd have taken me with you.'

'Yeah, that was a bit close for comfort,' Zak replied.

He and Dunk reached down and helped Sarah onto the path, before doing the same with Leah.

Soon, they were all stretched out on the ground, relief surging through them.

The ugly shrieks beyond the wall were louder than ever.

'I wouldn't be surprised if every Hellian in 'Demons and Demonilla' is less than a hundred metres away,' Leah said.

Zak couldn't disagree. He stared at the wall. At twenty feet high, it looked considerably easier to climb than the cliff. 'Let's see what we're dealing with then,' he said. Getting to his feet, he began to climb once more. This time, he made it to the top in seconds flat and dropped down on to a stone path on the other side, crouching low. He peered down into the monastery grounds.

What he saw sent a chill up his spine.

Avernon was burning, every building ablaze, shedding reddish light over the Training Yard, which was overrun with Hellians, some small, some large, some walking, some crawling, some on two legs, some on four: Reptilaks, Scorpoids, Mothmen, Arachnoids, Grippers and other species Zak had only seen before as illustrations in a book. Dead bodies of Templars and Hellians peppered the ground, alongside discarded Magnaswords.

Zak's stomach churned when he spied the lifeless form of Iccy and Izreal, Mister Gudrak's Hell Hounds, lying dead for all to see.

Surveying the area, he saw forty or so Templar Knights, kneeling, their arms tied behind their backs, positioned at the far side of the amphitheatre. They faced front as if watching a bizarre stage performance. Standing before them, William Brockenhurst looked broken, his long grey hair dishevelled and knotted with blood. To his left, Pottsy looked even worse, his forehead bleeding profusely.

Zak's stomach sank further when he saw the figure at the end of the line.

Mister Gudrak was bound by thick rope to a flagpole. His face was bruised and beaten, his naked torso covered in gashes and cuts, his yellow skin stained red with his own blood.

Rage burning within, Zak's eyes locked on the

creature standing beside Mister Gudrak. Tall and cloaked, it was a pale-faced humanoid with yellow eyes, pallid skin and small pointed teeth that glowed eerily as he grinned at the spectators.

'*Ballivan*,' Zak growled under his breath.

Zak scanned the Templars, and his heart flipped. Sid and Irene were on the front row, Anne kneeling beside them; all three looked exhausted, hurting, but very much alive.

Looking at the sheer numbers of Hellians, Zak's mind spiralled: *How on earth could Lord Ballivan be defeated?*

The others joined him on the wall.

'So I guess we are outnumbered,' Dunk said quietly.

'Just a bit,' Zak replied.

Lord Ballivan extended his arms to the crowd, demanding silence. Within moments, he got it.

'CHILDREN OF HELL,' Lord Ballivan yelled. 'THE NIGHT IS OURS!'

The Hellians went wild, filling the air once again with screeches, shrieks and howls.

Lord Ballivan turned to the Templars. 'And we shall await the arrival of your child warriors with great anticipation. I can only assume they have had some manner of victory in Wales but it makes no difference – the relic they have found at Saint Catherine's Chapel shall soon be mine. But for now, we shall enjoy a pleasant distraction.'

He turned to Mister Gudrak.

'Nathanaryn Gudrak – you are a traitor to your motherland and to your King. And for these, the greatest of crimes, I deem you should suffer for all to witness.'

'Just kill me now, Verekus,' Mister Gudrak said.

'The sound of your voice makes me suffer enough.'

Lord Ballivan leaned over and whispered in Mister Gudrak's ear. 'Oh, you shall die this night,' he whispered. 'But before you do know this: I shall be taking your wife as my own, and I shall raise your offspring as mine, too. Have visions of this as you die.'

Lord Ballivan smiled coldly at a trembling Mrs Gudrak, as she clung tightly to Garrick and Gibblon. He turned back to Mister Gudrak.

' I took your wife's horn years ago,' Lord Ballivan sneered. 'Now I should like to complete the set...'

Mister Gudrak remained silent, defiance etched on his face.

Lord Ballivan's laughter echoed through the yard. Then he pulled free a long serrated dagger from beneath his cloak, and seized Mister Gudrak's head. Then slowly, terrifyingly, he ran the blade along the length of the horn and back again. The smile on his face broadened.

Mrs Gudrak screamed. 'NO, PLEASE!'

Lord Ballivan laughed again, his yellow eyes finding Mrs Gudrak's. 'Surely you wish your husband to share your deformity?'

'Cut it off,' Mister Gudrak said. 'I care not.'

'Don't hurt him!' Mrs Gudrak pleaded.

'Hurt him?' Lord Ballivan grinned back at Mrs Gudrak. 'I intend his pain to be so great they can hear his screams of agony on the Ptheradax plains.'

'We need to do something, Zak... and fast!' Sarah said urgently.

Zak gave a decisive nod. 'No matter what,' he said. 'There's going to be a fight, and we don't stand a chance unless we free those Templars. Leah, it's your job to cut them free, even the odds a bit. Sarah, you have the dart gun and you're the best shot, so position yourself on the wall and do all you can to protect Leah as she does her thing. Anyone attacks her, turn them to dust.'

Sarah nodded.

'And me?' Dunk asked.

Zak glanced over at the Training Yard and looked at Mister Gudrak. 'I want you to do something else.'

Dunk smiled as Zak told him his plans.

'I like that idea,' Dunk said.

Leah seemed concerned. 'Surely the Hellians will see me freeing the Templars?'

'Not if they're concentrating on something else,' Zak replied. 'And they will be.'

'What?' Leah asked.

'Me,' Zak replied simply. 'I'll create a distraction.'

'What do you mean "*you*"?' Sarah asked, concerned.

'No time to explain, but wait for my signal before the fight back,' Zak replied. 'Now go... and good luck.'

Dunk nodded. 'Same to you, mate,' he said, patting Zak's arm. He and Leah sprinted off.

Sarah's eyes found Zak's. She opened her mouth to say something, but no words came. Aware time was against them, she raced after Dunk and Leah.

Zak's gaze returned to the Training Yard, before filling his lungs with air and shouted at the top of his voice.

'BALLIVAN!'

He vaulted the wall, dropping twenty feet and landed nimbly on the damp grass. He shouted again, louder this time. 'BALLIVAN!'

He drew his Magnasword from its holster. Then he took a step toward Lord Ballivan.

And then another.

- Chapter 35 -
The End of the Beginning

With each stride, more Hellians turned toward Zak. He scarcely noticed the hisses and snarls directed at him as he advanced coolly on, his mind fixed on one thing, and one thing only: *Lord Ballivan.*

Sensing the change in his followers, Lord Ballivan looked over and saw Zak approach. An ugly smirk curled on his mouth. He lowered his dagger.

'STEP AWAY FROM MISTER GUDRAK!' Zak shouted over.

Lord Ballivan ignored him. 'Judging by your skin colour, you must be the Watcher known as Zak Fisher!' he yelled back, his voice high and penetrating.

'I guess I must,' Zak shouted.

'And where are your companions?'

Zak's jaw tightened as he spat out the next words. 'Dead in a church in Wales... but what do you care? Surely this is all you're bothered about?' He raised his clenched fist high. Opening his hand, the Seal of Solomon cast a shimmering blue light all around.

Silence filtered through the yard.

'I think you should end this now,' Zak shouted, 'because if not I'll throw the Seal over that wall and into the Irish Sea... and you'll never see it again.'

For the first time, Lord Ballivan looked ruffled. 'You would not.'

'Try me,' Zak replied. 'And believe me... I've got a damn good throw.'

'Then what is it you want for the ring?'

'I *want* you to walk out of here with your little minions. I *want* you to not harm anyone else. I *want* you leave this world and not come back. That's what I want, but I know that's not going to happen, so instead I'll make do with - well, just *you*.'

'Me?'

'You and me, one on one. The winner keeps the ring. How does that sound?'

'NO, ZAK!' Irene cried, voice cracking.

Zak didn't take his eyes off Lord Ballivan. 'So do we have a deal?'

Lord Ballivan couldn't reply fast enough. 'We do.'

'I thought you'd say that,' Zak replied.

Mister Gudrak's expression looked desperate. 'He is a child, Verekus,' he said desperately. 'Kill me if you crave blood. Kill me but let him live.'

'It is the Watcher that has demanded blood,' Lord Ballivan replied coolly, 'not I.'

Zak felt countless eyes burn into him as he entered the amphitheatre. All the while, he held the ring above his head, as if a torch guiding his way. In the centre of the arena, he returned the Seal to his pocket, before drawing Kelly Barnes' Magnasword and extending the blade. With a Magnasword in each hand, he turned to face Lord Ballivan, who had pulled free a sword to complement his dagger.

Then, to Zak's amazement, Lord Ballivan's feet left

the ground and he flew into the arena, his cloak flapping in the icy breeze.

Ugly sounds of anticipation echoed off the perimeter walls.

Zak glanced at Sid, Irene and Anne. Almost immediately, he regretted it. Seeing their frightened faces only distracted him from his purpose, and he couldn't allow that. He had to give the others the one thing that could give them a shot at victory: *time.*

Zak turned back to Lord Ballivan and watched him land a short distance away. At once, he was shocked by Lord Ballivan's size. Easily as tall as Mister Gudrak with a body both lithe and powerful, his presence instilled awe and terror in equal measure.

'Watcher, I shall give you this one chance,' Lord Ballivan said. 'Give me the ring and perhaps you do not have to die this night.'

'We both know you'll kill me whatever happens,' Zak replied. 'And I'm fine with that.'

Lord Ballivan chuckled. 'Indeed we do,' he said, each syllable delivered slowly and with venom. Then his expression changed; his eyes glowed with rage and he leapt into the air again, rocketing toward Zak like a bullet. As he landed, he brought his sword down, targeting Zak's head.

Zak raised both Magnaswords in a cross pattern. The three blades collided in a deafening *clang* that shattered the night.

Zak felt the exchange reverberate throughout his body, attacking every muscle. Swiftly, he angled his Magnasword and counterattacked, with a strike at Lord Ballivan's chest.

Lord Ballivan blocked the shot, before attacking

again, this time directing the dagger at Zak's heart.

Zak defended the strike, and wheeled about, using Kelly's Magnasword to slash at Lord Ballivan's arm. Again, Lord Ballivan parried the strike.

Time and again, each of them attacked and defended. Unlike Dreanda, however, Lord Ballivan didn't tire. Instead, each passing second appeared to strengthen his mind and body.

But Zak didn't tire either. The shrieks of support for Lord Ballivan barely registered with him; his concentration levels were so high he felt like he was fighting in a soundless vacuum.

After minutes of battle, Lord Ballivan lowered his sword and said, 'Enough! Although your skills are great, Watcher, you cannot defeat me.'

'But I am defeating you,' Zak replied. 'Or are you too stupid to see that?'

Lord Ballivan's top lip curled with fury. 'You really have no idea what true power is, do you?' He stared at Kelly Barnes' Magnasword. 'Allow me to show you.' He blinked.

Zak felt the Magnasword fly from his hand, landing metres away. Stunned, he clasped his remaining Magnasword tightly with both hands.

A cruel grin rounded Lord Ballivan's mouth. His stared at Zak's sword and blinked again. The sword tore out of Zak's grip, landing far out of reach.

Suddenly weaponless, Zak look dumbfounded. *He had forgotten Mister Gudrak mention Lord Ballivan was telekinetic.* He heard Irene's terrified voice somewhere in the crowd. 'Please, stop this!' she yelled.

Ignoring her, Lord Ballivan's extended his knife-like fingers and focussed his energies on Zak. He blinked twice.

Zak's body went rigid, his arms flattened against his sides as if bound by invisible restraints. He struggled but it was useless.

With a flick of Lord Ballivan's hand, Zak rose two feet off the ground, hovering like a dragonfly. Then he was soaring toward Lord Ballivan as if on a wire, until stopping merely inches from Ballivan's face.

'Now, Angel, it is time for you to die,' Lord Ballivan hissed.

'Nah,' Zak replied. 'But you know, up close you really are ugly.'

Lord Ballivan's eyes blazed. Clenching his fist, he slammed it into Zak's right cheek.

CRACK!

Pain seared through Zak, intense, unimaginable pain. An image of Kyle Dobson's punch flashed in his mind, but this felt nothing like that. This felt like he'd been hit by a sledgehammer.

'And when I say ugly,' Zak said, doubled over, spitting blood on to the ground. 'I mean really, really pig ugly.'

Lord Ballivan let fly another punch, this time striking Zak's left cheek.

CRACK!

His cheeks swelling like balloons, Zak rasped, 'I-is that it? Is that all you've got?'

'No. You may have this.' Lord Ballivan raised his dagger and pressed its pointed tip against Zak's throat. '*I give you death.*'

Then Zak did the most unexpected thing: *he smiled*.

'Thank you,' Zak said.

Lord Ballivan looked confused. 'Thank you?'

'For talking too much,' Zak replied simply.

What Lord Ballivan didn't know was that seconds before Zak had delivered these words, Dunk had appeared behind Mister Gudrak. In his hands was a long shimmering object: *Mister Gudrak's family axe.*

With a powerful swing of the axe, Dunk sliced through Mister Gudrak's bonds, which fell to the ground.

Dunk pressed the axe into Mister Gudrak's massive hands. 'GO!'

With newfound vigour, Mister Gudrak charged at Lord Ballivan, the axe held high above his head. 'BALLIVANNNNNN!' he screamed.

Lord Ballivan barely had time to react when Mister Gudrak swung the axe head into his neck, severing his head, which crumbled to dust together with the rest of his body.

Suddenly in full control of his faculties again, Zak promptly ran over and scooped up his Magnasword. Ignoring the mass of astonished Hellians, he turned to the Templars and shouted at the top of his voice:

'TEMPLARS. TAKE BACK AVERNON!'

- Chapter 36 -
Goodbyes

From the far side of the Training Yard, the Templars leapt up with a new lease of life. All the while Zak had been fighting Lord Ballivan, Leah had been moving from Templar to Templar, stealthily and silently, cutting them free and whispering instructions.

Some Templars picked up abandoned Magnaswords; others tackled Mothmen, overcame them, and stole their weapons. In no time at all, the Templars were armed, dangerous and ploughing through their opponents like a whirlwind.

The Hellians didn't stand a chance.

Zak scanned the scene. Dunk had withdrawn his Magnasword and was cutting down Hellians two at a time. Sarah emptied the dart gun with astounding accuracy, then withdrew her Magnasword and leapt into the fray. Leah freed the remaining Templars and joined the others in the eye of the battle.

Cutting down a Reptilak, Zak's eyes locked on Anne. Through the chaos, he sprinted over to her and grasped her hand. 'Come with me,' he said.

Barely able to process all that was happening, Anne took hold of it.

Zak led her quickly through the battle, dealing

swiftly with every Hellian that posed a threat, and over to the far side of the Training Yard, some distance away from the fight.

'You wait here,' Zak said. 'I'll be back as soon as I can.'

Anne's fingers clasped his like a vice. 'P- please... d-don't leave me.'

'I need to join my friends,' Zak said. 'But you'll be safe here. I promise.'

He flashed her a comforting smile, and pulled his hand from hers, before racing back into the battle.

Within minutes, every Hellian had been eliminated. The Training Yard resembled a London fog, soupy and impenetrable.

As the dust settled, Zak looked around. Exhausted Templars were checking on their injured comrades, others grieving the dead. He searched out Sarah, Dunk and Leah. Thankfully, they were all unharmed. As one, they approached each other.

Sarah was the first to reach Zak. She flung her arms around his neck and pulled him close. 'You did it,' she said.

Zak smiled. 'We did it.'

As she released him, Sarah gasped at his battered face. Heavily bruised, his cheeks were enflamed and puffy, his lips split and caked in blood. 'Look what that monster did to you!' she said.

'And look what Mister Gudrak did to him,' Zak grinned.

'Ah, it's an improvement,' Dunk said. 'Seriously, buddy, well done.'

'Cheers, mate, but well done to you, too. You really are Dunk the Destroyer.'

'Yeah,' Dunk replied. 'I've decided that's a naff nickname. I'm gonna work on another.'

Leah pulled Zak close and kissed his cheek. 'You are one crazy dude, Zak Fisher, but we couldn't have picked a better leader.'

'Thanks, Leah,' Zak said, 'but if you hadn't freed the Templars we'd all have been dead meat.'

'We all played our part,' Sarah said.

'That's because we're a team,' Leah added.

'The best team ever,' Dunk said.

Zak was about to comment when he noticed Anne, sitting cross-legged on the ground like a small, frightened child, her face emotionless. 'I'll be back in a minute.'

Stepping away from the group, Zak heard a fragile voice.

'Zak... you brave, brave boy.' Irene said, weeping uncontrollably. She seized him in a powerful hug. 'You did it. You saved us all.'

Sid appeared at her shoulder. 'Well done, son, I am so very proud of ya.'

'Thanks, Sid,' Zak said. 'It was nothing.'

'You defeated a Hell-Lord,' Sid said. 'Trust me, that's something.'

'Yes, and you could've been killed!' Irene said in a tone that was both chastising and fretful. 'What were you thinking?'

'I didn't have much time to think,' Zak replied.

'Well, you need to find time,' Irene said, her voice quivering. 'I don't know what I'd do if something happened to you.'

'Zak did what needed to be done, luv,' Sid said, curling his arm around his wife's shoulder. 'You always said he was the most special boy in the world. And tonight he's proved it.'

It was then Zak's gaze found Anne again and concern lined his face.

Irene noticed. 'Go and see her, Zak,' she said softly. 'She's been so brave. I don't know who she is or how you know her, but she's a very special young lady.'

'She is,' Zak replied. He walked over to Anne, his movements slow for fear of startling her. Then he knelt down and said in a quiet voice, 'I know it's a daft question but are you okay?'

Anne didn't reply.

Gently, Zak placed his hand on hers. 'Are you hurt? Do you need to see a doctor?'

Anne still didn't reply as her eyes met his.

Zak was about to say something else when Anne flung herself into his arms and started to cry. Her body shook wildly as she spilled tears that came from the very depths of her soul.

Zak held her for what seemed like an eternity. Every now and then she would pull away as if her tears were fading, but then they'd start again.

Zak felt responsible for every single tear. She had become involved in all this because of him. It was his fault.

And nothing anyone could ever say would make him think otherwise.

*

For as long as he would live, Zak would never know just how long he and Anne sat there in a soundless embrace.

Eventually, it felt like Anne had no more tears to give.

'Please... take me home now,' she said.

'I'm not sure I can just yet,' Zak replied awkwardly. 'I think the Templar bosses may need to talk to you first. I'm sorry...' As the apology hung there, he saw William Brockenhurst kneeling beside a dead Templar, clearly distressed. He was holding something in his right hand, which he placed gently over the Templar's face, hiding him from the world.

It was then Zak recognised the object and his heart sank.

It was Pottsy's baseball cap.

Zak knew immediately Anne shouldn't be at Avernon a moment longer. She had seen enough of death to last her a lifetime. 'I'll get a car to take you home right away,' he said.

'No,' Anne replied quietly. 'Will you take me? I'd like to walk home.'

Zak thought about it for a moment. *How could he say no?*

'Of course,' he said.

Zak told Leah, Sarah, Dunk, Irene and Sid his plans and didn't hear a single objection. Within ten minutes, he and Anne were treading the beach road, heading to Beridian. For some time they barely said a thing to each other. However, the further they got from Avernon, the more a sense of normality returned.

'So you're an Angel?' Anne said. 'An actual Angel?'

'So they say.' Zak raised his hand and presented his palm. 'With a halo and everything.'

Anne managed a smile. 'So where are your wings?'

'I'm still waiting for them.'

'Have you always known that's what you are?'

'Only since I came to Avernon, just before I met you.

Before then I didn't know about Hellians or Templars or any of it.'

'That is a head mash,' Anne said.

'You could say that.'

'So why are you here... on earth, I mean?'

'To stop creatures like Lord Ballivan. There's supposedly a war between Hell and Earth coming. We're here to help win that war.'

Anne fell silent. 'But what have I got to do with all that? Why did they take me?'

'Because they discovered I cared about you,' Zak replied. 'They wanted to use you to get to me. But it's over now, and you'll never be bothered again.'

Anne processed this. 'What was it that creature wanted from you?' When you turned up you were holding something.'

Zak reached in his pocket and pulled out the Seal of Solomon.

In that instant, the Seal's soft sapphire light coloured Anne's face.

Despite how exhausted she looked, Zak had never seen her look more beautiful.

'He wanted this,' Zak said.

'A ring?'

'It's called The Seal of Solomon,' Zak said simply. 'It's some kind of doorway between our world and Hell. It's sort of a big deal.'

'How does it work?' Anne asked.

'No idea,' Zak replied. 'And I don't want to know. But what I do know is that many Templars have died tonight because of it.'

It was these last few words that suggested an idea of what to do next. He didn't even give himself time to consider whether it was the right thing to do or not.

Drawing back his arm, Zak threw the ring as far as he could into the sea. The Seal of Solomon shone brightly like a shooting star until it landed in the water a distance away.

'There,' Zak said, satisfied. 'No one will die for it ever again.'

The seconds became minutes as Zak and Anne stood there in silence, watching the first rays of sunlight paint the ocean, ushering in the dawn.

'I can never see you again,' Anne said quietly. 'You do know that?'

Zak nodded. 'I know.'

'I'm sad about that. We could've had something special.'

'I agree,' Zak replied.

They set off walking again. Soon, the Beridian skyline came into view.

Anne stopped and turned to Zak. 'I can make my own way from here.'

'If you're sure,' Zak replied.

'I am,' Anne replied. 'What will happen to you now? Will they try and rebuild Avernon?'

'I don't think Avernon exists any more,' Zak replied. 'We'll probably be moved to the mainland. There's a Templar castle in Wales that gets mentioned a lot.'

'Well, wherever you go,' Anne said, her body trembling, 'and whatever you do... I wish you the best of luck. I doubt there'll be a day I don't think about you.' Her eyes dampened. 'I once said you're my hero, but I guess the reality is that you're everyone's hero. A hero for the whole world.' She reached up and cupped Zak's face in her hands, then she leaned in and kissed him softly on the lips.

'Goodbye, Zak Fisher,' Anne said, unable to look him in the eyes.

'Goodbye, Anne,' Zak said.

'And be careful,' Anne said. 'With all that's to come. Whatever that is.'

'I will.'

And with that, Anne sprinted off.

Watching Anne disappear into the distance, Zak felt a deep ache form in the pit of his stomach. He knew he'd never see her again.

And that was how it should be.

Zak turned in the opposite direction and started to walk. As he trailed his steps back to Avernon, he thought about everything he'd been through in the last twenty-four hours, and more significantly the consequences of it all. Would he be moved to Perigorn Castle? Or would he be taken somewhere new?

Deep down, however, he knew it didn't matter. Although he'd relocated many times in his life, this time would be different, this time he wouldn't be doing it alone. *He'd be doing it with his friends, and they were the best friends anyone could wish for.*

With that thought firmly in his mind, he turned to the ocean, and allowed the morning sun to glaze his face.

After all, it was the beginning of a new day.

Epilogue
A New Hope

The Murdulan Wetlands, Hell.

John Kurnan looked up at the bright green sky and watched a flock of phoenixes fly overhead. After entering Hell undetected by hiding in a Pyrocopter delivery at a Stargate, he had made his way from the Templar fort at Akron across the planet to the Murdulan Wetlands, a region in Hell very few Templars had visited before.

He pulled the long wooden oar from the clear blue water, before ploughing it back in, propelling the small makeshift boat slowly along the Tamazai River.

He had travelled forever to reach this point, and was nearly at his destination.

After receiving Wilbur Combermere's cryptic note, he had embarked as soon as he could on the journey and only hoped he wasn't too late.

He prayed Wilbur wasn't already dead.

Of course, he felt guilty at leaving Zak, particularly so close to the Renaissance, but he really had no choice. He needed answers to the questions posed in Wilbur's note. *Nothing else mattered.*

In the distance, Kurnan saw fine wisps of smoke slinking into the sky. He knew at once he was nearly there. Moments later, a small makeshift house with a crooked chimney appeared on the riverbank a half-mile away.

Kurnan knew a tiny house on a river in Hell was not the usual place for a Templar to call home, but then Wilbur Combermere was not a usual Templar.

Increasing the power in his strokes, Kurnan rowed toward the house, before pulling up on the bankside and leaping out.

A small figure emerged from the high reeds and stood before him. It was a female anthropoid - a *Bulbian* - no more than three feet tall, with olive green skin and large, kindly eyes the size of saucers. He had encountered Bulbians before at a trading post at Annyx and found them to be genial, loyal and kind-hearted.

Fully aware of Bulbian etiquette, Kurnan gave a deep respectful bow.

The Bulbian smiled her appreciation and curtsied in return. 'You are John Kurnan,' she said. 'We have been expecting you. I am Elza, Wilbur Combermere's aid and friend.'

'Hello, Elza,' Kurnan said. 'Is Wilbur still alive?'

'For the moment, yes,' Elza replied, 'but he will be passing shortly. Your timing is fortuitous as I do not expect him to see a new dawn.'

'Then may I see him now?' Kurnan said.

'Of course. Please, follow me.'

Elza turned and disappeared back into the reeds.

Kurnan followed her onto a winding path, lined with green and orange flowers, which led to the front door of what looked like a fairy-tale cottage.

Elza opened the door and extended her tiny hand. 'Please enter, John Kurnan. You are very welcome here.'

'Thank you, Elza.' Out of respect, Kurnan bowed again.

Although returning a kindly smile, there was something in Elza's eyes that conveyed both concern and sadness. 'Now, whatever Wilbur tells you I beseech you to not let your anger taint his final night. The secrets he has guarded have caused him pain enough, it would be sad for him to undertake his final journey with the sound of fury in his ears.'

Kurnan wasn't sure how to reply to that. *What kind of secrets had Wilbur Combermere guarded?*

'I'm not here to upset him, Elza,' Kurnan said. 'I just want answers.'

'But it is voicing those answers that will upset him... *and you,*' Elza replied miserably. 'I am certain of it.' And with that, she turned about and retraced her steps down the path.

Kurnan watched Elza disappear into the reeds, before passing through the doorway and into the house.

Straightaway, he felt he'd entered a furnace. A log fire blazed on the right hand wall, sending an orange glow over the small room where an old man with long, straggly silver hair lay on a bed in the far corner. The air was thick and perfumed with a sweet scent Kurnan recognised as that of the Pterradyl flower.

Slowly, Kurnan crossed the room, collecting a wooden chair on the way. He positioned it beside the old man and then sat down. 'Wilbur?' he said softly. 'Wilbur, it's me... Kurnan.'

At once, the old man's eyes opened. Staring at

Kurnan, Combermere's bloodshot eyes dampened. 'J-John?' he wheezed, his voice weak and thin. 'T-Thank God you've found me.'

'It's good to see you, Wilbur.'

Combermere forced a smile. 'I-I'm g-glad you found me before I die. T-there are things I need to tell you... mistakes only you c-can make right.'

'What mistakes, Wilbur?' Kurnan replied.

Combermere coughed violently. 'W-what I'm about to tell you is to my eternal s-shame,' he rasped, 'and the shame of the Templars, b-but you can make it right. You must... for the sake of those beautiful children.'

'Which children? The Angels?'

Combermere clawed for air. 'The d-decision we made was wrong, so wrong, but we believed we had no choice.'

'What decision?' Kurnan said, losing patience. 'Just tell me.'

Tears pooled in Combermere's eyes, as his gaze met Kurnan's. 'The mothers are alive... all four of them. D-do you understand? You must find them John. T-they were taken from us b-but you can find them... and you can save them. W-will you do that?'

But John Kurnan didn't reply. In fact, he barely heard what Combermere had said. His mind was spiralling out of control, processing the four words that would remain with him forever.

The mothers are alive.

CARL ASHMORE

Carl is a children's writer from Crewe, England. He has written nine books for children: 'The Time Hunters,' 'The Time Hunters and the Box of Eternity,' 'The Time Hunters and the Spear of Fate,' 'The Time Hunters and the Sword of Ages', 'The Time Hunters and the Lost City' 'The Night They Nicked Saint Nick,' 'Rhyme and Reason, 'Bernard and the Bibble' and 'Zak Fisher and the Angel Prophecy'.

He likes chives, Naan breads and second hand shops.

He can be contacted at **carlashmoreauthor@yahoo.com**

Check out his website: www.carlashmore.com

Printed in Great Britain
by Amazon